# An excerpt from *Mercy*

"You can do that without even looking." He sounded impressed.

"Yes. I've tied these shoes thousands of times."

I looked up again and he smiled down at me, and I hated how I felt under that breathtaking smile. He offered me his hand.

"We haven't met properly, have we?"

I stood up then because he expected me to. It's more accurate to say that he pulled me up, although he did it so naturally that there was no hint of force. But I came to my feet as if something propelled me, and what propelled me was his large, impossibly strong hand. He introduced himself formally, in a deep voice that held only a trace of Midwestern accent.

"Matthew Norris. I'm a big fan of your dancing."

"Lucy Merritt," I replied. "Merritt with two t's."

That seemed to amuse him and he smiled.

"It's nice to meet you, Lucy Merritt with two t's."

I stood there feeling ridiculous, seeing Grégoire out of the corner of my eye, and a few other dancers eavesdropping on our conversation like a bunch of gossip whores.

"So what are you doing here again?" I asked, a little peevishly. "Don't you work?"

"Oh, yeah, I work," he said, and the smile he gave me then didn't quite reach his eyes.

"A busy patron of the arts... So you're here checking out your investment?"

"One of them, yes."

# Mercy

By

*Annabel Joseph*

Other erotic romance by Annabel Joseph

*Cait and the Devil*
*Firebird*
*Deep in the Woods*
*Fortune*
*Owning Wednesday*
*Lily Mine*
*Comfort Object*
*Caressa's Knees*
*Odalisque*
*Command Performance*
*Cirque de Minuit*
*Burn For You*
*The Edge of the Earth (as Molly Joseph)*
*Disciplining the Duchess*
*Waking Kiss*
*Fever Dream*

Erotica by Annabel Joseph

*Club Mephisto*
*Molly's Lips: Club Mephisto Retold*

Coming soon:

*Bound in Blue*
*Master's Flame*

*For Jeff, who saved me*

*And still saves me*

*Again and again*

# Chapter One:
# Lucy and Mr. Norris

The floor was hard and cold against my shoulders, under my ass. He couldn't get a carpet? At least an area rug?

I guess this is what he paid me for, this discomfort and chill. My muscles started to ache from lying still and holding the demanding pose. If I didn't love him so much I would never submit to this, but I completely adored him, so here I was. And yes, he paid me quite well for my services and regularly asked me back, which I found both flattering and reassuring.

I looked up at him from under my eyelashes but I doubt he even noticed my gaze. His eyes were fixed, as always, on my supple dancer's body offered before him. I watched his powerful strokes, vigorous and intense. He was quite robust for a man of seventy-five. His name was Pietro and he was an artist. And me? My name was Lucy, and unfortunately I wasn't quite sure from day to day who or what I really was. I guess if I had to choose I would say I was a dancer first, who happened to fall into nude modeling on the side. It was high art stuff, not porn, although I knew plenty of dancers who took the porn route to make ends meet. Like most dancers, I wasn't precious about my body. I knew it was nice and I used it when it suited me. But porn wasn't really my thing. It seemed so squalid, so I was glad for this gig, being painted by a real artist.

The broad strokes Pietro made scratched loudly in the silence, that abrasive sound of pencil on textured canvas that I knew so well by now. Sometimes it irritated me, but sometimes it relaxed me and I floated off into daydreams listening to it go on. Sometimes, instead, I pictured the lines of my body as he put them to canvas with his hands. Pietro made large works, sprawling and spare, all shading and lines, although my body and face were definitely there. No abstract, amorphous, unrecognizable figure. It was definitely me and part of me got off on that fact. He thought I was beautiful. He'd told me so when he hired me. "I need your beauty," he'd rasped to me outside the theater like a desperate man. The very next day, I'd knocked on the door of his studio. He'd guided me inside, coaxed me out of my clothes and said, "Beautiful girl." Then he turned me so my back was to him and started to sketch my curvy little ass.

But it wasn't about sex, not even for a second. Believe me, no sex was ever involved. Even though Pietro undressed me like the most solicitous of lovers every time I came over, we were not lovers. We were nothing more than friends. Not even friends really. He was more like a mentor. Or maybe a grandfather, a nice grandfather who gave me advice. I loved Pietro with my whole heart, loved him like the father I'd never had, and Pietro was always kind to me the many hours we spent together at work.

He scratched at a line with his finger, adjusting the shading with a frown. When I thought that my back would break from the strain of the pose, he smiled at me and sighed.

"It is time for a break, I think."

"How did you know?"

"The little lines in your forehead, they draw together like this." He made a funny face, an exaggerated imitation of my discomfort. I laughed, shrugging on the robe he handed me.

I looked at the canvas while we chatted and rested. It was almost done, I guessed. The last two works of me had been standing poses, which was much more relaxing. I could stand for an eternity not moving a muscle, piece of cake. But this pose had me on my back with my arms up over my head, and my legs curled loosely at my side. It was a lovely pose, I could see that on the canvas, but it hurt to hold it for such a long time.

Luckily, Pietro was conscientious about giving me breaks. He only refused to let me up when he was in the throes of "the muse." When I did take a break I felt guilty, because it always took time for him to get back into that same space he'd been. It always took five minutes or more just to return my arms and legs to that perfect angle he craved. I would let him manipulate me into position, loose and compliant. It was sort of like sex, only Pietro wasn't my lover.

No, my lover had left me last week. Did I say he was my lover? He was my fiancé, actually. The operative word being *was*. He *was* my fiancé, until he left me at the altar. He *was* my fiancé until he realized he was in love with someone else. He had never loved me even though he'd said he did, and I hadn't loved him, and that was the worst thing of all.

But I preferred not to talk about Joe. I'd finally reached a point where I could conjure his face without bursting into tears. And around the time I reached that point, I decided not to conjure his face anymore at all. I was a practical person in matters of the heart. I had never been in love. I realized that now, after the wretchedness of last week, that I had never been in love and probably never would be, because there was something wrong with me. I couldn't feel things right, or maybe I just didn't want to.

Not feeling things came in handy in many ways. As a modern dancer, you're grappled and grasped pretty regularly. You spend hours punishing your body at the barre, at rehearsals, at choreography, at nightly performances. As an art model, you're manipulated and posed. When you make your life by your body, it's actually better not to feel too much. To feel only what matters. *Stretch. Breathe. Turn. Soar.* I felt my body move in space and that was enough.

This would be the third work I'd done for Pietro. The first two had sold as a set to an anonymous buyer for an obscene amount.

After they sold, Pietro had given me five thousand dollars and said he felt it wasn't enough. I tried to refuse it because he already paid me an hourly wage that was more than fair, but he insisted, telling me it would assuage his guilt.

"What did you sell them for?" I had pressed.

"A lot. A bidding war. Two buyers." Then he'd told me the amount and my mouth dropped open. I pocketed his check without another word.

But Pietro was deserving of every success. He worked hard at his art and his vision was original and striking. I wondered as we worked what this one would sell for. To me, it was even more beautiful and provocative than the others. I wondered if he thought the same thing, if it mattered to him. *What will this bring me? How much money will I make?* I wondered if he looked at me differently now. When he looked at me, what did he see? Beauty, as he claimed, or something else? A naked, compelling body to sell for money? Lots of money, it seemed. But I was more than happy to be a vessel for his success.

I left Pietro's at four o'clock to go to the theater. We had no rehearsals on Tuesday, just a nightly performance at eight. I was meeting Grégoire for dinner beforehand. Grégoire, my dance partner, and my best friend.

Grégoire was a couple years older than me, thirty years old to my twenty-eight. He had cried on my shoulder the day of his birthday. "Thirty?" he'd mourned. "It's too awful to be true." And it was awful, because we were dancers. Our performance life spans were miserably short, especially with the kind of punishing dance we did. I already nursed aches and twinges that worsened by the week. I hoped to make it to thirty-five, but even that seemed an unlikely event. So I held Grégoire in total empathy that night, stroking his soft black hair and crying along with him. Life after dance was something I never thought of, something I hadn't planned for, at least not yet.

"Lucy!" He waved to me as I neared the stage door. He was leaning against the wall jabbering on the phone. Talking to his boyfriend no doubt, who he claimed to love desperately, but who was rarely around. "He works," he explained. "He's not in the arts." The sugar daddy, who had a real job. Every dancer needed one, just as I'd had, only I hadn't been able to hold onto mine.

I waved back to him and crossed the cracked pavement. The ground outside the theater was littered with cigarette butts and plastic water bottle caps. *Disgusting dancers*, I thought to myself. I went inside to drop off my bag in my dressing room, my eyes adjusting to the darkness from the blinding light outside. I was so sun-struck I almost collided with someone in the corridor. He steadied me and I looked up at him with an embarrassed grin.

"Sorry, I'm blind."

He answered with a smile and left his hand on my elbow just a little longer than seemed right. And I can't explain it, but the way he held my arm felt...well...almost inappropriate in some way. When he finally let go I scurried down the hall, fighting the urge to look back.

But it was hard not to, because even in my blindness I noticed he was an extremely attractive man. Even sun blind, he'd made me feel hot and agitated with nothing more than the strange firmness of his touch. Sandy blond hair, a broad face and mouth, and blue eyes that couldn't possibly have been as light as they looked. It was just the sun, I thought, that made them so singular. It was only the sun that made me feel so unglued.

I pushed into my dressing room and found Elinor there. I dropped my bag, and I normally would have walked right back out. But he might still be back there by the stage door, and for some reason I didn't feel up to facing him again. Instead I resigned myself to small talk with Ellie. Elinor was a dyed-in-the-wool dancer, artistic and pure. Talking to her was like driving wood chips under my fingernails. After five minutes of her prattle, I figured I'd rather face the elbow grabber in the hall.

But he was gone. I burst from the stage door and gestured impatiently for Grégoire to hang up. Grégoire, the blessed antidote to Elinor. Grégoire was as far from precious as they come, especially considering he was a gorgeous, gay euro-boy come over from Paris to the delight of us all. He spoke English like it was his bitch. I wished often that I was a man because I loved him so much.

"How are you, gorgeous?" he asked, ruffling my hair.

"I'm fine."

"How's Pietro? You posed today, huh?"

"Yeah, he's fine. He's good."

Grégoire was both fascinated and jealous of my art modeling. When I'd first begun as Pietro's model, he'd demanded blow-by-blow accounts of every boring session. Now he seemed to finally be getting over it. "How's Georges?" I asked.

"He's out of town for the week. I miss him already. He gave me quite the send off last night."

I braced, hoping he wouldn't go into details, but of course he did. I listened, half aroused and half aghast. Georges and Grégoire shared a pretty intense sex life, more intense than anything I'd ever had. I guessed it was a sugar daddy gay thing but yeah, it turned me on. I found my mind returning to the man in the corridor, the man of the insistent elbow grasp, and I wondered what his sex life was like. A garden of delights, like Georges and Grégoire enjoyed, or the bland but satisfying niceness that Joe and I endured? And yes, I had only endured it.

Outwardly, I guess most would have been happy. He made love to me with such care and attention, it would have made any woman pleased, but I faked ninety-nine percent of my orgasms. He made love to me with such careful attention that it crossed the line from erotic to clinical. Nothing was worse than when he went down on me. I shuddered just thinking of it, how considerate and solicitous he'd been. When I shuddered, Grégoire thought I was cold and pulled me closer.

"Let's pretend we're married," he said.

"Again? We pretend that every day."

He put his big hand on my ass and squeezed it. "This time, pretend like you mean it, Lu."

The sway of his hips matched mine as we walked together. Grégoire was not a swishy gay man, although he could be if he wanted to. He was actually quite proud of his straight act, which he honed and perfected. His lover, Georges, was not completely out of the closet. When he took Grégoire out around town, he was expected to act straight. And of course as a dancer, Grégoire had to be masculine and he was. Actually, people assumed we were lovers because he was so absolutely masculine when we danced together. And I suppose in a way we were lovers. There's no other way to express that dynamic between devoted partners who really know each other. Who know each other's center, each other's lines and planes and joints. Grégoire knew me like a ball player knows his ball, like a musician knows his instrument, like a carpenter knows his tools. He was attuned to every single thing about me and my body, and when he danced with me everyone could tell.

Of course, I had other partners. I danced with many partners in the company who were very good and skilled and knew me very well. But Grégoire was my partner, my best match, and I was his. It was a wonderful relationship, one I felt blessed to have.

\* \* \* \* \*

Later that night, I woke up at three A.M. from a nightmare. It was the same nightmare I had several nights a week, the feeling of having a hand clamped over my mouth so I couldn't breathe and I couldn't scream. I had the same unbearable feeling on waking, the desperate need to cry, to weep. I knew that if I could only cry, things might start to get better. The need for me to cry was so acute that it was painful. I screwed up my face, tried to force those wet droplets from the corners of my eyes. But nothing, no tears came. They never did.

These nightmares had been happening for months, long before my recent breakup with Joe. That dry tense feeling when the tears wouldn't come, it drove me to desperation. In the beginning I used to scream trying to bring the tears to my eyes, but all my screams brought were the police, yelling and banging on the door to see if I was all right. I assured them that I was fine, that'd I just had a nightmare. *Thank you, officers. Sorry. Good night.*

13

If you saw me from the outside, you would never suspect that I was a person who woke up regularly with the excruciating need to scream. That I was a person who couldn't bring tears to my wide green eyes no matter how hard I willed it. That I was a person who was dead inside. The truth hurts, but that's what I was. My body was the only thing that made me alive.

On the outside, I looked like a normal person. A dancer with a healthy body, muscular and lithe. I had very pale skin, the result of a life inside theaters and studios, hours at the barre. My hair was red, longish length, and waved into curls when I didn't have it up. And my dark green eyes, they were nothing spectacular either...not like *his*, I found myself thinking. No, I looked totally typical and normal from the outside. Not to say I was a depressed, unhappy person either. I don't know how to describe what I was. I guess I was someone who was waiting to become someone. Which was unfortunate, since I was pushing twenty-nine.

\* \* \* \* \*

On Wednesdays my company had a traditional class before rehearsals. I came in the stage door almost hoping to collide with the blue-eyed man again, but he wasn't there. Why couldn't I get him out of my mind? We had exchanged one touch, been in each other's space five seconds at most.

What had he been doing backstage? I knew he wasn't a dancer. He was too old, and had been wearing business clothes. I didn't recognize him as any of the administrative suits. He certainly wasn't the type of man who organized and ran small dance companies. What type of man was he, then? What did he do? Something very powerful, I thought, and I don't know why I was so certain of that. Had he ever seen me dance? And why should I care? I went into the rehearsal room and threw down my dance bag in frustration. I started to stretch next to Grégoire at the barre. *Reach. Bend. Breathe. Point.* I flexed my feet, went up on my toes, felt the strength in my muscles along with that faint but ever present twinge of ache. My mind emptied as the rehearsal

14

captain began and I soon lost myself to the push and pull, the straining and agony, the soothe and sweep of modern dance.

Our company was considered avant-garde, although we used classical technique and even sometimes danced *en pointe*. We used new and buzz-worthy choreographers and non-traditional music, and performed acrobatics that made people marvel, bringing more and more fans to our shows. We were a relatively small company, twenty-four dancers, but we were growing and had just moved into a larger theater space earlier in the year.

And my place in this scrappy little company? I suppose I was one of the stars, although when you dance for a small company and don't make much money, you don't feel like a star. Nor did I have much of an ego. I didn't dance for the ovation. I danced because I had to dance, because it was who I was. But I was able to do the more spectacular tricks of the choreography, which earned me respect and made the roses fall at my feet. It was a good life, and now, since my breakup with Joe, it had become my whole life, for better or worse.

These exercises were bone memory, a meditation. I could cycle through them half asleep. *Point. Reach. Turn. Bend.* It was so simple and precise. It was comfortable absentia, a mantra for the body that I couldn't live without. I leaned back into a graceful, languorous stretch. I smiled, catching Grégoire's eyes over my shoulder. Then my smile froze and I almost fell off balance, because there, over Grégoire's shoulder, my eyes found *him*.

It was all I could do not to whip my head around, turn back to take a longer look at him leaning against the wall. He stood casually, his arms crossed over his chest, but his eyes had been fixed on me.

I swallowed hard, tried to keep my mind on my work. A flush rose in my cheeks as I realized I'd flubbed a *tendu*. Somehow I knew without a doubt that he noticed. In fact, I pictured him smiling that same amused smile he'd given me in the hall. I fixed my eyes on some point across the room and kept them there. I refused to look at him even when I turned to work his way. I was so tired of thinking of this man and now he here he was, in class,

15

the one place I could usually relax. The whole time I fought with myself to put him from my mind, all I could think was that his eyes were really that blue.

When we finished at the barre, I turned to Grégoire."Who is that?" I asked, nodding over my shoulder.

Grégoire looked in his direction. "That, my dear, is a new patron of our company. Smile nicely for the very rich man." He gazed over at him with a broad, fake smile. I pinched his arm hard.

"Stop it, G! What is he doing here?"

"I don't know what he's doing here. Seeing where all his hard-earned dollars go. Watching class. Watching you, right now."

"Stop looking at him." I felt like I was back in middle school, in the cafeteria checking out boys.

"He's still looking at you," breathed Grégoire.

I looked over at the man finally, and his eyes met mine and held them until I flinched first and looked away.

"What is he, some kind of businessman?"

"Yes."

"He dresses like one. Is he gay?"

"He's a very rich and very straight developer," Grégoire chirped back. "His name is Matthew Norris."

"How do you know that?"

"Because I met him yesterday. We were all drooling over him. He was meeting with Maureen."

Maureen, the business manager of the company. I glared at Grégoire as he shot another admiring glance Mr. Norris's way. "I thought you had a boyfriend that you just *adored*."

"I do. I can look. He's looking at you again."

"So what?" I feigned disinterest but Grégoire saw right through me.

"You're not attached anymore," he said with an all-too-knowing grin. "He's still looking at you."

To my relief, the rehearsal master called us to attention and continued the class.

\* \* \* \* \*

After the show that night I went back to Georges's place with Grégoire. He'd begged me to come since Georges was out of town, but as soon as we got there, I figured out what he was up to. He immediately booted up his boyfriend's computer.

We searched using the keywords *Matthew Norris, developer, New York*, and I was amazed at how many results came up. I browsed over the pages for a while until I started to feel like a stalker, and then left with a show of boredom and went into the other room. But Grégoire kept at it, dug through articles and postings to turn up facts on him. He called out them out while I pretended disinterest in front of the TV.

"He's divorced," he yelled. "Years ago. And you wouldn't believe what he had to pay her to get out of it."

"Did he cheat on her?"

"It doesn't say. Hold on, I'll try to find out."

I rolled my eyes. Even if he discovered Mr. Norris was a cheating scumbag, he wouldn't have told me because he clearly wanted me to hook up with him. Even if he discovered he had leprosy, ate babies in satanic rituals, and ran a meth lab, he still wouldn't have told me on the off chance we'd go out.

"Damn, he has a girlfriend," he sighed a moment later. Then, "Oh, they recently broke up. Ha!" A triumphant laugh. "He's available, Lu."

I didn't reply but a part of me got excited. *He's available.* Did he want me? He was a single man, rich, handsome, a patron of the arts. Grégoire said he'd been watching me during class...

But what did he want with me? The way he'd looked at me... He'd looked at me like he already knew me. He'd handled me in the hall like I was already his. That's why it had felt so strange. It had been a possessive grip when he had no right to possession. He was clearly a man who was used to getting anything he wanted, but just because he donated to the company didn't mean he could choose a girl from the ranks for his pleasure. *For his pleasure.* Why did my mind automatically go there? Maybe he only liked my dancing. Maybe he just wanted to be friends.

17

No, I didn't get that vibe from him. When he looked at me, when he'd touched me, it wasn't friendliness I felt. My mind snapped from its train of thought when Grégoire started printing. "God, G." I sighed, rolling my eyes. "Why are you doing this?"

"For you, dearest," he said in my ear, and then dropped a photograph in my lap.

Yes, it was him, larger than life. The blond hair, the blue eyes that haunted my dreams. The broad face, the masculine features, the perfect smile. I shivered and felt strangely afraid. I handed it back to him. "I want you to have it. Something to stroke to while Georges is out of town."

"Oh, come on!" He shoved the picture back into my hands. "It took me fifteen minutes to figure out how to blow that up for you."

"I don't want it." I ignored him even though he was inches from my face, smiling his mischievous smile. "I have absolutely no interest in this rich prick."

"He's not a prick. I know you're not big on guys right now," he said, "but this guy! What do you think he's worth? How many millions?"

"Why does that matter?" I shook my head. "It probably just makes him weird."

"Weird?"

"Yes, weird. All rich people are weird. And he's totally weird. I can tell he is."

"Georges is rich, and he's not weird."

"Yes he is, if what you tell me about your sex life is true."

Grégoire laughed, jumped over the sofa and curled up with his head in my lap. "Oh, Lucy."

I didn't reply, just ran my fingers through his sleek black hair.

"You know what? I think you're really, really sad." He stroked my leg, soft and slow. "I think this thing with Joe has tripped you up."

"It hasn't. It's just made me realize some things about love."

"Love?" Grégoire snorted. "You don't know anything about love, Lucy Merritt."

18

He teased, but his words hit a little too close to home. Anyway, who was he to lecture me about love? "I'm going," I muttered, pushing him out of my lap.

"Aw, don't be mad."

"I'm tired. It's late, you stupid French pretty boy. I'll see you tomorrow. Have a nice night."

"Don't forget your photo," he said, holding out the picture of Matthew Norris.

"Thanks." I crumpled it into a fistful of paper before shoving it in my bag, feeling full of fear and frustration and lust.

\* \* \* \* \*

As soon as I got home, of course, I took out the photo, smoothed out the wrinkles as best I could. I lay on my bed and looked at it a long time, trying to inure myself to the beauty of his face.

And yes, I found him unbearably beautiful, which was strange, because he was far from a classically beautiful man. He looked rather coarse and rough around the edges. *Animalistic,* my uncooperative mind whispered. Yes, that was exactly what he was, animal male disguised in a suit. The proverbial wolf in sheep's clothing, and me, I was the sheep. I looked at his eyes a long time hoping and wishing it wasn't true, but then I remembered his hand on my arm, his look in the rehearsal hall, and I knew it was true. I was his prey.

As much as he compelled me, I was scared that he wanted me. Really scared. I was pretty sure he wasn't a criminal or a rapist, and the truth was, if I didn't want to see Mr. Norris, I didn't have to. I thought about all the trivia Grégoire had yelled out to me. *He mentors inner city children for Big Brothers and Big Sisters! He donates a ridiculous amount of money to charities. He owns that beautiful new skyscraper over on Marsden. He's made all his millions from nothing, he came from a dirt poor family in the Midwest!*

19

I looked into Mr. Norris's sharp, piercing eyes and tried to imagine him as a young child, poor and hungry. I studied his perfectly tailored suit and crisp white collar and tried to imagine him in ill-fitting clothes, no books or toys to play with, no trips to the doctor when he was sick. I thought I could see it there a little, in the small wrinkles around his eyes. Or maybe he was just tired. I didn't suppose rich, sexy businessmen like him had much use for sleep. I'd grown up poor too, in the Deep South. Raised by a single mother who'd sacrificed everything—her youth, her money, her happiness, so I could dance the way I'd been born to. Just after I'd finally "made it," been hired into a company in Atlanta, she'd been hit by a car walking to work.

I crumpled the picture back up. Ludicrous to think we had anything in common. Just because we were both born poor trashy people didn't mean we belonged together now. All we had in common was that he was a new patron of my dance company, and that he seemed to have a hard on for the talent, which was me. I uncrumpled it and tore it into a thousand pieces so I wouldn't be tempted to look at it again.

I lay in bed late into the night though, trying to erase the photo from my mind. Trying to erase the feeling that we had more in common than dirt poor beginnings.

* * * * *

I was really tired the next day and dragged myself to rehearsals in a funk. I avoided Grégoire and hid out in my dressing room until Elinor arrived, at which point I grabbed my pointe shoes and settled on the floor in the hall. I buried my face in the newspaper, working on the crossword puzzle. I was just tying my shoes, trying to figure out a nine letter word for love, when a pair of expensive loafers came to a stop on the floor beside me.

*Holy shit.*

I looked up at him. My heart pounded in my chest and I had to make myself breathe.

"Hello, Lucy," he said.

"Hello, Mr. Norris."

He frowned a little. "How did you know my name?"

"How did you know mine?" I said right back, before the politeness filter in my brain kicked into gear.

He laughed. "Please call me Matthew."

"Okay, Matthew." But it felt strange to call him Matthew. He looked like someone I should call Mr. Norris, especially looking down his nose at me as he was. I looked back at my puzzle and recommenced tying my shoes. My heart was beating so hard I was sure he would hear it.

"You can do that without even looking." He sounded impressed.

"Yes. I've tied these shoes thousands of times."

I looked up again and he smiled down at me, and I hated how I felt under that breathtaking smile. He offered his hand.

"We haven't met properly, have we?"

I stood up then because he expected me to. It's more accurate to say that he pulled me up, although he did it so naturally that there was no hint of force. But I came to my feet as if something propelled me, and what propelled me was his large, impossibly strong hand. He introduced himself formally, in a deep voice that held only a trace of Midwestern accent.

"Matthew Norris. I'm a big fan of your dancing."

"Lucy Merritt," I replied. "Merritt with two t's."

That seemed to amuse him and he smiled.

"It's nice to meet you, Lucy Merritt with two t's."

I stood there feeling ridiculous, seeing Grégoire out of the corner of my eye, and a few other dancers eavesdropping on our conversation like a bunch of gossip whores.

"What are you doing here again?" I asked, a little peevishly. "Don't you work?"

"Oh, yeah, I work," he said, and the smile he gave me then didn't quite reach his eyes.

"A busy patron of the arts... So you're here checking out your investment?"

"One of them, yes."

21

I looked down at my feet, hating the blush in my cheeks. I was irritated that he made me feel this way. I couldn't quite believe he'd come out and said that to me, especially with half the company watching.

"I find your dancing very inspirational," he continued. You're a true pleasure to watch."

"Thank you," I mumbled to the floor.

"Am I making you uncomfortable?"

"A little." I looked pointedly at the dancers milling around.

"I'm harmless, I promise." He leaned closer and I had to look up at him, look in those piercing eyes that seemed far from harmless to me. "I just appreciate a thing of beauty when I see it, Lucy Merritt."

I panicked. I threw a glance at the other dancers and blushed an even deeper shade of red.

"I'm not a *thing*," I finally managed to say. "And I have to go to class now. Excuse me."

I didn't wait for a reply, just shouldered my bag and practically ran down the hall. And prayed, really prayed that he wouldn't be watching class today. Thankfully he wasn't, although Grégoire frowned at me from across the barre.

"What is wrong with you?" he sniped while we stretched. "You really pissed him off, you know."

"So what? He's a big boy."

"Yes, he's a very big boy and he just donated a lot of money to the theater."

"So that means he can take his pick of the dancers?"

"Oh, come on. He's interested in you. What's so bad about that?"

"He's weird, G!"

"No, he's not. I talked to him after you left. He's a really nice guy. I tried to defend you, you know. I told him you were actually a pretty nice person. Which you used to be."

"I don't need you apologizing on my behalf. Anyway, he called me a *thing*."

"He was complimenting you, Lucy. I heard the whole conversation, believe me."

"Well, he looked at me like I was a thing. Like I was *his* thing. Just because he donates money to the company—"

"Oh, Jesus. A rich guy wants to ask you out. Cry me a river! Don't you see? This is what you need right now, a nice sugar daddy rebound romance."

I stretched with punchy intensity, leaning over to touch each toe. What I needed was for him to shut up, which he never seemed to do. "I don't need anything right now, okay? No men, no dates, no rich creepy guys looking down their noses at me."

"Whatever." He did some effortless jumps, then leaned down to hug his ankles with a sigh. "Lucy, I love you," he said, his voice muffled by his shins. "Don't be mad at me. I just want you to be happy again."

"I love you too, G," I finally muttered. "And I *am* happy," I lied.

# Chapter Two:
# Gala

Mr. Norris did not return to the theater the rest of the week, or at least if he did, I didn't see him. I wondered if he'd call me. I was sure he could get my number if he wanted to. But he didn't and I felt foolish for expecting it. Why would he call when I'd been such a raving bitch to him? I felt partly guilty and partly relieved that he'd disappeared. And yes, partly disappointed, if I was honest with myself. But I didn't dwell on him. I threw myself into my dancing. Harder, faster, more expressive. I pushed my body to quiet my mind.

Georges came back into town after the weekend and he and Grégoire had a passionate reunion. I found myself again on my own every night after work. I had other friends I could have gone out with, but instead I kept to myself. I felt confused about Mr. Norris, and now abandoned too. Abandoned by Grégoire and abandoned by *him*. I left the performance each night in a funk and retreated to my depressing apartment, alone.

I rented a room in part of a gentrified house, a charming old mansion that had been sliced and diced into lots of tiny efficient apartments. They were all weirdly shaped, and some had kitchens in the bedrooms. My room didn't even have a bedroom. It was just one large, odd shaped room. From the outside, the house was a beautiful house. But the inside was not beautiful at all, just strange.

I often thought it was just like people, just like me. Beautiful and impressive on the outside, but sliced and diced and strange within.

So it seemed appropriate for me to occupy this ugly house that, from the outside, appeared lovely and perfect. I stayed in that pathetic little apartment even though I hated it. I stayed long past the time I should have moved on. At least it was cheap and convenient to the theater. If I got out on time, I felt pretty safe walking home. If I got out too late, when the crowds had already thinned, I usually took a cab the few blocks. There were bars and restaurants all around and when they closed, drunk men poured into the streets. Not that I was afraid of a few drunk men, but they could be scary in the wrong time and place.

All that depressing week, during the day, we rehearsed hard for the Gala. We had two Galas a year, one in the fall and one in the spring. It was early October now, chilly weather and brown leaves blowing in the street, so Gala was in the air. Some of the dancers really got into it and worked with the office staff on themes and decorations. They brought in caterers, florists and planners, and in the end it was always a grand and impressive night.

The Gala was an opportunity for the richies to come out to see us. To rub elbows with us and make us feel like whores. They paid for some time with us, forced intimacy, and they got it because money can talk. It's not like they expected a lap dance or anything. Most of the big-money patrons were white-haired old couples, so a lap dance probably would have finished them off. But it felt icky in a way, to smile and socialize with them those two nights a year. Socialize with people we had nothing in common with except that they gave us money to do what they liked. But that was the life of the modern dancer and we were contractually obligated to participate and smile. The theater buzzed with plans and preparation while I obsessed privately about blue eyes and a hand on my elbow.

This fall it was to be a Greek theme. Grégoire and I rehearsed a new work that we would perform exclusively for the guests. I found myself getting caught up in the piece as we rehearsed. It was lyrical, sensuous, the story of a Greek statue come to life from cold, emotionless rock. I loved my costume, an ivory wisp of a gown that floated and spun when I moved. The dance would probably be performed as part of our next season, but for now, only our most generous patrons would have a sneak peek. Gala tickets were expensive because of this exclusivity, and somewhat scarce, which made them even more desirable. The Galas typically sold out before the previous one was even over. Did I expect Mr. Norris to grace us with his presence? Yes. In truth, I did.

That's why, the night of the Gala, I was totally stricken with nerves. I paced in my dressing room, hopped and turned and stretched endlessly. I ran through the motions and tricks of the dance in my head, over and over, and trusted in Grégoire to hold up his end. He watched me from the vanity, eating an apple in silence. I'm sure he knew that Mr. Norris was in my thoughts, but for whatever reason, he didn't tease or badger me about it. Maybe, like me, he was anxious to see him again. Maybe he still nursed the hopeless crush on him that made him push me his way whenever he had the chance. He was so quiet and calm, so unlike his usual self, that I knew he felt as anxious as me.

Yes, that's what it was. We were both *nervous*. How long since we had been nervous together before a performance? I couldn't remember the last time, and I guessed he couldn't either. It gave me a full and hyper feeling, like my chest was going to burst from excitement or dread. It took me back to ten years before, when Grégoire and I had been faceless dancers in the corps of the City Ballet. How far we'd come since then, how much we'd accomplished, and how much we'd aged. I started to feel almost wistful on top of all the nerves. Darling Grégoire, my lover of a partner. I couldn't wait to feel his hands on me, couldn't wait for us to move together, to bring the music and steps to life. But I couldn't say a word to him of why I was nervous and shaky, so we sat in uneasy silence and waited to be called to the wings.

Finally, it was time for us to take our places. This piece began on stage, no flourish of an entrance. We padded out behind the curtain and assumed our still positions. He put his arms around me as I arched into the lovely lines of the statue I would play. He looked at me and winked, squeezing my side with the faintest pressure. How I loved him. *Help me, G*, I said with my wide, frightened eyes. *Help me. I'm nervous. I'm scared. What if he's not here? What if he is?*

Then the curtain opened and between the both of us, the dance unraveled in a perfect arc. No missteps, no awkward lifts or late beats. Together we nailed it and it was intoxicating. When I reached for him, he was there. Always, with Grégoire, the perfect amount of pressure, the exact amount of force to propel me where I needed to go. As for me—my every line was perfection. I prayed that he was watching. He *had* to be. *Please.* I wanted him to want me again, to find me the thing of beauty he'd described even though I'd been so terribly rude. I selfishly wanted him to want me even though I'd pushed him away.

When the piece ended we received a standing ovation, and armfuls and armfuls of flowers that filled my nose with their sweet scent. These Galas were always over the top. Between graceful *reverences*, I scanned the small audience for Mr. Norris, but all I saw was a sea of bald heads and tuxedos, and old matrons in garish silk gowns.

After the curtain call, they brought up the lights in the theater. The wealthy guests swarmed the stage and the champagne and hors-d'oeuvres flowed. I went to the dressing rooms with the other dancers to change and tone down my stage makeup. By the time I returned the party was in full swing. Many deferential and polite patrons of the arts sidled up to me and complimented me. I smiled so much my face started to ache, but I appreciated their words. We had moved them emotionally and that seemed a worthy thing, and their feelings were honest and heartfelt. Grégoire hovered around me, playing the straight guy, except with the gay patrons, who saw through his act with a wink.

But even amidst all the glamour and champagne, the lovely Greek setting and the flattering praise, I grew melancholy because he had not come after all. Our wealthy patron Mr. Norris was nowhere to be found. Around midnight Grégoire brought me some champagne with a sympathetic smile, leaning next to me on the fake Greek balustrade.

"I thought your beau would be here," he said.

My *beau*. What a bizarre word to use for him. It was too gentle a word for what he was. Maybe Grégoire used it ironically, silly French boy. No, Mr. Norris was not my *beau*. In my fantasies at night, *beau* did not describe what he was to me. *Lover. Conqueror. Master. Animal.* Even, ridiculously and embarrassingly sometimes, *husband*. But *beau*, no. It was far too soft for what Mr. Norris was in my dreams.

"No, he's not here. I haven't seen him," I said, shaking myself from my reveries.

"But you wanted him to be here."

"Yes, and so did you," I shot back.

He smiled a wry smile. "You were great tonight, Lu."

"So were you. It was fantastic. It really was."

He took a deep breath. "I had that feeling I haven't had in a while, that something I did was truly beautiful. That something between us grew and developed and was...transformed."

"Oh, G." I hugged him hard. He held on to me as we hid back in the wings and I thought if I was able to cry, I would have cried in G's arms, for so many things. For happiness and sadness, for confusion, for disappointment that lodged like an awful lump in my throat until I thought I would choke.

He let me go and we peeked out at the glamorous spectacle from our hiding place. We lapsed back into our usual sneering comments when he returned with more champagne.

"To being dance whores." He held up his glass to mine.

"To being dance whores," I agreed. That was what it felt like, these events, one hundred percent, even if you'd danced better than you'd danced in your life. *If you pay for me to dance, I'll pretend we're friends.* Poor Grégoire had a suit jacket full of phone numbers, both male and female. I looked around at the blue-haired rich ladies and their pompous rich husbands. Where would I be at eighty years old? At a party like this? Living vicariously through others?

I grew more and more despondent the later it got. I wondered if Mr. Norris had withdrawn his association with the theater. Over me? Silly. But what if he had, because I'd been rude to him, because he scared me? And just as I was mulling over that unpleasant thought, I felt a hand on my elbow, a pressure I remembered. My blood rushed loud in my ears. I turned and there he was, a foot away. He wore that same unflappable, broad smile.

He nodded to my partner first. "Beautiful work tonight, Grégoire." He pronounced his name perfectly in French, the way I never could.

Grégoire blushed like a boy and stammered his thanks. They shook hands like straight men would do, and I worried for a moment that G might faint. But he didn't, and then Mr. Norris turned in my direction.

"And you, Lucy Merritt with two t's. Stunning. I really don't have words."

I didn't have words either. I stared at him, speechless, sick with embarrassment and lust. He may have been acting like our last conversation never happened, but I still burned with mortification over it. He turned from me, made more polite small talk with Grégoire, and then, with a strange subtle agility, he dismissed him. As Grégoire left us, he shot me a warning look. *Don't fuck this up, you little dork.*

I turned back to Mr. Norris. *Matthew.* I'd called him Mr. Norris so many times in disdain. I'd never remember to call him Matthew now.

"Mr. Norris?" I began. *Ugh, you idiot.* "Um, Matthew, the last time we talked...please forgive me."

"There's nothing to forgive."

"Yes, there is. I was so rude to you. I apologize, I really do."

He smiled, that kind, easy smile, and leaned close so my eyes fixed on his lips.

"I apologize for calling you a thing," he said. "Although, in my defense, I did call you a thing of *beauty*."

I looked up at him and somehow managed a smile. His own smile was infectious, but he still scared me. Why did he scare me so much? I couldn't put my finger on it. *Wild, animal male,* I thought. *Dangerous and unpredictable.* And here we were, alone together back in the wings where no one could see us. Mr. Norris, the wild animal, and me, his prey.

But he wasn't wild. In fact, his manners were impeccable. He took my glass and offered to bring me more champagne. He left, trusting me to wait there for him, and I did, although my brain was pleading with me to fly.

When he returned with our full glasses of bubbly, I waited for the typical moronic toast. *To dance whores,* I envisioned him saying, holding up his glass. But no silly toasts or comments were forthcoming. He only sipped his champagne and looked out with me as the room began to thin.

"Where were you?" I asked finally, to fill the awkward silence. "Earlier tonight? When the party began?"

"You missed me?"

I blushed a thousand shades of red.

"Well, you remember that I *work*," he said. "I had a phone call I had to take and unfortunately it went on and on. I did see your performance though, and I'm glad for that. It was lovely." And the way he said *lovely*, it wasn't gushing or fake, just hopelessly kind.

I turned my head away in self-preservation. If he didn't leave me soon, I would humiliate myself over him.

"How long have you been dancing?" he asked. He had a strange way of talking to me, sort of formal and stern, but his voice never rose above that quiet, calm tone.

"I've danced forever. Since before I can remember, I've been dancing."

"Did your parents dance, too?"

"No. Why?"

He shrugged. "I don't know. I just wonder where this kind of talent comes from. Genetics, nurturing? Or just hard work?"

I stared out at the rows of seats in the theater. "I've worked pretty hard."

"Hmm. I'm sure you have." He looked at me again like he was looking at a *thing*. "How long will you continue to dance, Lucy?"

"Until I can't anymore," I answered without pause. He looked hard at me then. Was he trying to guess how long I had left? "Have you ever danced?" I blurted out to distract him from thinking about my age.

That made him laugh, loud and hard. "Oh, no. Fortunately for humanity, no, I never have. And I never will."

His self-deprecating words made me giggle. "Maybe if you'd had lessons."

"Yes, maybe." He laughed with a nod.

I bit my lip. I had no idea what else to say. He rendered me speechless and I can't say how. I could see how he excelled at business. He had a manner about him that had me at his feet.

"So, do you like these things, these 'Galas'?" he asked.

I felt embarrassed, as if he'd somehow overheard the snide comments Grégoire and I had made all night.

"No, not really."

"Why don't you?"

I wanted to say something cutesy and glib, but the way he stared compelled me to absolute truth.

"Because they feel fake. Artificial."

"And you don't like that? Make-believe?"

He didn't say it suggestively, but my mind flew to the silly make-believe fantasies he'd spurred in my mind. Or maybe he did know. Ugh, why couldn't I stop blushing? I could feel it creeping up into my cheeks again.

"I don't know," I mumbled. "I like make-believe sometimes. When I'm in the mood."

"Hmm. And what puts you in the mood for make-believe?"

I didn't answer. I couldn't. I finally shrugged and said, "I don't know."

"I'm not big on make-believe," he said, looking out over the crowd.

"But dance is make-believe, isn't it?" I waved my arm around at the pomp and glitter that surrounded us. "And you're here, dressed up in your tuxedo and bow tie."

"Well, sometimes you just play along, don't you?" And by *you*, I guessed he meant people in general, but I felt it directed at me. *You just play along, Lucy, don't you?*

The champagne was making me warm. I rubbed my cheeks.

"Are you tired?" he asked in a strangely mesmerizing voice. It sounded like an inappropriately intimate thing to say, because what it really sounded like to me was that he thought I should go to bed. *His* bed.

"I'm just getting a little drunk. It doesn't take much."

"I guess not," he said, running his eyes up and down my body. "Someone as little as you."

"I'm not little."

"You're smaller than me." It was true, I was quite a bit smaller than him—the strong, tall, animal man beside me in his expensive shoes and bespoke designer tux.

"I may be small, but I'm strong."

"Yes. Strong, I believe. Perhaps even stronger than me."

I looked at his broad shoulders, his solid thighs. Even his hands were strong. Stronger than him? Not likely. He moved a little closer. He was so virile, so sexy. It had to be the alcohol that made me feel like throwing myself at him. Why had I drunk so much?

"Well, you're little and strong, and you're a hell of a dancer," he said, as if that settled things. I watched him sip champagne, perfect and rich, and I knew he thought for sure he would have me.

"Yes, I do dance," I said, shaking my head to clear it. "But I do a lot more than that. I'm a lot more than just a dancer, and I can do a lot more than pretty pony tricks."

He looked at me, his eyes narrowed. I quickly looked away. Why had I said that? "I think I'm drunk, Mr. Norris."

"Matthew."

"Matthew, I'm sorry. I'm just tired."

"Why don't you let me drive you home?"

"No," I said too quickly, then blushed red and hot again. "No, um...we're supposed to stay until the end."

32

"That's a shame. If you're tired." He spoke sympathetically although I'm sure he knew I lied. Maybe that's why he looked at me sympathetically. *Poor girl. Poor little cowardly liar.*

"Well, I won't exhaust you with more conversation." His tone was changed, distant and cool. He looked at me with muted reprobation.

"I'm sorry," I blurted miserably. "I really, really am."

"For what?"

"For being so rude, when you're just being nice to me. I don't know why I do it. I really don't."

"Oh, it's probably just a matter of being tired, and maybe a little nervous and scared."

"Nervous and scared about what?"

"Nervous and scared about me, I suppose, and what I might want from you. Yes?"

"I'm not nervous and scared," I protested without much conviction, because he was scaring me to death. His gaze pinned me and again I squelched the urge to flee. "I have nothing to give you, honestly. So, I don't know. I don't even know what you're talking about."

"Don't you?"

"No, I don't, Mr. Norris."

"Matthew," he said again. He looked at me, cool and thoughtful. "Okay, Lucy. Okay."

He rubbed his lips, the first nervous gesture I'd seen him do. "Okay, Lucy," he repeated again, and then he turned and walked away. I fought the urge to follow him, to run after him apologizing. Again, I'd repelled him. Why? Why was I such a mess around him?

Why did he make me so afraid?

As soon as I thought he wouldn't see me, I ran all the way back to my dressing room and slammed the door. I sat at the table where Grégoire had lounged earlier and put my head down in my arms. I couldn't face Grégoire or Mr. Norris or any of them. I couldn't face anyone out there in that crowd. I hid in that dressing room long past midnight, until I was sure every single one of them was gone. I waited and hid and trembled, coward that I was.

# Chapter Three:
# Coffee

When I finally left the theater, the cleaning staff had to let me out. It was late, dark and quiet. I think it was probably almost one. The bars hadn't closed yet so I decided to chance the short walk home. The way I felt that night, I dared anybody to come my way. I felt the way I felt when I woke up from my nightmares, like I desperately had to cry and scream when I couldn't do either.

I stalked down the empty sidewalk thinking about him, trying to understand why I felt the way I felt. And what on earth must the man think of me? That I was a train wreck, unbalanced and weird. That I was an immature bitch, not the talented dancer he thought I was at all. All the things I hated about myself, I was sure he saw them quite well.

I wrapped my coat more tightly around me. It had been a hard few weeks for me. I wondered about Joe, if he had married the love of his life yet. Kim, his ex. Did Kim know what love was? Joe said she did. Did she really love Joe? Kim and Joe both seemed like grown-ups, so much wiser and smarter than me. I could dance and I guess I was pretty, but what else was I?

A liar. A coward. A mess.

I heard some voices then, male voices, low and nasty. Dangerous laughter. I lifted my head to see a few men standing by a stoop between me and my house. I put my head back down. I wouldn't let them scare me, *I wouldn't*, but my body rebelled. My body felt fear. My heart pounded fast because of the way they looked at me, like they were going to *do* something. Like they were on the edge of action, making a decision. When I passed by, they fell into step behind me. My blood whooshed painfully in my ears.

"Hey," said one of them.

I kept walking.

"Hey, I'm talking to you, bitch."

My breath backed up in my chest. Should I start running? They would catch me in an instant and probably have a good laugh over it. So I didn't run. I just kept walking.

"Hey, you little bitch. You too good to talk to us, you skinny little whore?"

I kept walking, one foot in front of the other. I might have shaken my head, a pointless gesture. If they were going to do something, so be it. I wasn't going to run and I wasn't going to scream. I was just going to keep walking, one foot in front of the other, because I'd survive this or not, just like everything else.

Then I saw two more men approaching from the other direction. Oh great, it was a party now. Come one, come all, some girl is trying to walk home alone and it's after midnight, so she's fair game. But then the men behind me stopped and crossed the street. I soon saw why. The man coming toward me was one of the most threatening, muscular men I'd ever seen, and next to him, even dressed in a tuxedo, Mr. Norris looked pretty threatening himself.

"Come on," was all he said to me, and he put his hand on my elbow like he'd done twice before. This time he guided me over to a black SUV and pushed me into the back seat. No, he didn't push me. He just opened the door and helped me in. I guess it was the fury on his face that made me feel manhandled. He got in beside me and slammed the door. I sat in silence, not looking at him.

"Felt like getting raped tonight?" he finally muttered.

"There were no cabs. I left the theater too late."

"I offered you a ride home." I watched the muscle man leaning against the door outside, lazily rolling a cigarette.

"Who is that?" I asked.

"My driver."

We both sat there, two feet apart. It was chilly in the car and I shivered.

"Are you all right?" he asked.

"What are you *doing* here?"

"What do you think?" he snapped.

And that was enough. I started to cry. The sound of my sobs disturbed me but there was no way to silence them. I pulled my coat around me like I could pull myself together, but I couldn't. I couldn't stop. It had been far too long since I'd cried.

He sat still and silent next to me and watched me, his eyebrows drawn together in a frown. I cried forever, months worth of tears. I cried staring out his front window, then dropped my head in my hands until my fingers were slippery with tears. How long had I needed to cry like this? An eternity. I cried until I was breathless, until I felt weak. He didn't try to soothe me or hold me, although he did eventually offer me a tissue. I realized he had dug in my own bag to get it. He held it in his lap, my big ugly dance bag, while I dried the tears and blew my nose. After a moment he offered me another one, and then another again.

"Thank you for helping me," I said when I was finally calm enough.

"Are you finished now?"

"I don't know. I'm sorry. I don't know why I act this way around you."

"Don't you?" He flicked his wrist impatiently and looked away with a frown.

"What do you want from me?"

"Let's get some coffee, Lucy. We need to talk."

At some unseen signal, the driver walked off down the street, and Matthew climbed into the driver's seat while I stayed in the back.

"Why do you have a driver, if you can drive?" I asked.

37

"He's more than my driver." And he left it at that.

* * * * *

He drove me to a coffee house right near the theater. I'd never noticed it before but he seemed to know it well. I must have looked like a mess as we waited at the counter for our drinks, but I really didn't care. It was after two by this point, and the whole world seemed to have taken on an air of unreality.

He led me to an isolated table in the back. Low music played as we sat in darkness and clouds of cigarette smoke. There was a hum of people talking, laughing. They were night time party people, wide awake and full of life.

But not me. I was beyond tired. I was so tired that I was painfully and frantically awake. I sipped my coffee and stared down into my lap. He sat across from me, leaning back in his chair, looking like a million bucks. He'd taken off his jacket and loosened his silk bow tie so that it hung perfectly over his open collar. His short blond hair was ruffled just so. It looked like all he had to do to style it perfectly was to run his fingers through it. He watched me. Stared at me, really.

"You don't talk much," he finally commented under his breath.

"I don't know what to say. I'm sorry I cried for fifteen minutes in the backseat of your car."

"It was more like thirty minutes."

"It's been a really hard couple of weeks," I said.

"Has it?"

"Let me put it this way. I was supposed to have been on my honeymoon this week."

"Your honeymoon?" I could tell he was taken aback. "Well, what happened? Do tell."

"Do you want the long version or the short version?"

"The true version."

"Do you think I'd lie to you?"

"No, not really. I'm just a lover of truth. It thrills me," he explained in an ironic tone.

"Okay, then." I took a deep breath. "My fiancé invited his ex-girlfriend to our wedding. When she came into town, he fell back in love with her. He cancelled our wedding and took her on our honeymoon."

He thought a moment. "Was it to have been a big wedding?"

"No, a very small one."

"So he wasn't sure all along."

"No. I guess not."

"And neither were you," he said, and it wasn't a question.

"No."

"Why did you get married, if you weren't sure?"

"We didn't get married."

"You almost did."

"Are you really going to lecture me? You haven't exactly got a stellar marital record yourself."

His eyes narrowed.

"At least, I read online that you were divorced," I finished weakly under his darkening gaze.

"Well, that's not fair. It seems you know more about me than I know about you. Now you have to tell me something about yourself. Something deeply personal and humiliating, if we're going to be fair."

"I just told you I was left at the altar. That's not humiliating enough?"

"Did you love him?"

"Did you love her?"

He didn't answer me at first. Then he said, "Yes, I loved her very much. She didn't love me though. When you have money..." His voice trailed off, and then he looked right into my eyes. "There was no truth between us. Did you love your fiancé?"

I shook my head slowly.

"Why not? Why didn't you love him?"

"Because he didn't make me happy." I stopped and shook my head. "No. Because he didn't know the real me. Because there was no truth between us," I finally admitted.

He looked over at me, leaning forward on his elbows.

"Would you like to hear some truth, Lucy? Right now?"

"Yes, that would be really refreshing."

"I'd like to bend you over, stick my fingers up inside you, and see if you really can do more than pony tricks."

My mouth dropped open. I closed it a moment later and stood to leave.

"Sit down," he said in a way that halted me in my tracks.

I turned back. "You're being rude to me."

"You were rude to me too, weren't you? More than once. Now we're even. Sit down."

For some reason, I did as he ordered. I sat back down across from him, my gaze in my lap.

"Lucy, what do you think is happening here?"

"I really don't know. I wish I did!"

"I think you do know, but I'll play along. What did you think of me? How do you feel around me?"

"I... I..."

"Think first, and then tell me the truth."

"You scare me."

"Why do I scare you?"

I looked down at my hands, swallowed hard. "Because of how you make me feel."

"How do I make you feel?"

I shook my head. I couldn't admit it, never.

"Answer me," he pressed. "We won't get anywhere until you talk to me. Just say it."

"I...you... You make me... I want you to... I want..."

My voice trailed off, my face on fire. *I want you to be an animal. I want you to eat me alive.*

"Can't you say it?" he asked. "I'll tell you, Lucy, since you seem unable to form the words." He paused and looked right at me.

"You want me to master you. You want me to rough you up a little, don't you?"

I bit my lip. I had no idea what to answer to that. Again, I felt dangerously close to tears, even after all the tears I'd already shed. I brought my cup to my lips and drank the coffee to assuage the tightness in my throat.

"Your fiancé, he didn't understand, did he? What you like. What you need."

"I don't understand either."

"You will," he said.

I blinked, looking at him. He stared back at me without a hint of a smile.

"Do you know what a submissive is?"

*Breathe. Swallow. Don't cry.*

"Answer me, Lucy."

"I...maybe... I think I do."

"Have you ever been submissive to someone? Your fiancé?"

"No, I...no."

"No, he had no idea, did he, what he had in his hands? You've never been disciplined, trained? Controlled?"

His sharp perverse words brought a flood of warmth between my legs. My nipples tightened under my shirt as I shook my head.

"Answer me out loud, Lucy," he said. "Look at me."

I looked up in abject mortification. "No, I never have been."

"Would you like to be? Look at me," he insisted. My eyes met his and he held them hard. "Would you like to be?"

"I don't know!"

"*I don't know.* That means, *no, I'm too scared.*"

I closed my eyes and lowered my head. "I already told you I was scared."

"How long?" he asked then.

"How long what?"

"How long have you wanted it? To be dominated, to be tied up and beaten and fucked?"

I shook my head. How do you answer a question like that?

"A pretty little girl like you couldn't find someone to take you in hand? You'll settle for some vanilla fuckboy who was still in love with his ex?"

"Why do you care so much?"

"I'm sure you can puzzle that out if you try." His jaw clenched a little and he looked away from me, scratching his neck with a frustrated sigh. I looked at him, beautiful Mr. Matthew Norris, sitting there in his tuxedo and his unkempt tie. My mind spun with a thousand questions, but there was one question I had to ask right away.

"How did you know?"

"The same way you knew. And you did know, Lucy, from the moment you saw me. I can't explain how." He leaned very close, speaking low. "You set off alarms. Look at me."

I dragged my gaze to his.

"When you started talking about pony tricks, I nearly laughed out loud."

"I'm not into that animal stuff."

"I have no interest in playing ponies, believe me. I have no interest in ninety percent of the stupid games dominants play with their submissives."

*Dominants. Submissives.* I felt like I'd just fallen ass-backwards into the life I'd wanted but thought didn't really exist. I had no idea people really did the things I wanted. I couldn't believe he might want to do them to me.

"What *are* you interested in?" I asked.

"Owning your body and doing whatever I want to it."

There it was again, the hot rush of wetness between my legs. I looked at him from under my lashes while my cheeks burned crimson. He wanted my body, wanted to do things to it. That man sitting there, virile and dangerous, he wanted *me*. I shivered and pressed my thighs together. Somehow I couldn't phrase a response. I could barely draw breath.

"Is that something that might interest you, Lucy?"

I stared down at my hands twisting in my lap. "I don't know."

"No more *I don't know*'s," he said. "Yes or no?"

"Maybe. I can't say. I don't know what you want to do to me."

"I'll do a lot of things to you. I'm only asking you if it's something you'd like to try."

My mind raced in circles, stimulated by horniness and caffeine. All around us, regular people talked and laughed casually, but my life had changed. I scrabbled for words, my thoughts in a tangle. I lifted my cup to take a slow drink, buying time.

"Is this how you pick up all your partners?" I asked. "You give them this tough little talking to?"

He tapped his fingers on the table impatiently, as if he already owned me and I was already making him mad. "First of all, this is far from tough. And secondly, I haven't picked up a partner in six years. I had a girlfriend and we recently broke up. I would have thought you knew that from your reading about me."

"She was your submissive?"

"That's none of your business."

"What happened? Why did she leave you after six years?"

He frowned down into his coffee, then looked back up at me with narrowed eyes.

"She didn't enjoy it. Power exchange. I thought she did. But she did it for me, for my money, I guess."

"All those years?"

"Yes, Lucy. Now you see why truth thrills me. I've lived without it for far too long."

Truth. He talked about it an awful lot.

"If you're so rich, why don't you just buy a hooker?"

"Because I don't want a hooker. I want you."

"How do you know? You don't even know me."

"I know enough. I know that your body turns me on. I know you'd get off on submitting to me."

"That's all you need in a girlfriend?"

"A girlfriend?" He laughed. "Sorry, I don't want another girlfriend. I just want a submissive to put through her paces. I'm giving you truth here, Lucy. I'm not saying that to hurt you."

So it showed then, the hurt and humiliation I felt at his words. My face burned with it. I felt like I'd just been kicked.

"I want to use your body because I find it beautiful and perfect. I just want to play with you, but I think you'll enjoy it all the same. And if you want," he added as an afterthought, "I'll pay you for your time."

I made a nauseated face.

"Yes, I thought that's how you'd feel. Anyway, the pleasure will be payment enough."

My God. My God. My God. *My God.*

"Okay," I said. "Here's some truth for you. I've never fucked someone I'm not in a relationship with."

"Oh, we'd be in a relationship. Just a non-traditional one. Do you really want another boyfriend? So soon?"

I thought for a minute. God, no. I didn't.

"And it wouldn't just be fucking, Lucy. Exchanging power is erotically charged, yes, and it can be deeply sexual, but it's about much more than getting off. It will meet needs you didn't even realize you had. It will meet needs for you and me both. And it would be safe, of course. Everything we did together would be absolutely safe and consensual."

"Consensual?"

"Yes, it would have to be. You know what I mean by consensual? You would be there because you want to be. And we would use safe words."

"Safe words?" No explanation was forthcoming. "What are safe words?" I was a little afraid to find out.

"Safe words are words that keep people like you safe."

"Safe from what?"

"Safe from people like me."

He leaned back then, stretching casually, as if we discussed nothing more unusual than the weather. I sat across from him and wrestled with my feelings. Anger, indignation, shame, curiosity, lust. Then his eyes returned to mine and he spoke with intensity in his voice.

"You know, I want to own you and I want to use you. I want your obedience and beauty. But what I really want is for you to find joy in it too."

"Joy?"

"Yes, joy. And perhaps, at times, a little pain," he said with a faint smile. "I'm not going to lie to you. There's a good bit of the sadist in me. There will be times that I'll purposely hurt you, times that I'll try to make you cry. There will be ups and downs, and, well, a considerable amount of pain. But somehow I think you'll enjoy it."

My God, that I could even be sitting here considering it. But his warnings about pain didn't frighten me at all. In fact, he was right. The idea was exciting me. What kind of pervert was I? He must have seen that I was weakening, that even in my fear, my uncertainty, I wanted to say yes.

"We could start slowly," he said. "I would teach you and guide you. I know right now you're afraid of the unknown. You barely know me, I realize that. I barely know you. But there are some very elemental desires you and I share. And if we get to know each other better and discover that we don't suit each other, we'll be truthful to one another, won't we? Can you promise me that?"

I thought about six years of deception, the toll it would take on someone's trust. "Yes, I would be truthful to you," I said with conviction. "I would always tell you the truth."

His expression deepened as he looked at me. "You have no idea how those words make me feel. Because I believe you, little girl."

*Little girl.* He had no idea how *those* words made me feel, the tingle that raced across my skin. I desperately wanted to be his little girl, his lover, his toy, whatever he wanted me to be. But he'd warned me I couldn't be his girlfriend. Would everything else be enough?

"What do you think?" he asked.

"You drive a hard bargain."

He laughed, an exhalation of nervous energy. "I'm trying. I really am. I suppose this isn't what you expected."

"You planned all along to ask me this when you invited me here?"

45

"I started putting words together the very second I laid eyes on you."

That made me shiver a little. All that time, he'd been thinking of doing these things to me. "When was that? When you first laid eyes on me?"

He rubbed his forehead and sighed. "It was a while ago."

I stared into my coffee, overwhelmed by the moment, by the decision. It seemed to me that the next words I chose to say would alter my life in a significant way, whether they were *yes* or *no*.

"I know that I've shocked you," he said. "Why don't you take some time to think it over? Really think about what I've said, think about what you want to do. Next Saturday night I'll be sitting right here. If you want to give it a try, take a cab here and meet me. If you don't, then stay away and I promise I'll leave you alone."

I nodded. Yes. I needed time to think. Time to come to terms with the decision I knew I'd eventually make, but wasn't quite ready to make yet, not out loud.

"But Lucy," he warned, "if you show up here, I'll take it to mean that you're ready to begin. You'll need to bring your overnight bag. Do you understand?"

I nodded.

"Answer me out loud."

"Yes, I understand," I said, blushing hot. "But I can't get here before 10:45, after the show."

"Okay then," he said, nodding. "I'll meet you here at 10:45. At eleven o'clock, if you haven't shown up, we'll understand each other."

He reached out and cradled my face in one of his hands. His fingers felt cool and firm against my flushed skin. He looked right into my eyes. I felt a strange feeling of closeness to him, I suppose because he understood me so well. "Either way, I've really enjoyed this hour with you. Tears and all. I think you're ridiculously beautiful and sweet. Well, maybe not sweet," he said with a wry smile. "But honest. I appreciate your truthfulness. You have no idea how much."

He released me and I held his gaze, awed and confused. "I've never been so truthful to anyone in my life."

"Neither have I, in quite some time." He turned away, looking out at the crowd around us. "I hate to ask it, but in these matters discretion is very important. I'd appreciate very much if you wouldn't share our...truth telling with anyone who doesn't need to know."

"I won't. I wouldn't," I promised. "Although my mother told me never to keep secrets for strangers."

He looked at me very directly. "We aren't strangers anymore."

He drove me home then, and watched from his car until he saw my light come on. I looked from the window but I didn't wave. I watched him pull back into traffic and wondered what he was thinking at that moment, because my own thoughts were wild. It was 3:45 when I finally laid down, but sleep wouldn't come. I fantasized instead of his hands on me doing vulgar things. My fantasies were vague and salacious, because I had no idea what he would actually do to me.

And yes, I was quite certain that he was going to do something to me. Before we'd even left the coffee house, when he'd helped me from my chair and guided me to the door with his hand pressed to the small of my back, I had known. I had made up my mind. The words were right on the tip of my tongue, the words to plead with him to take me, that I wanted to be his, that I wanted him to use me, that I wanted him to take me right home. That I wanted him to hurt me with his big, strong hands, that I knew I would enjoy it, that I wanted to try. I didn't tell him though because he'd told me to think it over, and already I was anxious to obey. So I would think it over until Saturday, as he'd asked me to do, and then I'd go to him at the coffee house, and then...

Then what? What would go on between us? How would it feel? Would he hurt me? How much? Would I enjoy it? Would I feel, as he had suggested, *joy*? Finally, too tired to keep my eyes open, I started to drift into dreams. The strange fantasies subsided, replaced by one single word. *Matthew. Matthew. Matthew. Matthew.* I was already gone for him, totally gone. I was naively, desperately crushed on Matthew Norris even though he'd told me very bluntly he didn't want a girlfriend. And I believed he meant it when he said that to me, but I thought that would change. I was sure if I was good enough, I could change his mind.

\* \* \* \* \*

Oh, my fucking back. It was ridiculous. I looked up at Pietro toiling away at his canvas and I could tell he was in that zone, that place he went to sometimes. There was no way I could stop him now, although my muscles ached for relief. What kind of art model would I be, to interrupt him in his moments of genius? A less sore art model, I thought dismally.

I'd sat for him all day Sunday, then on Monday for a few more hours. Now it was Friday night and he'd called me, his voice filled with urgency. "I'm so close to finished," he'd begged. "Lucy, please, you must come!"

So here I lay at nearly midnight, aching and twitchy. I let my mind wander, a trick I'd learned from dance. When something was torturous and took excruciating effort, you just let your mind wander away from the pain. You can probably guess the place to which my mind wandered. It wandered to Matthew, who I planned to see the next night.

I was impatient, yes, but a little scared too. Would he be happy with me once he had me in his arms? Would he realize he'd made a big mistake and end things? I had no doubt he would end things abruptly if he wasn't pleased with me. I would do everything I could to prevent that from happening, but there was only so much I could give, only myself as I was. If he decided I wasn't good enough...

I daydreamed there on the cold hard floor of a painter's studio and pictured Matthew sitting somewhere more comfortable thinking about me. Maybe his mind strayed to me during some important developer business meeting, or as he sat in the backseat of his car on the phone while his beefy driver drove him around. That driver, I wondered what was up with him. Maybe he procured drugs for Matthew. Or women. Hookers. I couldn't imagine someone like him staying continent for long. If he'd broken up with his girlfriend, what had he been doing in the meantime? I would make him wear condoms, wouldn't let him near me without them, that was certain. There was no way I'd give in on that. Everything else, well...how far would I go for him? How far would he try to make me go, and what would he do? How much time had he spent since he'd met me, thinking about how he was going to *use* me, as he'd said? Did he already know what would go on? Had he long ago planned exactly what would occur? Or would he make it up as he went along, based on my reactions?

My reactions. What might those be? I had no idea, because I still had no idea what he would do to me. I'd read books about BDSM. I had a general idea of what people did in the world of dominance and submission, but he'd scoffed and claimed that most of those things didn't interest him. That all he cared about was using me, making me his own. His own *thing*. I smiled, remembering when he'd called me a thing of beauty. I'd told him peevishly that I wasn't a thing. He was probably thinking even then that he would have the last laugh. He had probably thought to himself, *well, Lucy, we'll see.*

# Chapter Four:
# Guidelines

I drifted through the Saturday shows lost in a world of my own. Grégoire knew I was meeting our rich patron for coffee, but I told him nothing else. I had actually planned to tell Grégoire everything, reveal everything we'd talked about that strange night, but in the end, I kept it from him. It wasn't that I didn't trust Grégoire to keep a secret. If I had asked him to, he would have kept any secret of mine to the grave. Nor was I ashamed to tell him. I shared everything with him, every humiliation and every triumph. In fact, I shared so much with him, I couldn't quite believe I was keeping something this big to myself. I guess I was afraid he might tell me not to go, that I shouldn't let him use me, that it wasn't safe. That something was wrong with me for wanting a relationship like this. All of the things I wouldn't let myself think. All those things that were probably, unfortunately, true.

So I said goodbye to Grégoire by the stage door and climbed in a cab at 10:40 sharp. I had showered and carefully shaved, and scented and perfumed every inch of my body. I'd painstakingly made myself up to look alluring and sexy. I had applied my very best dark red fuck-me lipstick, and put on jeans and a sweater that hugged my curves. Under my clothes, I had on things I hoped he'd find exciting and beautiful. A black silk thong, a matching black balconette bra. I could have dressed up in more risqué trappings but I had a sense it might upset him, to take that initiative myself.

All too soon, the cab pulled up at the coffee house. I paid the driver with bills rustling in trembling hands. I stood in the cold night air for a couple of minutes outside on the sidewalk, then I just couldn't bear the anxiety and I went in.

I was assailed right inside the door with the familiar smell of smoke and coffee, the sickly sweet scent of clove cigarettes. I swallowed hard and started the long walk to the back. What if he wasn't there? What if he was there, watching from some hidden place, laughing with friends as I made a fool of myself returning to report to him? I looked around furtively, embarrassed and agitated. I took in all the happy people talking and laughing with their friends and for one split second of a moment, I almost turned and ran.

But then I neared the table and he was there, and it comforted me greatly that he looked nervous too. He sat rigid and still, looking down into his coffee. On the other side of the table was another cup, presumably for me.

He looked up, and my heart leaped. *My heart leaped.* So trite, but that's actually what it did. My breath caught and I had to choke a little to get it going again. He looked stunning dressed in casual clothes, jeans and a sweater. I'd only ever seen him in business suits and tuxedos, powerful clothes of status and formality. But in jeans and a sweater, you could see he was a man, just a beautiful man, potent and attractive. He looked up at me, and in that second the worry left his face, replaced with something else, something priceless—a broad smile of palpable relief.

He wanted me. *He wanted me.* It was written clearly all over his face. I walked the rest of the way to the table, propelled by sheer gladness, and I returned his smile with an uncontrolled smile of my own. He stood up to pull my chair out when I was close enough. So formal and old fashioned. I turned to mush. He sat back down and gazed at me. I waited for him to say something but he just stared.

"Is this for me?" I asked, gesturing to the cup in front of me.

"It's what you ordered last week. You can get something else if you like."

"No, it's perfect. Thanks." He'd remembered what I ordered and ordered it again for me. *Sigh.* I picked it up, warming my hands with it, and my face, which was still cold from outside.

"You should wear a coat," he chided. "That little sweater wouldn't keep Satan warm."

I laughed, breathing in the coffee and letting it warm me, the coffee he'd gotten for me.

"So you came."

I nodded.

"When did you decide to come?"

I thought of my recent impulse to flee.

"About a minute ago."

He smiled, and his eyes moved over me slowly. "Are you scared?"

"Yes."

He fidgeted and rubbed his cheek.

"Drink your coffee," he said.

I added some sugar to it and stirred. He watched, taking a deep drink of his own.

"I went to the show tonight."

"Did you?"

"Yes. I often do."

"To see me?"

"Yes. To look at you." The way he said it made me wet. He watched me. *He wants me, that man right there.* Oh my God. He smiled, perhaps sensing my anxiety. "Tonight, Lucy, we'll mostly talk. Nothing too wild."

I nodded, thankful to hear it.

"Answer me out loud," he said. "I prefer it."

"Yes, Matthew," I amended, blushing.

"You have a lot to learn but I think you're a pretty smart girl."

"I hope I'm good enough for you."

He took a deep breath, a very loud one. From the look on his face I half expected him to stand up and walk out. But instead he reached across the table. "Give me your hand."

I did, and he took it, and we could both feel it shaking in his grip.

"Don't be afraid." He spoke so quietly it was hard to hear above the hum around us. He turned my hand over in his palm, studying it like there were secrets there. "Just always tell me the truth. Okay? Always."

"I will."

"Are you finished?" he asked, letting go of me. "I'd like to go somewhere more private before we really talk."

\* \* \* \* \*

We went out to his car, and again his driver was missing in action. The first thing he did was roll down the windows.

"Lucy Merritt, if you ever show up to see me again smelling like a French whorehouse, you'll be sorry you did."

How embarrassing. I was already a fuck up. He kept the windows down the whole way to his house. When we arrived he pulled me to the sink in his kitchen. "Wash it off. I want to smell you, not some perfumed-up whore."

I tried to wash it all off, which wasn't easy, partly because I was so distracted by his spectacular house. It was difficult too because it was mostly on my clothes, but I did my best. I guess it was all right, because when I came out, he sniffed me and muttered, "Good enough."

Then he took my arm and led me to a door in the hallway. "We'll always play in the basement," he explained. We made our way down the carpeted stairwell, and I guess I expected him to take me to a dungeon of sorts. Black and forbidding, tricked out with crosses and beams and chains hanging from hooks in the ceiling. But the room he took me to wasn't a dungeon at all. It looked more like an art salon. Or a really cool and modern funeral home, done in crisp and textured neutrals.

He told me to look around, to look at everything. I walked around but I didn't dare touch. The walls were upholstered with fabric, velvety drapes in taupe. There were huge, comfortable sofas that I tried out, sitting down on them, and as it turned out, that was the only chance I'd get. I didn't know it yet, but only Matthew ever sat on them, while I knelt or lay supine at his feet, or bent over an ottoman with my ass in the air. But they were very nice and comfy, the matching ottomans scattered around the room in several heights and sizes. He pointed out the eyebolts near the bottom of each one. "I'll strap you to these when I beat you or fuck you, sometimes." I just nodded when he said it, like that was perfectly great. *Oh, wow, Matthew, bolting me to an ottoman. That's a spectacular idea.*

When I was done drooling over the cushiony sofas and ottomans, he took me over to a large armoire in the corner. It had drawers full of leather restraints, straps and cuffs, sex toys and paraphernalia that made my eyes go wide. The many things he showed me in that armoire both shocked and titillated me. I was so hot by that time, I wanted him to take me then and there. I was really close to begging for it but I managed to keep quiet, the obedient little slave. He showed me paddles and crops and canes, and tooled leather straps just as thick as the paddles. He showed me delicate but painful looking clips and clamps. He put one on my finger to give me an idea how it would feel. It pinched a little, but nothing I couldn't bear. "It will feel different on your nipples and your clit," he cautioned me. I swallowed hard. Of course it would.

Then he showed me dildos and butt plugs and other toys that terrified me. They were far too large to ever fit up inside me. "You'll like these best of all," he said with a smile. He showed me a shelf full of lubricants, all different types. Scented, flavored, heavy duty, light duty. He showed me one bottle with a gleam in his eye. "This kind will make you itch, for when you've really been bad."

Yes, my eyes must have been like saucers looking into that armoire. He showed me everything proudly, like the curator of some perverse museum. When I'd had a good look at it all he tilted my face to his. He looked into my eyes and I felt shy and exposed. It was very, very hard not to look away.

"Look at me," he insisted. When my eyes were fixed on his, he spoke in a low voice. "So what do you think, Lucy Merritt? If you're going to be my lover, you'll have to endure all these things."

And the way he said *lover* made me absolutely thrill, and then that word *endure*, it sounded sexy as hell to my ears. I searched for my voice, for what to say. He pressed me some more, his voice goading me.

"Are you sure you don't want to run home? Climb back into bed with your worn out copy of *The Story of O*?"

"No. I want to stay here."

"Okay then. Let's stay."

He led me to the center of the room, then walked away, talking over his shoulder. "Face me. Take off your clothes. Everything. Put them over by the door."

I stood still for just a second, and then I did exactly as he said. I took off my sweater, my jeans, my shirt and socks and shoes, until I wore only my thong and bra, and then I looked up at him, my face flaming red.

"Everything but the panties," he said from the sofa, where he sat watching every move I made. I removed my bra and placed everything by the door, thankful at least for the small scrap of fabric between my legs. As I walked, I had to make an effort to move my limbs. I had been naked for Pietro so many times, practically naked in dance costumes which left nothing to the imagination. But never, never had I felt as naked as I did now, and that was even wearing the panties he'd so graciously let me keep on. His intent gaze was terrifying and yet thrilling. I desperately hoped he liked what he saw.

He stood up and beckoned me back to the center of the room where he met me, looking over me long and critically. I burned and blushed. It was so intimate and embarrassing. My hands came up of their own volition to cover my breasts.

"Don't," he warned. "Don't ever try to hide your body from me. In this room, when we're together, it's mine. Understand?"

I nodded and put my hands down, and felt my nipples grow hard under his gaze. I didn't know whether to look at him, or look away, or look at the floor, or what. Then his hand touched my buttock, and I flinched.

"Stand still."

Again he reached out to touch me, and this time, I was still as a statue for him. He ran his hand slowly all over my bottom, down to the underside of my cheeks and then further down to my upper thigh. Finally, he was putting those beautiful hands on me. He stood close, in my space, and I could smell him, feel him, his incredible maleness sending my own body into a chaotic, hypercharged hum. His fingers crept under my thong and he slowly pulled it down to the tops of my thighs, where he let it rest. He moved closer behind me and pressed against me. I stifled a moan. Though he was still fully dressed, I could feel his rigid erection against my ass.

His hands moved over me with maddening deliberation. His fingertips traced my shoulders, my belly, the curve of my hips, while I stood as still as I could manage. He cupped the heft of each of my breasts, squeezing and caressing them, then closed his fingers on my nipples until I gasped, pinching them even more brutally before letting them go. My pussy flooded with wetness for the things he was doing to me, and the thoughts he was making me think. He leaned down and breathed right against my neck, his rough cheek pressed to mine.

"Lucy. How do you feel?"

I swallowed. "I don't know."

"If you say 'I don't know' again I'll give you twenty with the cane. Think before you speak, and then answer. How do you feel?"

I might have sobbed then, one quick sob. "Exposed."

"Do you feel like putting your clothes back on?"

I shook my head.

"Answer me, goddamn it."

"No," I said quickly.

He walked away from me, went back to the sofa, sat down and looked at me.

"Stand up straight. Unclench your hands. Look at me and listen."

I obeyed, my pulse pounding loud in my ears. I tried to relax, tried not to look scared.

"I want you to feel exposed, so if that's how you feel, we're off to a good start. You won't wear clothes in this room. This is a room where I own you. When we're in the confines of this room, you belong to me. If that's not something you can agree with, you're free to leave at any time. But I have to warn you, and I'm completely serious about this, if you ever leave this room before I'm finished with you, then you and I are done. Do you understand?"

"Yes."

"As you see the walls are upholstered, and this is the basement of the house. It's completely soundproof, so you can be as loud or as quiet as you like. I don't really care if you scream or grit your teeth in silence. But I don't use gags."

I didn't know what that meant, although he said it like it was important. I stood silently, taking it all in.

"What you'll need to remember and think of always, is that in this room, you exist for my use. You won't have much cause to talk, but if I ask you a question, you'll answer respectfully, using proper address. Do you know what proper address is?"

"Um...no."

"*Um* is not proper address," he frowned. "Shrugs, grunts, and headshakes are not proper address. *Yes, sir* or *Yes, Matthew* will suffice in the vast majority of situations. You will avoid using the word *no*, of course. You'll do whatever I ask the moment I ask it of you and you won't balk. If I don't tell you what to do, you'll stand or kneel and wait until I do. Do you understand?"

"Yes...sir." The word *sir* felt strange on my lips. I couldn't remember the last time I'd addressed any man as 'sir,' but it felt more appropriate than calling him Matthew at that point. We were no longer equals, not now. He went on in his cool, authoritative voice.

"If you don't please me for whatever reason, you'll be punished and it will hurt very much. Even if you please me, sometimes you'll be punished because I'll enjoy watching you endure it. But I'll never injure you and I won't draw blood. Same thing when I fuck you, the same rules apply. It won't always feel good, but I won't injure you and I'll never draw blood. Do you understand?"

Again, I whispered "Yes, sir."

"We'll use a safe word in the beginning, and that word will be 'mercy.' 'Mercy' makes it end. But I warn you, don't dare use it unless you're desperate. If I catch you using it when you don't really need to, whatever punishment you were getting, I'll visit it on you ten times worse. I don't tolerate lying well, as I've told you, to include the misuse of safe words. Lying and hiding sends me into a fury. You won't ever do either. Do you understand?"

"Yes, sir."

"After our sessions I'll expect you to sleep over. If you're not to sleep over, I'll have Davis drive you home. When we leave this room, our scenes will be over but your body will still be mine to use. The rules relax, but you'll remain my submissive, and when I want you to take my cock, you will. And this will be our agreement, Lucy, until one or the other of us decides to terminate it."

I took a deep breath. To *terminate* it. God.

He stood up and crossed to the armoire.

"But punishments will usually only take place down here. I've already shown you many of the things I'll use to discipline you. As I've said, I can do whatever I want to you, and I will. You're permitted to feel all the pleasure you wish, whenever you wish, but you may only come with my permission. Do you know why?"

He looked at me. I swallowed the *um* that came to my lips and thought hard. "Because I can only do as I'm told?"

"Yes, that's part of it. The other part of it is that you belong to me when we play. *All* of you. Your body, your feelings. Even your thoughts. Sometimes I'll ask for your thoughts, Lucy, and you'll give them to me. I'll ask you to do things you don't want to do and you'll do them for me. And your pleasure, your orgasms..." He paused for effect. "Mine, not yours. Do you understand?"

"Yes, sir."

I had understood submission on the surface, in the simplest form, but it was becoming clear that the submission Matthew expected was a lot more involved than it had been in my erotic dreams.

"The pleasure you feel will come at my hands always. You won't touch yourself without my permission. Coming without my permission is a serious infraction, a punishable offense. To complicate matters," he continued with a smile, "if I tell you to come, and you don't, I'll punish you for that as well."

"But—" I clamped my mouth shut.

"Go on. If you have any questions, better to ask them now."

"What if...what if I just can't come?" Like most women, it was never a sure thing for me.

"Trust me, if you're with me—*with me*, you understand—then you will. If you aren't with me...if you aren't giving yourself up to me, that's your problem, your infraction, not mine." He looked at me hard. "You see?"

"I think so. Yes, sir."

As I said this, he lifted some nipple clamps from the armoire.

"Have you worn clamps before, Lucy?"

"Yes, once," I admitted.

"By yourself, or with a lover?"

"By myself."

"Did you like how it felt?"

I burned with embarrassment. "Yes. But I didn't make them very tight," I added as an afterthought.

That made him laugh. "Adjustable clamps. I don't use those. Mine hurt. What about toys? Have you ever worn a plug in your ass?"

"Yes, sir." It was too humiliating.

"By yourself, or with a lover?"

"By myself," I whispered. "I was curious."

"Don't be embarrassed. You'll wear them all the time here. They're excellent for keeping subs in the right headspace. Have you ever been spanked?"

"No. Well, just play stuff."

"A hand?"

"Yes. And a hairbrush one time."

"Your fiancé? You tried to clue him in, didn't you?"

"Yes. But it didn't really take."

He put down the clamps and picked up one of the canes, a small whippy one, and walked over to me.

"Bend over."

I hesitated. He looked at me hard. I wanted to obey, but...if I bent over, he would *hit* me. He would hit me. It would hurt. Maybe I wouldn't be able to take the pain, and then...

"It's scary, isn't it, the first time?"

I nodded, and he nodded too.

"I know. Now, bend over. I don't like to say things more than once."

I bent forward slightly, and before I even finished, he striped my bottom with the cane, just once. I yelped in pain and reached back to shield myself, frantically rubbing the fiery stripe he'd left. He took my hand hard in his.

"Give me the other one."

He secured both my wrists in front of me in a firm grip while my mind was still stuck on the throbbing pain of what he'd done.

"You will never put your hands behind you. Never, never, never. You'll never try to protect yourself. In the beginning, I'll restrain you for your own safety, until you learn to control yourself on your own. Canes can draw blood pretty quickly on a hand. A paddle can break one. Do you understand?"

"Yes, sir," I said, and then I shrieked as he brought the cane down on my ass again. I tried to pull away from him but found I could go nowhere. He had me held tight. I gasped for breath. I couldn't do it. I couldn't do it after all. After all this, I would have to tell him it wouldn't work, that I couldn't do what he wanted. But

I was doing it, wasn't I? He'd hit me twice and I'd lived. But how many would I have to take? While I was wondering that, he hit me once more. I yowled and struggled, but again, I was held fast.

"Okay," he said. "Take some deep breaths. You survived some of the worst pain I'll visit on you. You did survive, didn't you?"

He looked at me and I blinked back through tears.

"It hurts, I know. I told you. This isn't a game. Have you had enough, little girl? Do you want to leave?"

"No, sir," I whispered. "I don't." I wanted him to hold me, I wanted him to soothe me, but no, I didn't want to leave. He pulled me close and looked down at my ass, smoothed his rough hand over the aching sting. "You have three beautiful welts now, Lucy. Look."

I did, and the welts looked angry and red. Beautiful? I wasn't sure about that yet, although I felt a strong, unexpected ache between my thighs. Surely that hadn't turned me on, had it? I watched with relief as he put away the cane and didn't pull out any other toys. Instead, he cupped and fondled my breasts, holding them in his hands while my bottom burned and the throb between my legs ratcheted up. "These are lovely. Real. The perfect size." He pinched my nipples, even harder than before, and I moaned. Then I blushed.

"It's okay," he said with a smile. "It's good that you enjoy it. But you may not come, not unless I say."

I bit my lip as he continued to toy with my nipples.

"You like this," he said. It wasn't a question. "You have sensitive nipples."

"Yes, sir."

"Have you ever had a clip on your clit? Between your legs?"

"No, I haven't."

"I bet you'll like that too. Very much. Spread your legs."

I did, but not enough, because he nudged my feet impatiently. "Wider."

He pulled the panties down and off and pushed my feet apart until I was spread wide open, and then he put one hand on the front of my waist to hold me still, and with the other hand, thrust two fingers up inside me. I was mortifyingly wet, but he didn't say anything about that. Instead, he asked, "How many partners have you had?"

"Four." *And not one of them ever touched me like this.*

He sighed, wiggling his fingers around inside me. "I believe you. You're small. Tight." He pulled out his now sopping fingers and without any warning at all, thrust one of them deep into my ass. He slid it right in to the hilt, lubricated as it was with my pussy juices. I held my breath as he pressed it into me, hard. I fidgeted a little as he tried to put in another finger. It wouldn't go. He didn't force it, but he did tsk at me.

"Have you ever had anal sex?"

"No, sir."

"Never? Not once?"

"No." My voice sounded strained. He didn't try any more to insert the other finger.

"Well, you will," he said. "Are you on the pill?"

"No, I can't take it. It makes my periods go on forever."

"We don't want that, do we? Where are you in your cycle?" he asked, pulling out his fingers and walking away.

Oh, Jesus Christ. "I had my period last week."

"Okay. You'll let me know when you have your period and we'll do other things. Are you clean? No sexually transmitted diseases?" While we discussed this, he washed his hands at a sink in the corner. The fully equipped playroom.

"God, I hope not," I think I said.

"I'll use a condom every time, although I'm clean. You've never had unprotected sex with your partners?"

"No, I never have."

"Even your fiancé?"

"No. I was saving that for my wedding night."

For some reason that made him chuckle. I suppose he thought it funny, that I'd almost married some vanilla fuckboy, as he said. I wondered what Joe would think of me if he could see me now. He'd probably think, *God, I almost married a freak.*

"Well," he said, "for now, anyway, we'll use condoms. Maybe, eventually, we'll get some blood work done. But if you can't take the pill..." His voice trailed off, and I stood thinking how bizarre it was, to be discussing these things in such a businesslike way, and then I stopped thinking altogether, because he was walking toward me, starting to strip. The animal way he moved took on a whole new meaning as he revealed his body. Each limb, each muscle seemed perfectly formed and proportional, superbly male. His broad chest tapered to muscular hips and thighs and the most beautiful cock I'd ever seen. The natural, easy way he walked, even the way his arms swung at his side as he approached resonated in some unconscious part of me.

"Get down on your knees," he ordered, fisting his cock. It was huge and purplish red. "Kneel up straight and keep your eyes on my cock while I speak to you."

Not a problem, I thought to myself as I stared. It would be very damn hard to ignore, especially jammed right up by my face as it was.

"Have you sucked a lot of cocks, Lucy Merritt?"

"Not very many."

"You'll suck mine a lot, and you'll swallow my cum. You'll suck mine like there's nothing you enjoy more on earth, and you'll savor my cum like it's the nectar of the gods. Do you understand?"

"Yes, sir."

"Open, and keep your hands in your lap. Open wider," he said as he guided his cock to my mouth, so I did, and without preamble, he shoved it in. I choked and gagged from the shock. "Relax." His fingers held my head steady. "Get your mouth wet, open your throat for me."

I tried, I desperately tried to fellate him, but I was clumsy and hopelessly inept. Tears came to my eyes from all the gagging, but he didn't withdraw, he just stroked my hair. "It's okay, don't give up. It takes practice. You'll get plenty of it. Just relax and try your best."

And actually, it did get a little easier. My mouth filled with saliva, which helped him slide more easily in and out. My throat became used to the steady thrusts, or perhaps numb to them, and I only gagged from his thrusting every few times. He drove me on, firm and encouraging. "It's okay, you'll get better. Pay attention. Try."

He sighed then, and I felt a bolt of pleasure, that I was somehow moving him with my clumsy attempts. "Be open," he breathed. "Accept me. You have to learn to be open to me." He picked up the pace, fucking my mouth, holding my head in his hands. By now, tears of strain were streaming down my face.

"Now," he said, "lick my balls. Put your hands on my thighs, put your face right up in there." I tried my best to do what he asked. I lapped at his balls carefully, lost in new sensations, velvet skin and rough hair tickling my nose. The masculine scent of him permeated my senses, made me feel wild and wanton. "Harder," he coached, "broad strokes with your tongue. Oh Jesus," he said, his fingers twining in my hair. "Yes, just like that."

Soon afterward, he thrust back into my mouth and came in my throat with a growl. Just as he'd told me to, I swallowed every drop of his cum as if it was the most delicious nectar on earth.

"Jesus Christ," he muttered when he finally pulled away from me, whether in frustration or appreciation, I had no idea. He yanked me to my feet and looked down at my wide eyes, my damp cheeks.

"Are you turned on?" he asked.

"Yes, sir," I said breathlessly, and I was.

"Lie down on your back. Part your legs, put your fingers on your clit."

I did, and he knelt down next to me. "Masturbate," he said. "Don't be self-conscious. When I tell you, you're going to come."

I took a deep breath and closed my eyes, played with myself nervously.

"Look at me. Open your eyes," he snapped. "You're coming for me, not for yourself."

And I remembered then what he'd told me. *If I tell you to come and you don't, I'll punish you.*

I was going to disappoint him already because I couldn't do it. I knew that I couldn't.

"Do it. Play with yourself," he said. "I want to watch. Make yourself come."

"I don't know if I can," I whimpered.

He stood up and crossed to the armoire, which made me panic. He didn't bring anything too scary though, just some small silver clips. I watched him, going still.

"Don't stop." He put his fingers over mine, making them move. Then, while I watched him, he tugged and flicked my nipples, making them taut and hard as stones. I held my breath as he opened the clips, attaching first one, and then the other to my sensitive peaks. My pelvis came up off the floor and I moaned like a wild thing. I'd never felt anything so erotically painful in my life.

He looked at me, bemused, and whispered, "Do you like that?" Then he put his hand over mine, over my clit, and thrust his fingers in and out of me, and put his lips to mine and whispered to me, "Come." And with a helpless cry of relief, that's exactly what I did. I came like crazy, came like I'd never come in my life. I bucked against his fingers, completely gone. My vision blurred, my blood sang in my veins and my whole pelvis seemed to contract and release in excruciating pleasure.

When I came back to earth from the place I'd gone to, I saw him watching me, his lips curved in a satisfied smile. Then slowly, with his free hand, he undid first one clip and then the other, lowering his mouth to each nipple afterward, sucking away the sting. Then, only after that was accomplished, did he withdraw his fingers from inside me, and then held them to my lips and whispered, "Lick, until they're clean."

I savored his powerful, thick fingers, marveled at how big they felt in my mouth. I licked my scent, my juices from him with earnest appreciation. I licked eagerly and thoroughly and delicately until he was satisfied, and then I waited to be told what he wanted next.

But finally, for the first time all night, he had no words. All the guidelines had been laid down and he'd given me my tests.

Now all he did for many long minutes was look down at me, stroking my thigh.

"Little Lucy," he said finally. "Beautiful girl. What do you think about this? Did you find it too difficult? Too scary?"

"It was difficult and scary," I answered. "But I liked it very much."

"So did I," he said with a frown. And the frown, I wasn't sure where that came from, but I didn't care a second later, because he lowered his lips to mine and kissed me long and hard. His fingers, still damp from my lips and tongue, buried themselves in the hair at my nape and pressed into my scalp. I felt his chest against mine, his rock hard stomach against the arm at my side. I hadn't been sure if he would kiss me, non-girlfriend that I was, but he kissed me as if he treasured and loved me, and for those long moments he kissed me, I let myself pretend he did. He kissed and nuzzled me for what seemed like ages, and then pressed his cheek against mine. Rough stubble across my jaw, soft breath against my ear.

"Beautiful, beautiful Lucy," he murmured, and I thought, *here then, here is the joy.*

# Chapter Five:
# Hands

Finally he helped me up, and I gathered my clothes near the door. "Don't bother to put them on," he said. "You'll sleep in the nude when you're here." He left his own clothes lying on the floor. I followed him up the two flights of stairs to his bedroom, both of us silent. What was there to say? I just stared the entire time at his awe-inspiring ass and thought that something like that was probably a punishable offense.

He guided me into his bedroom. It contained a huge wrought iron bed and two nightstands and not much else. It was stark white and gunmetal grey, modern and formal and fastidiously clean. The bed was just as massive as I'd imagined it, and I looked at that bed for a long lascivious moment, pictured him fucking me on it. Then I turned and I froze stark still.

On his wall were two large canvases. In the first, a girl stood casually, one hip turned out, her eyes downcast. In the second, she looked backwards over her shoulder, her hair falling down her curved back and heart shaped bottom. You could barely see her face, but I didn't need to. Because the girl was me.

It frightened me to death. I suppose it was the knowledge of what he'd paid to have them. The fact that they were in his bedroom where he slept. The fact that he had bought these paintings nearly a year ago. Everything, every word and action between us suddenly took on a twisted, stalkerish slant.

He stood still and let me look, although he seemed less at ease. He stood between me and the door as if he feared I might bolt. He watched my face closely but didn't say a word in explanation, as much as I felt I deserved an explanation of some kind.

"So it was you who bought them."

"Yes, it was me."

"Did you...did you know they were me? All along?" I asked stupidly. As if this was all some great coincidence.

He tilted his head, a patient smile. "Of course I did. You don't pay that much for paintings and not get a tip about the model."

"Pietro told you who I was?" I asked incredulously.

"And where to find you."

"So you...so you donated to the company..."

"Because of you? I suppose. In a way. Does that bother you?"

"It creeps me out a little bit, yes. He sold these paintings to you months ago. Last year."

"Yes, I know. I thought about taking them down so you wouldn't know I had them. But I didn't. Do you know why?"

My voice trembled. "Because it wouldn't have been truthful."

"Yes, Lucy, it wouldn't have been the truth. The truth is that first I procured the paintings, and then, I decided to procure you. I'm a collector of beautiful things, and I find you so beautiful that I have to have you. I need you to be mine. I thought it might be enough to own paintings of you, but it wasn't. And so here we are."

Yes, here we were, indeed. He watched me while I tried to still my beating heart, quiet the adrenaline roaring through my veins. Fight or flight? Why do either? He had already hurt me, and I'd liked it, and I knew he would do it again. So he had Pietro's paintings...it was actually kind of flattering.

"I've never seen them up close. The finished ones."

"Look all you like," he said, nodding towards them. "Beautiful art is for looking at."

I sidled closer, looked up at the curves and lines of my body.

"I wish I had a camera," he said.

I laughed softly. I was standing exactly as I was in the first painting, looking up at myself on canvas as if into a mirror. But then my eyes moved to the second painting, and I thought to myself, I don't look like that anymore. Because in the painting my ass was white and unmarked, and now it had three vivid stripes across it that I could feel whenever I moved.

"I'm glad they went to someone who appreciated them. Who wanted them," I said when I finally looked away.

His eyes flicked from the paintings back to me. "They're certainly worth what I paid. And I'm grateful for what they resulted in."

"You mean...me?"

He laughed, but the way he spoke kept me always off kilter. His compliments were delivered in the same cool, impersonal tone as his threats.

"Yes, you, Lucy Merritt with two t's. I'm grateful you're finally here with me, and that you're as submissive in real life as you are in those works."

My eyes flew back to the paintings. Submissive?

"Don't you see it?" he murmured. "Ah, well. I did. And I was right. Things went well for us the first time. You still feel they went well?"

He wanted truth from me. He was checking one more time. My answer hadn't changed. "Yes, sir."

"And what about you, Lucy?" he asked. "What exactly do you get out of all this?"

"Good sex," I lied to him, even though he'd cautioned me so many times already to never, ever lie.

His eyes roved over me, silent and appraising, looked at me standing naked in front of his naked paintings of me. All his valuable acquisitions in one place.

"You know, they're beautiful, Lucy, but nowhere near as beautiful as you. I wouldn't have thought it possible, that you'd be so much more beautiful in real life. The first time I saw you by the stage door, I was too shocked to speak. Do you remember?"

"You demand truth, but you're feeding me lines."

"Not lines, believe me. You're the most beautiful girl I've ever known."

I looked at him then, looked at him watching me, and I remembered how he'd run his fingers over me downstairs when I'd first undressed.

"So that's what matters most to you? Truth, and owning beautiful things?"

"Yes, I suppose."

I suddenly had a ghost of a memory, a high school lit class, a Greek picture on the cover of a report. "I think there's some kind of poem about that. *Beauty is truth, truth beauty, and that is all you need to know.* Something like that. I studied it once." I tried to remember the exact words of the poem, remember more about it, but he was staring at me with a look I didn't understand.

"Keats," he said after a moment. "Lucy, it's time for bed."

\* \* \* \* \*

I followed him into his bathroom, which was just as gray and stark as his chamber of a room. The surfaces and fixtures were spotless, and the towels hung from the towel racks folded perfectly as sculptures. I felt like I was in a museum, and I might have been. He certainly looked like a Greek god of a statue standing there beside me, and I stared at his reflection in the mirror as we brushed our teeth. He went through all the motions of a normal human, tooth brushing, flossing, taking a noisy piss with the door wide open. Then he pulled me into the shower with him, holding me by the arm and washing me perfunctorily, like I was a dirty window or a dish in the sink.

When we got out, he handed me a towel and I dried myself, wondering at his sudden change of mood. He had gone from being warm and complimentary to being brusquely and puzzlingly cold. He took my towel away and pulled me into the bedroom, leading me straight to the bed. He had a condom in his hand that I hadn't even seen him pick up, and he put it on with practiced finesse,

70

using only one hand. With the other, he pushed me onto my stomach and held me there, bent over the bed. He used one of his legs to part my thighs, then placed his cock at my entrance and forced his way inside. I gasped, shocked, because it hurt, and I thought then that he wasn't *cold*, he was *angry*.

Was it my reaction to the paintings? That I'd accused him of feeding me lines? The poem I'd recited to him? He fucked me roughly, pounding me hard. My pussy ached, and I felt strangely detached from what had been for me, previously, a romantic act. Lovemaking. This wasn't lovemaking, this was fucking, and I wasn't sure if I liked it or not. I'd never been with a man as large as Matthew, and I felt battered rather than sensuous. I lay still and pliant and I didn't think of coming, not even once. No, the whole time he fucked me, I just stared at the paintings, and I thought, those paintings are beautiful, but this, what he's doing to me, is not.

I heard him grunt, felt the last thrust, felt him hold himself tense against my back. He pulled away as soon as his orgasm was over.

"Up. Into bed," he ordered, slapping me once on the ass. I crawled quickly onto the bed and moved to the side where he nudged me. He went to discard the condom and then got in on the other side. He pulled the covers up over us, turned his back to me and turned out the light, settling down with a sigh. The silence was deafening. I would have given anything just to hear him mutter goodnight. So that was the first time we had intercourse together. To say he'd made love to me would be a laughable deceit. He had used me, exactly as he'd told me he wanted to, and while I knew this was what I'd signed up for, I started to cry.

After a moment, he turned the light back on. "What? What is it?"

"I don't know," I sniffled through tears.

"I'm going to hang you from a hook and flay you alive next time you say 'I don't know' to me."

"I'm confused!"

"Why?"

71

"I don't—" I stopped myself just in time.

"You didn't like what we did tonight?"

"My ass hurts," I finally said, and the welts did hurt a little, but that wasn't why I cried.

He watched for a long time in silence, just watched me cry as he had that night in his car, as if I was some kind of museum exhibit. *What do we have here? This is fascinating. Intense.*

"Are you really hurt, Lucy? Or are you just ashamed? I thought you said you liked it."

"I did like it."

"So you cry then, when you like things?"

"I've just never...felt anything like this. I don't know how to feel about this. And I do feel a little ashamed about it all."

He was quiet for a long time, and then he sighed again.

"Listen to me, Lucy, I'm not a big fan of shame. I know I'm kinky. I know I'm crass. But I'm not ashamed, and I don't want you to be."

He lifted my chin, made me meet his eyes. One broad thumb swept the tears from one cheek and then the other as he spoke.

"So you like to get roughed up, get fucked, get ordered around. So what? I like doing those things to you. So you being ashamed around me is both annoying and ridiculous. Just go to sleep, instead of lying there crying like an idiot."

"I'm not an idiot." I tried to say it respectfully, but I guess I failed from the look on his face.

"Listen to me," he said, his fingers digging into my chin. "You're whatever the fuck I say you are when you're with me." He turned away from me again. "You'll learn," he muttered, and turned off the light with a snap of his wrist.

\* \* \* \* \*

When I woke the next morning, it was because his hand was jammed between my legs. His fingers spread me deftly to find my clit, and began to trace slow circles there. I was still groggy and achy from the night before. I pressed back against his front, half expecting him to shove me away. He didn't though. He pulled me closer, molding his body to mine and nibbling on my neck.

"Good morning, Lucy."

"Good morning."

"Do you want to fuck?"

It was a rhetorical question since he was already sheathed and nudging his cock into my wet slit from behind. He drove in, holding my hips still, pulling me back against him. The whole time he never stopped the slow circles on my clit, slow rhythmic circles that made my thighs clench. I leaned my head back and he nuzzled me with his rough morning stubble. The sensation was overwhelming, and I feared he would stop what he was doing before I could come. I put my hand back on his thigh, and the other over his hand on my clit, but he made a disapproving sound and I took them away. He caught both my hands hard in one of his and held them trapped between my breasts, and the whole time, the slow circles never stopped. I felt like I was melting right into him, the delicious heat of him. The pleasure he was giving me crowded everything else from my mind.

I moved back against him restlessly, never wanting the sensation to end. I could feel the sparks and tension building inside me. I wanted him to make me come, but knew very well he might choose not to. He kept on driving me, driving me to the very edge of that cliff. Finally I whimpered, a sound of entreaty, begging for release.

"Yes, okay," he said, driving deeper. "You can come." The moment he breathed his words in my ear, his fingers found the very part of my center to trigger it, and so, that instant, I did. My walls contracted and I shuddered, pushing back against him, riding out the molten waves of pleasure. He grunted and bucked jerkily through his own orgasm just after mine. Our soft feral noises blended together in the silence of the morning, and his hot, strong hands didn't let go of either part of me. He still kept my hands captured tightly in his left hand, and his right remained between my legs, possessively stroking my mound.

"Little girl," he said, "who taught you to come like that?"

"I thought—you said—"

"Yes, I said you could come. And you did. Jesus Christ."

"I've never come like I have...last night...and now..." I stammered, totally at a loss for words. Or more accurately, I was afraid to spill out words I shouldn't say.

"Well, I like it," he said. He stretched beside me, warm and masculine. Hard muscles, soft, ticklish chest hair. I lay still in his arms shivering from aftershocks. I looked over at the paintings and unexpected tears came to my eyes. I'd actually had no intention of crying again. I was terribly embarrassed that I was, and steeled myself for another lecture. Where the tears came from now, I had no clue. I thought of all those nights before I'd met Matthew, when the tears wouldn't come. But I couldn't talk to him about that, I couldn't explain that to him no matter how hard I tried.

He turned me back to face him. Again, that look of detached curiosity.

"I'm sorry. For crying again. I...I don't know why. I can't help it."

"You're allowed to cry. It's pretty common in relationships like this."

I brushed at the tears. "I guess it's because I don't know how to feel."

"What do you mean, how to feel?"

"I don't know what I'm allowed to enjoy."

"You're allowed to enjoy it all. I told you that yesterday."

I could barely meet his eyes. What I really wanted to ask was, *am I allowed to fall for you?* But I didn't ask that, of course. I tried to turn off those feelings that I suspected were leaking out from my eyes in those undisciplined tears.

"It's always an adjustment in the beginning," he said. "It will get less confusing. At least I hope so." He kissed my forehead and, slowly, both of my eyes. "You can leave after breakfast," he said, and got up and dressed and went downstairs.

\* \* \* \* \*

My muscles protested as I climbed down from his Mount Everest of a bed. I took a quick shower, even though I wasn't sure if it was allowed. I felt the need to wash myself off. I needed to wash off all the depravity of the night and that morning if I would be expected to face him over breakfast.

I was shocked at how my muscles ached, muscles I didn't know I had. It had been so long since I'd felt aches like that, being a dancer. I maintained a relatively standard level of fitness. Matthew had somehow exercised muscles my body didn't use in dance, or perhaps, exercised them beyond what they were accustomed to.

As quickly as I could, I got ready and went down the stairs to the modern kitchen where Matthew was eating. Not just Matthew, but the driver too, whom he introduced as Davis. Another woman, Mrs. Kemp, bustled around serving everyone. I soon learned that Mrs. Kemp cooked for Matthew and kept his house, while Davis ran his errands and was his "jack of all trades." I also discovered later that these two people knew everything about his proclivities, but that morning, I only wondered, and felt humiliated as I took a seat at the table. Mrs. Kemp brought me piles of pancakes, eggs, and bacon. Matthew looked at my plate over his paper and snorted.

"Mrs. Kemp," he said. "Lucy is a dancer, not a farmhand," to which she laughed. And yes, I could eat probably a fourth of what was on the plate, although Davis and Matthew ate twice my serving and more. I guess it took a lot of energy to fuck the way he did. There wasn't an ounce of fat on him, so I guess he burned it all.

Davis and Matthew had some cursory conversations about current events, household issues, errands he would need to run. I sat and ate, tasting nothing, wondering what the point was in this breakfast table charade. To show off his new lover to his household staff? The dancer he'd acquired, just like the paintings up in his room? He said nothing to me the entire meal, until the end when our plates were cleared away. Then he turned to me in full hearing of Mrs. Kemp and Davis and said, "Lucy, I'd like to set up a schedule for us."

"A schedule?" I choked out.

"Yes, a schedule of times to see you. For you to come over and play in the basement with me."

I blushed, but neither Mrs. Kemp nor Davis batted an eyelash.

"What is your schedule during the week?"

"I...I have rehearsals from twelve to four, Tuesday through Friday, and then shows from six to ten forty-five or so, and two shows on Saturday."

My voice trailed off. He was thinking.

"So you're off Sunday and Monday?"

"Yes, si—Yes, Matthew." I couldn't bring myself to call him sir in front of them.

He thought some more.

"I'd like to see you two weeknights, and then perhaps a day on the weekend. All day. How about Tuesday and Thursday nights, and then Saturday night and Sunday, until the afternoon? Would that schedule suit you? We could try it, and add more time if we need to."

I ground my teeth listening to him schedule me, schedule visitation time with the little dancer he owned.

"It sounds okay," I said unenthusiastically. I was so embarrassed that he would discuss all this in front of them. It was as if he did it precisely to humiliate me, in fact I knew he did. It was so draining being with him, an endless rollercoaster of highs and lows. He would kiss me, speak to me affectionately, and I would melt for him, and then he'd devastate me with heartbreaking ease.

"So you'll come here then, next Tuesday after your show. Davis will pick you up by the stage door."

"Why won't you?" I asked rather crossly.

"I may or may not," he said with a shrug. As in, *I may or may not bother to come get you. I care for you so little, I may just send someone else.*

But Jesus, he was just getting started. While Davis and Mrs. Kemp looked on, he continued to talk.

76

"You can leave whatever you want here, toiletries, clothes and personal items. I'll have Mrs. Kemp clear out some drawers. And of course I'll expect you to be impeccably groomed whenever you're here."

"Of course," I muttered.

I could feel his displeasure at my tone, just feel it in waves, but I didn't look up. I was afraid he'd bend me over the table and beat me right there, in front of the strangers who were so obviously meant to witness all this, whatever this sick thing was going on between us.

He let it go. "I like your manicure," he said. "It's perfect as it is. Don't change it."

I looked at my hands in confusion, at which point he laughed. Even Davis's poker face betrayed a snicker. "Not that manicure. Your wax job. I assume you wax?"

"Oh, yes," I said, hating him. "I have to, for work." What were we going to do next, start discussing my period again?

"Your cunt looks nice. I don't like hairless. Feel like I'm fucking a twelve-year-old girl. You're little enough as it is."

*I'm not little*, I wanted to yell, *you're big!* He was the one here with all the power, and I, the hapless one twisting and turning for his amusement.

Davis drove me home shortly afterward. I sat in the back seat, embarrassed beyond words. I had loved Matthew so much when he kissed me on my eyes, and then one conversation over breakfast had ruined it all. There was no way I was ever going back there. When Davis came to fetch me on Tuesday, he'd be returning to Matthew alone. I pictured that awkward conversation with injured triumph, imagined how embarrassed Matthew would be when Davis told him I wouldn't come.

But yeah, that conversation never happened, because next Tuesday night I climbed into that black car, and Matthew greeted me with a broad smile when I arrived at his house.

"Hello, Lucy," he said.

"Hi, Matthew." I just couldn't stay away.

I had wrestled with my conscience all week. I knew this would end badly, in a world of hurt. I knew there was only one way for this to play out. But I longed to be near him, for him to put his hands on me. I craved his handling like a drug.

So on Tuesday, after the show, I had washed and dressed and put on no perfume, and got into that car, just as I'd sworn I would not do. Now I was in his darkened house trailing behind him through the kitchen. He looked back over his shoulder. Intent eyes, ice blue and possessive.

"Are you ready to go downstairs with me?"

"Yes." *Of course I am.*

\* \* \* \* \*

He took me downstairs and again led me to the center of the room.

"Take your clothes off."

I fumbled with the buttons on my blouse, then jumped when he barked, "*Yes, sir!*"

"Yes, sir!" I parroted frantically. Had he asked a question? Was I supposed to respond to everything he said? He stalked back to me and ripped off my shirt. The buttons I hadn't gotten to yet went skittering across the floor. He unbuttoned my jeans roughly and pulled them off me, berating me the whole time.

"*Yes, sir!* You'll answer me respectfully. It's not hard. Two words, you little slut."

"I'm sorry," I cried over his tirade.

"*I'm sorry, sir!*" He took my face roughly between his hands. "You will never interrupt me again. Never."

"I'm so sorry. I'm just—I'm trying—"

"I'm sure you are, but you'll be punished just the same."

He pulled me over to the nearest ottoman and pushed me down until my knees buckled and I fell over it with a gasp. My mind was racing. What was I doing here? Why was I letting this happen? I looked up at his determined face as he cuffed each wrist and buckled them to the bolts. He stood and unbuckled his belt, pulled it from his pants, doubled it over.

"You'll get fifteen, five for each offense. You'll count each one out loud."

"Yes, sir," I answered, already tearful.

"You may cry as you wish, Lucy. And yes, this will hurt."

With no more warning than that, he landed the first blow. And yes, it hurt, it hurt like hell. It hurt so much that all I did was cry, and I forgot to count.

"One!" he reminded me.

"One!" I sobbed.

"You just added five more."

He whacked me again, and I managed a "Two!"

"You know, it really isn't that difficult, Lucy."

"Three!"

"You just need to pay attention, you little whore."

And this little whore counted every blow up to twenty. I didn't miss one, even when the pain was so great that I screamed.

When he was finished, he dropped the belt, tore his clothes off and knelt behind me. For a moment, he caressed the welts on my bruised ass while I tried to stop sobbing. I was terrified, and yet burning with need for him at the same time. He thrust his fingers between my legs to find me sopping wet.

"Lucy," he breathed, his voice thick with lust. What was happening? Was this sex? Punishment? Or something else entirely? He spread my legs with his knees and fumbled with a condom. Again, I had no idea where it had come from. I felt his hard cock at the back of my thighs. I strained back against him. He made a soft sibilant sound and stroked my neck, as if to soothe me, calm me. I was shaking.

"Breathe," he said. His fingers threaded up into my hair, then closed and pulled hard as he thrust deep inside.

He had me so completely under his power at that moment. I was so completely his, lustful and broken and hurting and hot. When he pushed inside me, started to fuck me, it was unbearable. It hurt but I never wanted it to end. My wrists were still fixed to the ottoman, and my hands clenched and unclenched as he drove into me. While he fucked me, his hands caressed my ass cheeks, making the ache smart and burn hotter. He squeezed them and traced the welts there, and then he thrust one of his fingers into my ass.

"Oh God!" I cried out at the wicked sensation of it. *Mercy. Mercy. Mercy.* God, if he didn't let me come... I bucked and strained under him, desperate for release.

"No, you may not come. You're still being punished."

I tensed all over. I held my breath. I writhed back against him in entreaty.

"Do not, Lucy. I'll tear you up if you do."

I cried, tensing every muscle in my body, and by some miracle, I managed not to come.

But oh, I cried. I sobbed and I shuddered that he wouldn't let me have my release. He pulled away after he finished and went to sit on the couch. I suppose he looked at me, but I was facing away from him, so all he got was an eyeful of my sore, red ass.

"Do you think you can remember the rules now?"

"I...I'll try."

"No trying. Yes or no?"

"Yes, sir, I'll remember the rules."

"I'm very proud of you for not coming, for not breaking that rule. I know it wasn't easy, especially when I played with your ass. You loved that, didn't you, you little slut?"

I whimpered softly.

"Answer me. Whining is not an answer."

"Yes, sir," I admitted, blushing red.

"*Yes, Matthew, I loved when you played with my ass,*" he prompted.

"Yes, Matthew, I loved when you played with my ass." Always truth with him. My clit was teeming. I was absolutely aching with unsatisfied lust.

"I love your ass. I can't wait to fuck it. I'm seriously going to love fucking your ass, but you're way too small. I can hardly get one finger in there as it is now. I'm going to have to train your little asshole to take my cock."

"Thank you, Matthew," I said. I don't know why. It seemed like an appropriate response.

He laughed in appreciation. "Good answer. Don't move." He got up and got a plug from the armoire. Not too big, nowhere near as big as his cock, but when he lubed it up and began to work it into my ass, I moaned, afraid.

"Open. Open," he breathed, pushing it in slowly, forward and back. "It's going in one way or another. This is how we begin. This is how we train your tiny little asshole for bigger and better things."

I pressed my face to the ottoman, clenched my helpless fists where they were cuffed near the floor, tried to be open as he said. The encouraging sounds he made barely registered over the moans he wrenched from me, the strange feeling of being pried open there for the first time. I writhed and shivered while he seated it inside me, slowly, inexorably to the hilt. My clit felt huge, distended with excitement and pleasure, oozing with lust. I ground it against the ottoman, feeling every bit the whore he'd accused me of being. Then he leaned forward over me and reached around to pinch my nipples. He pulled and teased until they ached, until my entire body was one huge, shuddering throb of need and tension. Then he pressed against me and whispered, "Lucy, come."

*Thank God.* I came like a lost, crazed maniac, struggling under him. He firmly held me down. I was his creature, his whore. I was at his mercy, remade by him into something completely new and shameless. As I lay gasping, turned inside out by his power to transform me, he leaned down and bit me on the neck hard and whispered, "Good girl. You're such a beautiful good girl."

# Chapter Six:
# Good Girl

Yes, I was his good girl, at least I tried to be. From that first nasty session, it got nastier fast. Every time I visited he was more depraved, more inventive, kinkier. And me, I looked forward to our times together with a lust that threatened to overpower my mind. I let him do anything he wanted, anything he could come up with, and that simple, informal arrangement defined our relationship. There were only two things I didn't allow him: to fuck me without a condom, and to mark any part of me but my ass.

He couldn't mark my legs or back because of dancing. "Oh my God," Grégoire had hissed the first time he'd seen the marks. It was the day after a particularly brutal session. "Oh my fucking *God*," was all he could spit out. He didn't do any lecturing, didn't even ask for details. He'd just said, "I don't want to know," and that was probably for the best.

I had to wear flesh colored dance panties under my tights and leotards, thick enough not to be seen through. But an allover body stocking would have raised some eyebrows, so I begged Matthew the very first week we played not to mark my legs or back. "Of course I won't, Lucy," he'd said, "if it will interfere with your work." So while he owned me, it was a fluid ownership, one where he did not always make all the rules.

And there were so many rules on his side, rules that changed all the time. New rules that were made, old rules he got tired of and discarded, that I was then punished for continuing to follow. But he followed my two rules without complaint and I was thankful for that, because I didn't get fired, and I didn't get pregnant.

It turned out to be true, what he'd said about not being interested in most aspects of BDSM. He didn't do collars or gags or leashes, or any S/M rituals or verbiage. His only agenda was using my body as he wanted to, as his vessel, his object, his tool. His tool for fucking, inflicting pain, caressing, his tool for holding beauty always within reach of his hands.

He did eventually develop some very specific demands about my appearance. I had to wear dresses or skirts with stockings, and no panties to get in his way. I was permitted to wear only one shade of expensive lipstick, a shade called Nutmeg. It was darkish purplish red, and I felt like a naughty little slut when I wore it. I felt like a vamp, a harlot, but he liked it because it made my lips stand out against my pale skin. I think he strove always for the china doll look for me. He was a collector, after all.

But not a doll collector, no, he had no dolls except me. He collected many other things, though, like sex toys and dildos, the more invasive and threatening the better. Paddles, whips and crops, canes, he collected those too. He collected sexy panties and lingerie, which always fit me perfectly. I suspected he had them custom made, the fit was so true. He bought me stockings of all types and colors, plain or back-seamed, and embellished with all manner of things. Bows or rhinestones, fur and lace, soft French stockings that felt like a caress on my leg.

Of course, whatever he collected, it was classy, of the utmost quality and beautiful design. He never put me in degrading or slutty lingerie, and forbid me to wear anything like that even when we were apart. The sex toys he bought were top class also. They were never cheap latex or rubber. They were always artisan pieces, sleek metal or glass. One day when he revealed a new and shiny plug to me, I asked jokingly when he'd buy me a solid gold one. *Or platinum*, I'd snickered, *even better*. I couldn't help it, the irony

83

of it made me laugh. He laughed a little too, before he thrust it up inside me and punished me for disrespect.

But it was patently clear from the beginning that he needed his base and vile desires to be somehow made into something elegant and fine. I thought sometimes of his dirt poor beginnings. His deep obsession with elegance and beauty made me think he must have come from a very ugly place indeed.

I was taught exactly how to address him, and it colored the way I related to him all the time. Always deferentially, always formally, the same quiet way that he spoke to me. It didn't come naturally. I was not a mannerly person. I hung out all day with a bunch of rude, egotistical dancers. Sometimes I spoke to him in ways he didn't like and he quickly let me know. My inflection, my accent, all of it was criticized and improved. If I spoke in a way that annoyed him, he would slap me sharply or give me a shake and I'd have to speak again, better, more politely, more deferentially, just as he liked. And although we practiced BDSM together, I was cautioned to never call him *master* or *daddy*, nor, for that matter, any vanilla endearments like *honey* or *dear*. I was only permitted to call him *sir* or *Matthew*. *Mr. Norris* was strictly off limits. He said it made him feel old, although he was only ten or so years older than me.

As for me, he usually called me Lucy, but he had his own favorite terms for me which he used whenever it pleased him. *Slut*, *whore*, and *tramp* were the favored ones. *Dirty little whore, slutty dirty tramp*, there were endless permutations. Occasionally he'd call me my favorite pet name, *little fuck*. As in, *you little fuck, that's not nearly good enough. Kneel up straighter and try it again.* Perhaps you don't see these as endearments, but I did, because when he said these words to me, his voice resonated with lust.

I became less skittish with each subsequent session, and more open to the pain which I actually came to enjoy. I guess once I realized he wasn't going to hurt me, really *hurt* me, it made it easier to bear. With Matthew, the pain was always tempered with pleasure, so the two things began to seem one and the same, two facets of one thrilling experience, two sides of the same coin.

For his part, he moved me very carefully along a continuum. As demanding as he was, I could see a painstaking and wonderfully protective method to everything he did. That made me adore him more than anything, the mindful way he trained me to do the things he asked.

And he asked for things I never would have considered doing before I met him. Usually, I ended up liking them very much. My favorite activity with Matthew, despite my inexperience with it, was getting fucked in the ass. I took to it like a fish takes to water, which was a good thing because he used me there a lot. He trained me to it slowly, teased me for three whole weeks with ever-widening dildos and butt plugs. By the third week, he'd progressed to making me sleep with one all night. I would writhe and fidget beside him, burning with lust, desperate for him to take out the plug and just fuck me there already. He would feign impatience. *Go to sleep, Lucy.* But I know he loved how horny he made me feel, loved the fact that I was, surprisingly, quite the anal-craving slut.

It was on one of those torturous nights I lay fidgeting, that he turned me to face him and looked at me hard.

"Lucy, please. Is it that uncomfortable?"

"It's just...invasive."

"Yes, it's meant to be. In the morning, I'm fucking your ass and I don't want to have to fight my way in." Then he'd turned his back on me with a great sigh. Tomorrow, tomorrow...*tomorrow*!

I squeezed my legs together. I was so horny for his cock and morning was still hours away. Soon, I heard his breathing get slow and regular, and I shifted ever so slightly and put my hand between my legs.

My clit was wet and swollen. My fingers caressed it furtively, sliding over the slickness. I barely moved, tensing my body. I only tapped at it lightly, but I knew I would come. I almost did, I was so close, when I heard Matthew shift and felt his big hand close hard over mine.

"*So* against the rules. Did I tell you to touch yourself?"

"No, sir." *Shit.*

"Did I say you could come?"

"No, sir," I almost sobbed, my near orgasm of relief ebbing away. He pulled me close against the front of him and whispered against my ear.

"I put that little toy in your bottom to remind you all night that you belong to me. To remind you that you're going to take my cock in your ass soon—and often, little one. If you have an orgasm, it's because I gave it to you and I want to enjoy watching it. I'm sorry you're a little anal-erotic slut, but you've been naughty. What happens to naughty girls?"

"Punishment," I whispered.

"Tomorrow you'll take twenty before I fuck your ass. I'm sorry, but that was a very poor choice in judgment."

"I know, sir. I'm so sorry. I...I was...horny."

"Yes, clearly. Even so, I'm surprised you'd try it lying right next to me. You know the rules."

"I thought you were sleeping." I could be sassy now. I was already getting punished in the morning.

"You just added five," he snapped. "Now go to sleep, and keep your filthy hands out of your crotch, you horny little slut."

I almost laughed, but I'd already pushed him pretty far, so I smothered my snort of laughter with a fake burst of coughing.

"You're really pushing it now," he said, and pinched my ass so hard that I started to cough for real.

As promised, the next morning, he shook me abruptly.

"Wake up, Lucy. You have five minutes to meet me downstairs and I wouldn't be late if I was you."

I scampered off to pee and brush my teeth. I tried to fluff up my hair but I still looked a mess. I ran down the stairs stark naked, blushing as always when I ran past Mrs. Kemp. I burst into the basement room to find Matthew waiting, completely nude as well. Each time I was confronted with his naked strength, his masculine power, it started hot drumbeats in my veins. I stared a moment, transfixed.

86

"Come on," he called to me at the door. He already had the leather paddle in his hand. He pointed to one of the sturdier ottomans. "This one."

I walked over with as much dignity as I could manage. I knelt over the ottoman he indicated like the graceful dancer I was. "Hands." I offered them obediently and watched him snap the cuffs onto my wrists, already shivering inwardly with lust.

He was in a good mood because he gave me a few warm-ups before he started to land the ones that really hurt. He snapped at me not to tense, but it was hard not to. The pain was so sharp, so stinging, it was hard not to clench and try to evade the blows. Halfway through, he started to lecture me.

"Who do you belong to?"

"You, Matthew. Eleven!" *Ouch!*

"Who does your pussy belong to?"

*Ouch!* "Twelve! You, Matthew! Thirteen!"

"And who does your clitty belong to?"

"Fourteen! You, Matthew! Fifteen!" I started to cry as he laid them on harder. My toes curled and my legs tensed as my eyes flooded over with tears. The broad, thick leather paddle was one of the worst things he used on me.

"And you'll find out shortly—"

"Sixteen!"

"—who your asshole belongs to."

I sobbed from seventeen to twenty, choking on the words while I creamed on myself at the same time, thinking of him fucking my ass. Afterward while I composed myself, he stood over me, tapping the paddle against his muscled thigh.

"You are never to touch yourself without me. Even when you go home, you're still mine. Here..." He prodded my soaked pussy with the side of the implement. "This is mine and only mine. Do you understand?"

"Yes, sir," I said, fidgeting at the crass caress of the paddle. I felt so horny and shamed.

"And if you slip up, Lucy, if you wank yourself at home, you'll tell me as soon as we're together and you'll be punished. Do you understand?"

"Yes, sir."

"And if you ever, ever give yourself to another man without my permission, I'll invite over fifty of my most horny friends to use you like a whore and fuck you in every hole, one after the other. Do you understand?"

"Yes, sir."

"I know you're a horny little bitch, but you'll fucking control yourself or you'll fucking know pain. Do you understand me, Lucy?"

"Yes, sir." The endless mantra. *Yes, sir. Yes, sir. Yes, sir. Yes, sir. Yes, sir to everything you say, forever and ever and ever, amen.*

He went to the armoire to throw down the paddle and sheathe himself. He looked at the various types of lube, noisily trying to decide which one would best help me accommodate his "fucking massive cock." Then he pulled the toy out of my ass and jammed copious amounts of lube up inside me, slick and hot. I was excited, but absolutely terrified. I moaned and he slapped my sore bottom.

"Control yourself, you horny little tramp."

I buried my face in the upholstery as he parted my cheeks, then I felt him against me, pressing against me with the thick head of his cock. Slowly he rocked at my entrance, but he couldn't get in.

"Open, Lucy."

I drew a deep breath, clutching at the bottom of the ottoman, my hands still tightly restrained. It hurt like hell, but I wanted it. I desperately wanted him to slide up inside my ass. *Open, open...*

"Open," he coaxed me. "Open. Open. Open. That's right." I could feel myself finally relaxing as he thrust just the head of his cock inside. He stopped, waiting for me to adjust. It was so tight, the pain so sharp. He was still so much bigger than any toy I'd endured.

"Jesus, Lucy," he breathed. He pulled out and slathered more lube on his cock. He squeezed my sore ass cheeks. "Settle down and relax. You've wanted this for a very long time." He rubbed my lower back and held my hips. Again he breathed, "Open..." and again pushed the head in. I tried with every fiber of my being to be open, and with a sigh, he carefully slid deeper into me. Centimeter by centimeter, inch by inch, he slid into me. It felt horrible and yet wonderful at the same time. My entire body tensed and shuddered from the unfamiliar pressure.

"Fuuuuccckkkk..." he groaned. He pulled out a little and then went deeper still. "Ahhh...good...that's right, Lucy," and he drove almost to the hilt. "Tell me if it hurts."

"It hurts!"

"Tell me if it really hurts," he said sternly. "If I'm *hurting* you."

I knew what he meant, because between us, there was hurt, and then there was *hurt*, and while he gave me hurt with the focus of a zealot, the other kind of *hurt* was not his thing. He went on fucking me slowly, ascertaining that the hurt he was giving me was the okay kind.

"Just relax..." He massaged my hips, pulling me back onto his cock. Again and again he withdrew, then drove deep again. Each time, I felt invaded anew. "Feel me fuck you. I know it feels different. Try to get used to how I feel in your ass." He ran his hand up my back, twining his fingers in my hair. "Your ass feels so fucking good to me, Lucy. I'll be fucking it all the time."

He rode me slowly and thoroughly up the ass for what seemed an eternity. I think he truly did it to fixate me to it, to burn the sensation on my brain. Then, with that accomplished, he decided, being my first time assfucking, that I should definitely come. He instructed me clearly that I would come soon, and he pinched my nipples, fucking me hard. I made a desperate sound, moaning and bucking back against him.

"Yes, you like that. I know." Then he told me, "Now. Now, Lucy, you little whore. You delicious little slut. Come on, come for me. I want to feel your ass clamp down on my dick."

And my ass milked his dick exactly like he wanted it to, and I came hard and fast. The orgasm seized my entire body, and I gave myself up to it, all of it, burning and rocking and crying out like a harlot on fire.

\* \* \* \* \*

I sort of liked that he forbade me to touch myself without him, because it was hard. It was *really* hard, because I always wanted to. Since meeting Matthew and being introduced to his particular brand of power exchange, I drifted through life on a high of carnal lust. I danced and I ate and I slept and I thought of him and the nasty things he did to me, the nasty things he made me do. It was really *really* hard.

Honestly, I didn't always manage it. The nights I didn't see him, I thought of him and dreamed, and sometimes it just seemed worth it to jack myself even if it meant some pain later on. Maybe you wonder why I told him at all, since he had no way of knowing if I touched myself or not. But I was a terrible liar, and he asked me every time, and I was terrified of getting caught in a lie. *Truth, beauty. Beauty, truth.* We had made our pact, after all. Aside from the one big lie we lived, I tried to be as honest as possible with him.

And we lived a gargantuan lie, at least I did, because he didn't want a girlfriend, and I was utterly, completely in love with him. I would never have said so to him because I think if I had, he would have ended us at once. So I was truthful as I could be with him within that restrictive framework of deceit.

Yes, I adored Matthew completely, and grasped at all the small, caring things he did for me. I treasured those fleeting moments of affection like jewels, beautiful sparkling jewels among the many harsh rocks he threw at me. Rocks and stones and boulders, I got it all from him. I never knew exactly what I would get each time I showed up. Sometimes he was easy-going, others he was harsh. Sometimes the rules seemed to relax into comfortable play time, and sometimes the rules brought nothing but pain.

One night Matthew picked me up at the stage door instead of Davis. He told me he'd been at the show. "I love to watch you dance," he'd said with true admiration. The way it made me feel, I thought I would float away. Then he said, "I'm feeling really nasty tonight. I hope you're ready."

"Yes, Matthew, I'm ready." By that point I was ready for anything, and the idea of him feeling nasty...well, what else was new?

As soon as we got to the basement, he started to strip. "Wait and let me undress you," he said. When he was naked in all his tall, strong beauty, he crossed to me and undressed me, taking his time.

"You look cute tonight."

"Thank you, Matthew."

"Do you know what rimming is?"

"Yes, Matthew."

"Have you done it before?"

"No, sir."

While he talked to me, his hands roved over me. He ran his fingers along the marks that still lingered from our last session. He slid his fingers between my legs, gathering the moisture there, then drew them up to finger my asshole.

"Did you touch yourself while you were away from me?"

"No, sir." He looked at me to ascertain that I gave him truth. He nodded, convinced.

"Good girl. Come on then. I've been hard for you since you left. And I *have* been touching myself," he added with a smirk. "Come here and kneel between my legs. Kneel up straight and listen to me."

I knelt in front of him and he scooted to the edge of the sofa, his thighs spread wide on either side of me.

"Look at my cock while I talk to you, Lucy."

Obediently, I did as he asked, and then he schooled me in the finer arts of fellatio while I explored his cock and more. I learned the precise and ticklish way he liked me to lick his perineum, and practiced some more at licking and sucking his balls. Then he fed instructions to me as I lapped at his asshole, and all the instructions were gratefully appreciated because I would never have figured out how to do it on my own. These were all things that I never would have done, that I never would have even considered or even known about, if I'd been married to Joe. Or maybe he would have eventually asked for them, but I didn't think so. For Matthew, they were just more of what he liked.

I was rewarded after his very instructive session by his cock shoved down my throat, a couple of thrusts, and loads and loads of cum. As usual, I savored it with a moan.

"Thank me," he gasped when he was able to.

"Thank you, sir."

"You like to swallow my cum?"

"I love to."

"You liked to jam your tongue in my ass?"

"Yes, I did."

"Come here. Lay across my lap."

I did, and at once, he started to spank me. He'd never spanked me like this, not over his knee. His hand hurt like crazy. I was shocked it could hurt so much, just as much as the harder implements. I kicked my legs a little just to work through the unrelenting stinging pain. It was so hard not being restrained. He put up with my fidgeting for a while, but then ordered me to be still. It was too difficult. I flinched and tensed from the fiery slaps to my ass. He pulled my arm back hard.

"Stop it. Don't tense, it makes my hand hurt. Let me spank you." He pulled at my hips, making me arch to him. "There. Now behave."

But it was hard to behave, really hard. I still tensed under the blows, and finally, with a frustrated exhalation, he pushed me off him.

"Stand up. Look at me." I did, apologetic and ashamed. "Go to the armoire and bring me the toy you wore Tuesday night, the cinnamon lube, and the hairbrush."

"Yes, sir."

"Hurry."

So I hurried to get them, and returned. He pulled me back over his lap. Again he forced my hips up so my ass was thrust out in front of him. He lubed up the toy and tried to shove it in, but I tensed again. I couldn't help it.

"Open, open up," he ordered, slapping my ass.

He thrust some lube inside me and tried again. This time, with steady pressure, the toy entered me. It was one of the bigger ones, though still not as big as him. Right around the time he got it inside me, I realized that the cinnamon lube stung. I started to squirm with rising panic as he whacked away at me with the hair brush.

"Matthew!"

"Hush." *Thwack. Thwack. Thwack.*

"Matthew, it stings!"

"Yes, it's meant to. You need to learn not to tense and clench when I spank your ass."

I moaned plaintively, squirming away from the blows, begging for respite.

"Enough," he snapped, and paddled me harder, lecturing in a stern voice. "When you clench, it not only hurts my hand, but you bruise more. You're the one that always complains about the marks with your dancing. You'll do better if you learn to relax and accept the pain. That goes for assfucking too, while we're on the subject."

I whimpered, kicking my legs like a naughty little whore. He continued paddling my ass to molten fire with the hairbrush while my asshole stung horribly from the sensation of the lube. Finally he put the brush down next to him.

"Now you lie still. I have some reading to do."

I lay there across his lap for fifteen minutes while he read some developer's report. My ass was throbbing and so hot with pain it felt like it radiated heat. If I tensed or fidgeted against his thighs, he picked up the brush and cracked me again. I tried to be good, I lay as still as I could, but I ended up getting quite a few swats, each one more excruciating than the last on my tender ass cheeks.

Finally he pushed me off his lap and had me kneel in front of him, and then he reviewed everything I'd learned earlier by having me rim and lick and suck him all over again. I was still distracted by the sting in my asshole, so he pinched my nipples hard and held them that way to make me concentrate.

"For fuck's sake, Lucy. Some enthusiasm. Open your throat. Get your tongue wet for me. Poke that wet little tongue of yours right into my asshole." The orders came hard and fast, just like him. When I'd swallowed his cum, and he'd finally released my aching nipples, he looked down at me with an approving smile.

"Good girl. You're a quick learner. I told you I felt nasty tonight." I felt nasty too, with the toy in my ass, stinging and throbbing, making me feel so full. "Stand up," he said, looking me over. "Don't move." He got a scary gleam in his eye. He went to the armoire and returned with a massive dildo. I watched warily. It would never fit.

"Come here. Come on." He put the dildo down, pointing up, on one of the smaller ottomans. "Sit down on it," he said. "Straddle the ottoman and work your hot little cunt down on this. I know you'll like having both your holes stuffed. Won't you, Lucy?"

"Yes, sir," I said obediently.

He held my hand to help me balance as I did what he asked. "All the way," he said. I slowly took it in, my legs trembling. I took my time, and he waited patiently, but once it was fully seated, he pushed me down on it even more. He parted my legs wider, pulling my hips yet again to arch my bottom out. Then he fastened my hands together with cuffs at the small of my back and left me, returning to the sofa to pick up his report. I looked back at him for a moment, my eyes pleading.

"Keep your back straight. Turn around," he said, not even looking up from the page.

So I sat there while he did his work. My cunt burned from the dildo and my ass burned from the plug. I could feel that I was soaking the ottoman too, absolutely soaking it with the lust between my legs. I was facing away from him so I couldn't tell if he watched me, but even so, I kept my bottom thrust out the way he liked. I'm sure it was fiery red from the spanking, I could feel it throb, the endlessly erotic sting. I had no idea how long I sat there. It felt like forever as I tried not to come.

"Lucy," he said finally.

I turned to look back at him. I can't imagine what my expression was. Desire. Desperation.

"Do you like that?"

"Yes, Matthew."

"Don't you dare come."

"No, sir."

He got up, the bottle of lube in his hand. He squirted a generous dollop of it onto his fingers. Then, holding my eyes with a knowing look, he reached down and parted my pussy lips, and deposited that stinging lube right onto my engorged clit.

"This should make things interesting for you."

All I could do was look at him and let out a soft sob. He ambled back to the sofa.

"Don't come, Lucy."

I clenched my hands into fists, dangerously aroused. My hips began to move an infinitesimal amount, against my will, just carnal, irresistible drive. I looked back at him, my eyes wide and begging as my clit caught fire.

"Don't. Dare. Come. Don't do it, Lucy. You know it means twenty. I'll use the crop on you this time."

I sighed and turned away from him. I would have given anything to touch my burning hot, wet clit, to rub myself into oblivion. It would have taken me seconds to come. I was almost to the point where I would have taken twenty with the crop just to have that release.

But he wasn't finished with me yet. No, not Matthew. After five minutes or so of that torture, he crossed to the armoire again. He returned with some tiny silver clips in his hand. I shook my head in denial.

"You are not to come from these clips on your titties. Do you understand?"

I gave a quick sob at the same time I whispered, "Yes, sir." Then I begged. "Please, Matthew—"

"No. Control yourself. I said no."

He caressed my taut nipples, then took the first between his fingers and put the clip on. I gasped, short frantic breaths. He caressed the other, then squeezed it and clipped it too. I tried, I really did try, but a moment later, I came. I came like a volcano, utterly out of control, my eyes squeezed shut, my hips jerking on the ottoman, pure mindless physical reaction. The orgasm went on and on as my walls clenched around the toys inside me, my nipples aching from the bite of the clips. When I finally came to my senses, I looked up at him, tearful and ashamed.

He looked back, shaking his head and tsking. "You naughty, naughty girl." He took my chin in his hand and squeezed it, his thumb caressing my cheek. "Naughty little slut, always coming without permission."

I sobbed guiltily because I knew that was what he wanted me to do, just as I knew that he'd actually expected me to come. Wanted me to come, because then he could punish me, exactly the way I liked.

"I'm sorry, sir," I moaned. He ignored me and went to the armoire for the crop. He held it in front of my face and tapped my cheek lightly with it.

"Twenty. You'll count."

Then he started to crop me, hot, merciless slaps of pain, and I counted, helpless, still stuffed in both holes. My hands made fists and I was glad that I was cuffed because it would have been impossible not to shield myself. Halfway through, he grabbed my hands and pulled them up so my back was even more arched, my bottom even more exposed. Each stroke of the crop was a lick of white fire. I counted, half gasps, half shrieks.

After he finished he released my hands and slathered more of that devilish lube on his cock. He pulled out the toy in my ass, and then he straddled the ottoman behind me and shoved his cock in. I sobbed the whole time he fucked me, pressing back against him to take him deeper. He held my hips hard and controlled every movement I made, reaching around every so often to press on my stinging, aching clit.

Finally he growled in my ear, "Okay. You have thirty seconds to come before I finish. Otherwise, you're out of luck."

With a grateful sob of relief, I bucked back against him, coming hugely before the words were even out of his mouth. He may have chuckled at my uncontrolled howling and shaking, but I was too far gone to know for sure. After that, he put his arms around me, pulled me close, and shuddered against me as he drove deep with his own release. He lay limp across my back for a long time, licking my shoulder, kissing and nibbling my neck. Finally, he released my hands from the cuffs, rubbed my wrists gently in the places they were red. He pulled out of me, helped me up off the dildo, and turned me around to face him.

I was wobbly and drained. Mindless. He kissed me and hugged me close.

"You are such a lovely girl. You're such a good girl, Lucy. And I really love it, the way you come."

I shone from the praise, even though my eyes were tired and sex-glazed.

"Now, kneel down here. Look at this." He pointed at the surface of the ottoman. "You'll need to clean this up before we head up to bed."

I looked at him from my knees, and he gestured again to the upholstery. "Hurry, girl."

So I crawled closer and lowered my mouth to the slick surface and licked that ottoman clean of all my juices, cinnamon flavored juices, like the good girl I was.

# Chapter Seven:
## Used

That night I dreamed I lost my legs, not in an accident or anything like that...my legs just started to disappear. I watched in disbelief as my ankles, my shins, my knees, my thighs each vanished gradually into thin air. I cried bitterly at the injustice of this. I was a dancer, after all. Then my vision started to go black around the edges, again, so gradually that the horror of it was prolonged. My crying turned to pleading, and then to screams of panic, because my breath was cut off as if a hand was clamped over my mouth. I screamed, but nothing came out, because I had nothing, no legs, no vision, and no breath to give my horror voice.

Well, in my dream, nothing came out, but there in Matthew's bed, I must have really screamed because next thing I knew he was shaking me awake with a look of consternation on his face.

"Lucy! What the hell are you yelling about?"

"What? I don't know." I gasped, pushing at him. "Stop."

He stopped shaking me, but he didn't let me go. "Are you okay? What the hell?"

"What happened? I was yelling?"

"Yes, you were. Very loudly. Screaming actually."

"I'm sorry." My eyes were already closing again. It was so cozy, being cradled in his arms.

"Lucy!" He shook me again and my eyes opened reluctantly. "What were you dreaming about?"

"Matthew... Nothing. It was nothing."

"You were screaming, *'No, no, stop.'* Were you dreaming about me? About us? What I do to you?"

"No."

"Tell me the truth."

"I am telling you the truth. I wasn't dreaming of you. If I was dreaming of you, I would have screamed, *'Don't stop. Harder.'*" I smiled at him. I thought that was really funny, but he didn't smile back.

"I was dreaming about dancing," I said. "I dreamed that my legs disappeared."

He looked down at me with a frown. "Why did you dream that?"

"I don't know. I can't control my dreams."

"Don't be a smartass. If you're having nightmares about me, I want to know."

"It wasn't a nightmare about you. Can I sleep now? I'm sleepy."

"I don't want you to sleep. I want you to talk to me. Do you like what we do?"

"What are you talking about?"

"What we do. What I do to you. What we do in the basement."

"Of course I do. If I didn't, I wouldn't be here."

"You wouldn't just go along with it to please me?"

I frowned. "No, I'm not her."

His face got hard then, angry. I would never have talked to him that way if I wasn't so tired.

"Matthew," I said, stroking his cheek. "Don't be angry with me. I'm telling you the truth. I love the things you do to me."

"Why? Why do you love them? Tell me why. Explain to me."

*I don't know* was on the tip of my tongue, but he was already wrought up enough. Instead I said, "Right now?" to buy myself some time.

"Yes, right now," he insisted. Okay, no time.

I looked into his intense blue eyes. "It's hard to explain, but it makes me feel safe."

He looked at me like I had completely lost my mind. "Safe in what way?"

"Safe in a way that I'm completely under your power, but I trust you not to hurt me. *Really* hurt me."

He looked at me a long time. I was so very tired by now.

"Matthew, may I please fall asleep again?"

"Okay," he grumbled. "But no more screaming."

"I'll try." I wanted to ask him to hold me until I fell asleep but I wasn't brave enough, and soon he let me go and turned from me. I looked at his back and wondered what he'd do if I scooted over and pressed against him. I imagined myself snuggling against him, my arm coming over his waist to rest around his perfect flat belly, my fingertips tracing up and down his trail. *Matthew*, I wished I could say to him, *I love you so much*. But I didn't dare. I didn't dare do anything like that. It would have been the end of us. So I just lay there and thought about it, and wished that he would fall in love with me too.

I can't really say why I loved him, and why I loved the things he did to me, why they made me feel protected and safe. I think some things you'd just rather not think about too deeply, and for me, that was one of those things.

\* \* \* \* \*

I got pretty good at hiding my feelings from him, but it was never easy because he read me like a book. I tried to guard the things I said to him, and I never, ever looked him in the eyes, at least not for very long. Sometimes he insisted that I look at him, that I look him right in the eyes, and I hated those times because it was hard to keep my feelings to myself. Surely he realized I hid from him, but for both our sakes, I suppose, he didn't press.

But while sometimes my feelings were allowed to be my own, one thing that was never my own was my body. I learned to be always, *always* available to him, and there was a kind of security in that arrangement. In fact, the most miserable times between us were when I struggled against him. I rarely did this, and when I did, I hated myself. Only now and again did I resist him, and those moments always made both of us hold our breath.

There were those moments when he asked me to do something especially coarse or intimate, something beyond what my mind was comfortable with. He searched for those moments, pushed me toward them, because I think he most loved to watch me struggle with myself. Struggle to persist, to overcome my fears and inhibitions, for no other reason than to please him and his lusts. Just as I lived to make him happy, he lived to watch me fight with myself to do as he asked. He lived to watch me try to make him happy, and to touch and own me, and feel me against his skin.

Therefore, nothing made him more furious than me withholding my body. Not my actual body, because he took what he wanted whenever he pleased, but my body's *reactions*, which he felt he owned too. If I tried to own them, tried to control my own sensation and pleasure, a punishment was given, and I was quickly trained from such folly. If I tried to touch myself, to arch my body the way I wanted, I was slapped or pinched and told to behave. I was expected to do only what he wanted, and I was supposed to find pleasure in that, and not seek my own pleasure or let my mind wander from him. It was actually a lot easier than it sounds because he knew precisely what would make me thrill and burn even better than I knew myself.

I think in a strange way that was my only power in our relationship, that power to be aroused, to go wild from his hands and his cock and his mouth. It was a power I had that both threatened and excited him. I was expected to always very clearly express my pleasure, as well as my nervousness or pain.

Only once did I try to resist reacting to him, resist feeling the pleasure and pain he visited on me. He was already in fine form that night. He had stood me against the wall and wielded his belt until I screamed, then pushed me to my hands and knees and fucked me hard from behind. I thought he was so wild that night that even if I shut myself off, he was unlikely to notice. *Wrong.* He knew the very second I left our dance, and he became enraged. I whimpered, stifled stubborn fear, and twisted away as he tightened his hands on my shoulders. He'd pressed against me, pressed my clit, pinched it hard.

"Come, damn you. You come." But I couldn't. Somehow, I had completely turned off. He pulled my hair hard. "Don't. You don't do this. I told you to come."

"I can't." He was really hurting me. He let go of my hair with a frustrated exhalation and pulled out of me. He turned me over, spread my legs wide and pulled me under him again. He drove back into me, lifting me from the floor with the force of his thrusts.

"You'll do as I say," he said, and his voice both scared and aroused me. He fucked me hard, like the sheer force of it could snap me back to him, back under his power. "I can fuck you like this for two hours, Lucy. You fucking come, or else." And he knew how to make me come. He did exactly what he had to do. The exact pressure, the quick tug on my nipples, the press of his hips. He knew, he *knew*. I did finally come for him, even distraught as I was. I realized then for the first time this bizarre dynamic between us. If I didn't enjoy what he did, he was lost.

The realization of that fact terrified me. The fact that I could hurt him, that I had a way to cause him distress. After I came, he fell away from me, and he gave me a look that threatened annihilation.

"Go to bed," he growled, and in tears of misery and shame, I ran from the room. I was still sniffling and sobbing when he came up nearly an hour later. "Just go to sleep," he'd sighed, and that had made me cry harder still, because his disappointment and true displeasure was the most painful punishment he ever doled out.

The next morning he had been cold to me still, and distant. I was afraid he was thinking of the words he needed to end us. Instead he asked, "Will I see you on Thursday?"

"Yes, sir," I replied, and what my voice said was, *I'm so sorry, I'll never do that again.*

And on Thursday, I climbed out of his car with my bag in my hands, nervous and breathless as always. He met me at the door, pulled me close and rubbed his cheek against mine and said, "I'm glad you came. You ready?"

\* \* \* \* \*

That Matthew cared deeply for me was never in question, even when his lovemaking pushed my limits. Even when his eyes seemed to both caress and revile me, I knew he cared. Some nights he flat out worked me over. Those nights were always a jarring shock. Almost always, those nights were followed by something akin to coddling, subtle rewards for being brave and steadfast.

Then there was one strange night that confused and unnerved me, a night when I'd taken a hard fall at practice and been laid up in my apartment. I let him know I'd be unable to play, that I couldn't come over. An hour later, he was knocking on my door.

I'm sure he partly came by to be sure I wasn't lying, to be sure there wasn't another man in my life, but I hoped he came to check on me too, to be sure I was all right. And to be honest, I wasn't all right. I was lonely, and scared like any dancer nursing an injury, no matter how small.

"Matthew!" I was shocked to open the door and find him standing there. He'd never been to my place. It was a mess. I looked like hell in my ratty pajamas, my eyes red and swollen from crying. "I really can't play."

"I know." He breezed into my apartment, a market bag in his hand. "I haven't come to fuck you."

He reached into the bag with a flourish, like a magician about to pull a rabbit from a hat. Instead he pulled out a pint of ice cream. I burst into tears.

"I swear I'll throw this at your head." He turned his back on me. "Get into bed." He rooted through my kitchen drawers until he found a spoon and returned, crawling under the covers beside me. It was just a twin, which made him seem even larger than usual, and he had to scoot close to me to not fall off the edge. He looked out of place in my tiny, messy apartment, and yet, right at home.

Thinking about that, how easily he adapted to my squalid little surroundings, made me burst into emotional tears again.

"Enough. Quit your crying. What happened?" I think he thought I was crying about my knee. I explained how I'd fallen, that I wanted to stay off my knee as a precaution. He was highly suspicious even then of my injuries, the pain he suspected I felt.

"How long will you be off?"

"Just tonight. Long enough for it to rest. To make sure there's no serious damage."

He looked at me still, hard and assessing, and then decided not to speak. Instead, he pressed the freezing pint of ice cream to my nipple, and smiled broadly when I shrieked.

"Are you hungry?"

"Yes," I said, although I wasn't. He ended up eating most of the ice cream himself. Ice cream wasn't something dancers ate before bed, but I took a few small bites to mollify him.

"Look at you. Take a real bite."

"I am."

He scooped a huge spoonful from the bottom of the carton. "Open up."

I laughed as he brandished the spoon at me. "Matthew, stop."

"Open your fucking mouth." He fed me the spoonful, letting me lick it off slowly instead of shoving it all into my mouth the way I think he wanted to. I teased him a little, using my tongue to do things to that ice cream that I usually only did to him. He chuckled. "That's right, you eat it all, you little fuck."

"You're trying to make me fat."

"Yes, that's exactly what I'm doing."

We laughed there together on my small, lumpy bed. I looked over at him, Mr. Matthew Norris sitting in my pitiful apartment, and I thought I would just die. I was so hopelessly in love with him. I looked away, because his blue eyes were bright and burning. *Don't look at me. You'll see.*

"I wish we were down in my basement," he said in a voice gruff with lust.

"I do too, Matthew."

He looked down at my knee. "Can't I fuck you here?"

*I don't know*, I wanted to answer. *Can you? How many of your rules would that break?* It seemed to me we were recklessly breaking them all, as he pulled me close and held me in his arms. The carton of ice cream was put aside, forgotten.

"Can't I fuck you here, if I don't jostle your knee?" His fingertips trailed slowly down my arm. I felt so warm and protected in his embrace. I basked in the smell of his aftershave, the feel of his fingers moving over my skin.

"Mm. I'm sure you could find a way."

"If I was so very gentle...?" he breathed against my ear.

"*Can* you be gentle?" I felt his soft laugh against my skin.

"I wonder how a sound spanking would affect your knee. Take your top off. I want to suck on your tits."

I took it off with his help and he fondled me, kissing and licking my nipples.

"Does that feel good?"

"Yes, sir."

"Am I hurting your knee?"

"No. No..." *No, don't stop.*

He pushed off my pajama bottoms and put his hand on the inside of my thigh, parting my legs, his fingers going right to my clit, then deeper into my pussy. I was already wet and hot for him.

"Am I hurting your knee?" he whispered again.

I made a helpless noise of denial. His fingers left me, and I watched in fascination as he lowered his mouth to my pussy. *Oh, my God.* I moaned under the manipulations of his talented tongue. He brushed his lips against my clit with a sensuous skill that had me trembling. I had never enjoyed receiving oral before. When Joe had gone down on me, it felt so submissive on his part that it wasn't sexy at all. The way Matthew did it, there was no question he was in charge. He held my thighs hard and had his way with me. Just as I reached the point of climax, begging for release, he stopped. He only smiled at my frustrated wail, looking down at me with those piercing, intent eyes. When I returned from the brink, he started all over, and did it again. And again.

"Tell me if it hurts..." he whispered. *Sadist.*

I urged him on with a moan. Finally, when I thought I would die from the hot ache of my unsatisfied passions, he gave me permission to come. He held my hips and pressed his tongue against me, licking all the way up my slit, before sucking my clit between his teeth and nipping it. It felt like he was eating me alive. I was the prey, caught and consumed by the predator. I almost screamed with the force of the orgasm that overtook me.

Afterward he licked and caressed my now sensitive pussy until I begged him to stop. When he finished tormenting me, he licked all the way up my belly and breasts and then licked right up my cheeks to my eyes. He rubbed his rough cheek against me and whispered against my temple.

"Do you have condoms here?"

"Yes."

"Where?"

"In the bathroom, in the drawer."

Again, after he'd been to the bathroom drawer, and rolled a condom onto his cock, and pushed inside me, again he whispered, "Tell me if it hurts."

*Tell me if it hurts.* It didn't occur to me until later how ironic it was for Matthew to so persistently protect me from hurt. He cradled me, half fucking me, half coddling me, hard and soft, until I shuddered under him and came on waves of endless, unfocused pleasure. I was fuzzy and helpless, in deep, deep submission to him. Afterward, I couldn't look in his eyes. I felt so much love for him, with his ice cream and his tender caring whispering fuck. Instead, I hid my face in his neck, and he let me. He didn't turn away or push me from him, just held me close and still.

"You know," I finally said against his skin, trying not to tremble. "You can be really gentle. I never suspected."

"Strange, huh?" He took off his condom and tossed it away, then lay back beside me. I looked at him and wondered how he'd come to be the man that he was, wondered that he had this tender, nurturing side he'd never shown me before. I was unbalanced by it, and yet fascinated. The rules that ordered our world were suddenly undefined there in my bed, and I took advantage, trying to draw him out at the same time I was afraid of what I'd learn.

"Did you used to be gentle, always? Before you got into rough sex?"

"Rough sex? Is that what we have?"

"Isn't it?"

"Because I restrain you? Because I beat your ass?"

"Because you beat my ass hard and often."

He laughed. "Well, then, I've always liked rough sex. But sometimes I like gentle sex. It's like...my kink." I laughed, and he smiled back, and so I kept on.

"When did you first spank a woman?"

"Oh God. Long ago, when I was a teenager."

"I mean, serious spanking. Scenes like you do with me."

"Oh. Yeah. I was older. Late twenties probably, before I screwed up the courage to try it. I was probably your age."

"Did you try it on a vanilla girl? Or you found a submissive?"

"All these questions, Lucy. I hardly remember. I think I started very clumsily with a vanilla girlfriend. I've mostly just been with adventurous vanilla women. You're the first one I've ever met who's really into it like me. And you, you were vanilla before you met me."

"Yes."

"A closet submissive."

"I guess."

"Fortunate for me. I got to train you up from scratch, just as I like you."

"You're not bored of me yet?"

"Not even close. Do I appear bored?" His cock was growing hard again. He stroked it, looking at me. "Do you ever wish I was your vanilla boyfriend?"

"Yes, sometimes." I wish I could have lied to him, but he would have known and that would have been worse. "But it goes away. I'm not vanilla anymore."

"So, what am I to you then?" he asked, looking me right in the eyes. I wanted to counter, *what am I to you*? But even then, it wasn't something I would dare.

So I just shrugged, defeated. "I've given up puzzling out what I am to you. What you are to me."

"Have you? Quitter."

He seemed to shake himself back to reality then. He stood up from the bed and told me he had to leave.

\* \* \* \* \*

One night soon after that, when it was almost Thanksgiving, he came to pick me up at the stage door himself. I asked where Davis was, and he told he was waiting down in the basement to watch me get my ass beaten and fucked.

And sadly, that made me wet. He was so evil, so perverted. And yes, Davis was there in the basement waiting, and when I stripped for Matthew, Davis watched me too. A few moments later I was sucking Matthew off. I was getting better at it, gagging less. I still gagged though, which was a convenient thing because it gave Matthew an automatic reason to punish me. When Matthew came in my throat, I tasted him and swallowed him, never forgetting for a moment that Davis was there watching this whole scene.

"Over the ottoman," he said the moment I finished. "I'm so fucking tired of you choking on my cock."

I went to the ottoman he pointed at. Davis watched all this from his place by the door. He didn't sit down. He just stood still and watched me. He was only there, of course, to humiliate me with his gaze. And yes, the old me would have been humiliated beyond measure. I would have felt sickened to be debased in front of this man. But by now I was so used to humiliation, had been so trained to enjoy it, that Davis's presence only worked me up more.

"Give me your hands." Matthew buckled them hard, angry because he could tell I was turned on. He knew every subtle signal of my body. Yes, he was pissed that Davis's presence wasn't hurting me as he'd hoped, but I was sure he'd find another way to make me cry. He walked to the armoire, got a huge butt plug. "Put your ass up in the air."

I squeezed my legs together and arched my bottom to him. He lubed up the toy and began to press it into my asshole.

"Open," he said, slapping my cheeks. "Don't tense up and make me shove it in." He finally drove the toy home deep inside me, so I was stretched open and totally in thrall to him.

He got the crop next and whipped me hard, to punish me, yes, but for the sheer fun of it, too. No lectures, no frowning, no deriding my oral sex capabilities. He whipped me just to see me jump. Blow after sharp blow fell. I cried eventually, even though it wasn't a long beating. I almost always cried, even with my tolerance for pain. But as usual, I was so turned on by the end of it that my pussy was dripping with lust.

He sheathed himself, then knelt and thrust into me from behind, coming over my back, his weight pushing me down. His cock inside me rubbed up and back against the anal plug. I moaned like a slut at how decadent it felt. Within minutes I was trembling, tensing.

"Do you want to come?"

"Yes, Matthew."

"Beg me."

"Please, please, let me come, Matthew."

"Try again. That's pitiful."

"Please, please let me come with your cock inside me, and the toy in my ass. Please, Matthew. It feels so good. It makes me feel like a whore—"

"Because you are a whore." He whacked my ass with his hand.

"I know, Matthew. I am." Davis witnessed all of this but I didn't care.

"You wait until I say, you slutty little tramp." He fucked me hard then, hard and brutal. "You like it in both holes?" he asked hoarsely.

"Yes, Matthew."

He undid the cuffs and pulled me to the floor. He took the toy from my ass and worked his dick in. I moaned from the rough pain and pleasure.

"Spread your legs wider. Wide apart."

I complied, and he drove deeper, so deep I thought he might split me in two. The orgasm came over me like wildfire, hot and searing. He held me down as I shook myself free of every last vestige of my pride and identity. I was his fuck toy, pure and simple. He came less than a minute later, jerking against my ass. It was then I realized I hadn't asked permission for my orgasm.

"I'm sorry, sir," I said when I could breathe again. "I'm so sorry I came." But I wasn't really sorry, even when he brought out the cane. He handed it to Davis.

"Punish her," he told him. "Not too hard, though. She's a hell of a fuck, and you can have what's left of her when you're through."

Ever the obedient lackey, Davis started to cane me. It was the first time Matthew had someone else join us, and while I'd liked having Davis watch, I liked less having him join in. I realized quickly how careful Matthew was, that I'd never appreciated Matthew's finesse at giving me pain. Davis beat me like a dog. I screamed each time his arm fell, and it only took five excruciating blows for him to draw blood. Matthew stopped him then, taking the cane and handing him a condom.

"We can share her now," he said. "You can use her cunt and I'll use her mouth. You saw how she likes having all her holes filled."

I lay still, reeling as they discussed how to take me. I watched from some kind of dissociative state as Davis picked up my legs and thrust deep into my still slippery pussy. Matthew knelt with one thigh on either side of my head and jammed his cock deep down my throat. They both fucked me, and I lay there like a good girl, like the good girl he'd trained me to be.

And as I lay there still and quiet, I thought, *this, this is what he meant about using me. This is what it really feels like to be used.*

# Chapter Eight:
# Shame

He pulled me upstairs afterward, showered me off under water that was barely warm. He waited long enough for me to brush my teeth, brush the taste of his cum away, and then he pushed me toward the bed.

He was furious. I didn't know why. I'd done what he asked, even let Davis fuck me and draw my blood. I didn't understand the scene that had just happened, and I felt I had no right to make him explain. And honestly, I didn't want to know why he had wanted it. So I just lay silently beside him, traumatized and numb.

Had he expected me to rebel against him, refuse to let Davis use me? There were so many rules I didn't know or understand. I thought again of how it had felt, pinned by both men, used as an abject receptacle. Shared. *Abused.* My mind whispered the word again and again. *Abuse.* Had he crossed a line? Should I have stopped him? Could I have stopped him? I could have. But what upset me the most was that he'd wanted to share me and treat me so cruelly in the first place.

My mind raced, replaying the scene again and again in my mind, and then a small rebellion, a tiny spark of rebellion began to grow. I could hear him breathing steadily beside me, feel the bed shift under his weight. I thought of the quiet, calm way he'd invited Davis to have me, the cold way he'd knelt over me and

111

shoved his cock down my throat, and it suddenly seemed that Matthew was someone I should hate. I started to tremble from the horrible need to act, and then I did act. I decided to leave.

Well, I decided, but I didn't just get up and do it, not right away. No, I started to inch, millimeter by millimeter, to the edge of the bed. When I was far enough away where I thought he wouldn't grab me, I lay the sheets back carefully and rolled onto my feet. I got probably four feet away before he said to me, "No." He said "no," but it sounded more like *don't you dare*. The ice in his voice was enough to freeze me. He put on his bedside light and sat up, frowning at me, cool determination in his icy blue eyes.

"You come now, Lucy, and you get right back into bed."

I was shaking so hard I thought my legs would give out, and I suddenly felt very naked, more naked than I'd been in my life. I wrapped my arms around my front, tried to cover myself the exact way he'd forbidden me to the very first day, and started to cry.

"Stop it," he snapped, but I shook my head.

"I can't," I bawled. "I can't."

He crossed his arms over his chest. He didn't move or speak, because I think he realized that if he pushed me any more right then, I would have snapped. And strangely enough, through all this, I went nowhere. I just stood there like a statue in front of him and continued to cry. I didn't make any more effort to leave, nor did I return to his bed. I just stood. It seemed like I stood there for an hour in time, but it was probably only five minutes, five silent minutes of trembling, passive revolt.

"You're shivering. Just fucking come back to bed."

"I hate you." It felt good to say it even if it was a lie.

He looked away from me and bit his lip. Trying to keep his temper? Or had I actually hurt his feelings, my indefatigable tyrant?

"There are a lot worse things I could do to you, Lucy. A lot worse things!"

"Why do you do it at all? Why do you do these things to me? Why did you share me with Davis, humiliate me—"

"Humiliate you? I promise you, I've not even begun to humiliate you. I'm ridiculously soft on you—"

"Why? Just tell me why," I interrupted him. At any other time, he would have beat me silly for that. But now, our rigid rules seemed suspended, put aside for something more important and raw.

"That's none of your fucking business. I don't have to explain myself to you."

"It's because you hate me," I screamed at him.

"I don't hate you. That's fucking ridiculous."

"You hate women," I insisted, and then he threw off the covers, walked over to me, and grabbed my face.

"Don't you ever, ever presume to tell me what I hate," he said through tightly clenched teeth. "Now you listen to me, you stupid little fuck. You can either get back into bed with me and shut your fucking mouth, or you can walk out that fucking door and go home." He looked hard into my eyes, squeezing my chin between his fingers. "But you think first. You think really hard, Lucy Merritt. Because I promise you, if you walk now, you're never coming back."

He let go of my chin, and not gently either. My head snapped back and I bit my lip. He walked back and got into the bed, pulling the sheets down roughly, while I stood, mute and stupid, rubbing my lip.

"Get over here," he barked. "Do not make me drag you."

I stood still, looking at him. What would he do if I came back to the bed? It seemed all of a sudden that I was standing on a precipice, one of those cartoon types, where there was nowhere to go but down. Just one tall rock in the middle of the desert, with only enough room for my two feet to stand. All around, a sheer drop off, like a cliff.

Well, hook an anvil to me. I was going down.

I walked over to the bed, never taking my eyes off him. As soon as I was under the covers, he grabbed me and pulled me under him. His cock reared between my thighs.

"Don't you even move, you stupid little fuck."

He rolled on a condom and kicked my legs apart with his knee.

"Look at me." My eyes flew to his, because there was a tone to his voice I'd never heard. He grabbed my hands and pulled them taut over my head, and he just fucked me, his face inches from mine. As he fucked me, he started to talk to me, low and threatening, in a strange icy cadence to the punishing force of his thrusts.

"Don't you ever yell at me like that again. Don't you ever ask me questions. Don't you ever tell me how I feel about you." Then his eyes got even harder, narrowed dangerously. "Don't you ever try to steal away from me in the night, just don't. You're mine, Lucy, don't you realize that? You're mine and you always will be." Then he repeated it to me again and again, in time to his fucking, as if he was trying to burn it on my brain. *You're mine, you're mine, you're mine, you're mine, you're mine.* Then he pinched my nipples hard, so hard that it took my breath away, and he licked at the pulse in my neck and said, "Come for me."

All he ever had to do was say it. Barely a moment later, I came apart in his arms. I felt punished and helpless, the orgasm racking my body even as hot tears wet my cheeks. He clasped me close when he came, while I was still shuddering. I thought I felt him shudder a little too.

When our breathing slowed, he stood and left me. I thought he was going to punish me then, which I fully expected. When he came back to the bed, I braced for clips, restraints, and pain, but he rolled me over and put his hand on my back.

"Lie still."

He began to rub my bottom, my painful striped cheeks. The small amount of blood that Davis had drawn had long ago scabbed over, but it still smarted, it still ached. Slowly, gently, Matthew applied salve to it, rubbed soothing cool salve all over my ass. Who knew he even had salve in the house? He'd never so much as offered it to me. I started to cry just because he was being tender. He hated it when I was emotional like that, but he didn't reprimand me. What he actually said to me was, "I'm sorry."

He said it so quietly I almost didn't believe my ears. But then he said it again, louder, "I'm sorry," and my tears flowed hopelessly then. "Not sorry about Davis," he qualified. "You agreed to let me use you in that room however I liked. No, I'm sorry because I broke a promise to you, a promise I made to never draw blood."

"But you didn't draw it, Matthew." I was so sick for him, I would excuse him, even now.

"No, I didn't, and I wouldn't. But when I handed someone like him a cane, I might as well have." He put his hand on my back and rubbed me all over, lazy and slow. "Anyway, I'm sorry, Lucy. I hope it doesn't leave a scar."

I hadn't even thought of scars. Was that the point, no scars left behind? No souvenirs to remember him by?

"I'll have to punish you tomorrow," he said as he rubbed the knots from my neck. I moaned softly, maybe from fear, maybe from pleasure. Who knows, at that point?

"I'm sorry, Matthew," I whispered through one last gush of tears, and I meant it. I didn't say it to try to get out of being punished, because I knew I wouldn't. "I'm so sorry I said those things to you. I didn't mean them."

"I know it, Lucy. I know." His hands were so strong, so firm and so warm. He massaged and stroked me from my shoulders to my thighs. He didn't do it to soothe me or stop my tears, I knew. He did it because he liked to feel my curves, liked to hold them under his hands. *These shoulders, this waist, the flare of hips, it's mine.* Even so, I loved every moment of it, and basked in the sensation as long as it went on. I stretched a little the way he liked, flexed my dancer's muscles beneath his fingertips.

"You know," he said as I did this, "my rules, my requirements, they aren't always easy. But they're important. They're there for a reason."

*What reason?* I wanted to cry out. *Why won't you love me? Why do you hold these rules between us?*

But what I said instead was, "I wish I could be more perfect for you."

"Oh, Lucy," he said after a moment. "You're more perfect than anything I have."

\* \* \* \* \*

The next morning he dragged me out of bed before dawn and hauled me down to the basement without a word. He bent me over one of the ottomans and cuffed my hands in perfunctory silence. I put my head down on the cushion, resigned. Yes, I'd behaved terribly and I deserved severe punishment. Davis was there too, looking tired and annoyed. Must suck, to be dragged out of bed only to witness me get my ass beaten. Well, maybe he'd be invited to fuck me again now that Matthew realized how much I hated it.

Matthew lectured me first about tantrums and rules, then dropped his many spanking implements in front of my face, then gave me a lengthy and businesslike disciplinary beating that came very close to being more than I could take. Ten with the paddle for disrespect, ten with the crop for raising my voice, ten with the strap for covering myself from him and crying like a baby, ten with the cane for just generally being a stupid fuck, as he so colorfully put it. I screamed and I begged and I cried up until the end, but his only response was to kneel down behind me and lube up my ass. He fucked me then, steady and hard, not brutally, but not gently, no. As always during punishments, I was not allowed to come. Then he invited Davis to fuck me in the ass as well, and he did. Thankfully, he did not again invite him to wield the cane.

When Davis was done fucking my then tender ass, Matthew pulled me up from my knees, shaking and weak. He had me thank him for disciplining me, and thank Davis for fucking me. Then he lightly kissed my wet, tearstained cheeks and sent me upstairs to his bedroom.

I came down afterward for the obligatory uncomfortable breakfast, now cleaned up, dressed, and all made up. Human again, not a toy for beating and sex. My ass was so painful, sitting down was its own punishment. I fidgeted helplessly even though Matthew snapped at me to stop. Mrs. Kemp bustled back and forth without so much as a glance. Davis ate with us too, which was excruciatingly weird and awkward. Near the end of breakfast, Matthew told me to tell Davis goodbye, that he would not be back with us again.

* * * * *

The incident with Davis actually turned out to be a good thing because it opened my eyes, snapped me back to reality. It was Matthew's way of telling me that what I was doing was not okay, that it was absolutely not okay to fall in love with him. Letting Davis abuse and fuck me was an explicit way to tell me that I needed to fucking get my head straight. Of course, I thought, *of course* Matthew had known exactly how I felt, exactly what false hopes I harbored. What a dork he must have thought me, to believe I loved him, to think he might one day love me back. To think we might one day marry and have babies, be a happy family during the day, and spend each night behind a locked basement door. By inviting another man into our insular world, he got his point across with clarity and élan. *Don't fall in love with me, Lucy, or I will hurt you. Don't fall in love with me or I'll show you that love hurts.*

So, yes, as much as the Davis incident hurt me, in the end, it helped me infinitely more. I returned to our next session with a new attitude, new conviction. New promises to myself that I was determined to keep. I would no longer let myself crush on Matthew. I would not harbor silly, girlish fantasies. I would not imagine him confessing his true and undying love for me. I would not picture him pining after me when I was gone.

After that, things got much easier. A new silent and burly driver was hired to shuttle me back and forth but he never joined Matthew and I downstairs. Putting pointless hopes of love and affection from my mind, I focused only on pleasure and pain. I developed into a perfect little sex slave, with my lust-laden mind trained only on pleasing him. Matthew commented on it often, praising me for the progress I made. I even stopped gagging when

I sucked him and he had to find other reasons to punish me, which he effortlessly did.

In turn, Matthew began to beat me less cruelly, or maybe I just got more used to the pain. And he gave me more pleasure, more delicious pleasure than I thought I could bear, and almost always, he let me come.

Eventually, too, the marathon sessions of depravity altered, commuted into something less frenetic and more refined. He always still hurt me, and he always still fucked me soundly, but he began to spend a lot of time just looking at me too. Sometimes he'd make me stand there for an hour with my hands at my sides, my legs spread, and a toy burning in my ass. All the while that I stood there facing him, he'd sit on the couch and stare with an unfathomable look, a look that would make me want to fidget, although I could not.

Sometimes he put clips on my nipples and on my clit, and made me lie still in front of him, wet and desperate, but untouched. Other times he would pore over work contracts, take phone calls and send emails while I stood with my ass to him and my hands cuffed at the small of my back. At first I worried that he was getting bored with me, and I tried harder to please him when we played. I moaned louder, wiggled more frantically under his beatings, debased myself even beyond what he asked of me. Of course this only incensed him, and he snapped at me to cut it out.

Over time I came to realize that he wasn't planning to get rid of me, and in fact, one Sunday, he requested to see me more. I was so happy about it that I almost wept. He added Sunday night and part of Monday, so that the only day off that I had to myself was Monday afternoon and night. That was really good for me because when I was alone, without rehearsals or shows or Matthew, I was completely lost. I withdrew from my friends and I soldiered through work. I still loved to dance, and I still did it well, but it was only something I did until I saw him again. Grégoire snapped at me more than once after we danced, to come back from wherever the hell my mind was.

Poor darling Grégoire. Our deep connection suffered, and in turn, our dancing partnership suffered as well. Our ten-year friendship began to degrade. He tried to hold onto me, and I to him, but we just grew apart. I couldn't share with him anything about Matthew because he so thoroughly disapproved, and it made me sad because up to that point, Grégoire had been so much a part of my life.

Whenever he tried to bring his concerns up to me, I gave him stony silence. "He's taken over you," he said to me once. "He's completely taken over your life. What will you do when he drops you, Lucy?"

"I don't know, G," I had answered, shutting out his words.

Because that was the truth. I really didn't know what I'd do.

\* \* \* \* \*

I had another relationship that suffered, and that was the relationship between me and Pietro. He called me to sit for him and I agreed to, and I begged Matthew not to beat me the session before. "He won't like the marks."

"The marks are part of who you are now."

"I know, but there's just one more painting. One more of this series. Please, Matthew, please."

He sighed. "I've been waiting all day to mark you. Two days. Since Thursday night."

"Can't you just hit me softly?"

What a face he made then. "You tell me."

In the end, he didn't beat me at all, but he used me for sex that made my toes curl. Even so, the marks from Thursday were still visible on Monday when I showed up at Pietro's studio. To me, they looked rather mild, considering the bruises and welts I normally had, but to Pietro, I guess they were something else altogether, and there was a horribly awkward moment as I tried to explain them to him.

"It's totally consensual, Pietro. It really is."

"Consensual? You do this consensually with who?"

"You know him," I said, a little piqued. "You're the one who gave him my name."

His eyebrows shot up. "Do not say such a thing. I promise you, I give no one your name who treats you this way."

"The man who bought the first two paintings, Pietro. He told me you gave him my name when he asked."

He frowned, caught, and his teeth ground together. I felt bad for him, and I quickly spoke again.

"I don't mind. It's okay. We've been together since October."

"Since October? He does this to you since October? What of that very nice boy you were to marry? James or John...?"

"Joe. He left me."

He began to draw me as I was, standing there looking at him with my hands in fists, embarrassed and defensive.

"How do you want me to stand?"

"I want you to stand just as you are."

He drew for long moments in silence, and his strokes were angry and quick. Then he said, "You like this, really, Lucy? To be beaten this way?"

"Yes I do."

"Why?"

"I don't know why. He makes me feel protected."

He snorted, an ugly, derisive sound.

"If this makes you feel protected, there is something wrong with your brain."

"Pietro, it's really none of your business."

"If I want to draw your body that you abuse, then it is."

"Fine. Then don't pay me. If you're so unhappy with me, you can draw me for free."

He closed his notebook with an angry snap.

"Put on your clothes and get out, please. I can't paint you anymore, not like this."

I stared at him. "Pietro! Why? You can't even see the marks in this pose."

"No, I can't see them, but when I look at you..." His voice trailed off, and his shoulders slumped. "I used to look at you and see amazing beauty. Now I look at you and see only a stupid and beaten girl. Please get out of my studio. Please leave now. Here, take this with you." He tossed the drawing he'd done to the floor.

He turned his back on me and went to wash the charcoal off his hands, wash them off violently as if he washed his hands of me. My face was hot and I felt numb and cold all over. I put on my clothes quickly, not wanting to be naked anymore. I glanced down at the drawing, and it was me, cloaked in shame and sadness. I left it lying right where it was and walked, blind with tears, out the door.

In all the time I'd spent with Matthew, he had never, ever come close to making me feel shame like this. Coming from Pietro, it devastated me.

He might as well have settled himself over my shocked face and shoved his cock right down my throat.

# Chapter Nine:
# Dinner

I walked home from Pietro's studio bawling my eyes out. Blocks and blocks along city sidewalks, but no one stopped me to ask if I was all right, which was just as well, because I'm not sure how I could have explained to them. When I got home, I crawled into bed.

I pulled myself together for work the next afternoon. I didn't tell Grégoire what had happened, though he worried about me when he saw my swollen eyes. Maybe he thought I'd finally broken things off with Matthew, which would have been a great relief to him. But no, I pulled myself together to see Matthew too, climbed into the back seat of his car that his new driver, Kevin, held open for me outside the stage door.

If Matthew noticed my red eyes and listless sadness, he made no comment, and if anything, used me harder than he usually did. I needed that pain though, desperately needed it, if only to feel something other than shame. I didn't tell him either about Pietro, although seeing the paintings up in his room made my eyes blur again with tears.

It was December by then, a couple weeks before Christmas. Like most dance companies, we'd added extra holiday shows and rehearsals, and my body ached from the strain. I would be twenty-nine in early January, and I could feel my ability to dance slowly ebbing away. My hips and knees screamed in protest when I leaped and kicked, and my ankles gave me constant needling pain.

So, during this time just before Christmas, I started to feel like my life was falling apart. My joints ached, my best friend judged me harshly for my choice to keep seeing Matthew, and an artist who once found me beautiful now found me stupid instead.

Only Matthew remained unchanged and consistent in his actions towards me. He treated me with the same affectionate scorn, the same rigid horniness as he always had. I fought as hard as ever against the impulse to love him in this time when I felt so needy and bereft, because if I lost him too, I thought that probably would have finished me off.

In the week leading up to Christmas, though, I was unable to see him. I had extra shows to dance and Matthew had obligations to keep. But on Christmas Eve morning, he called and asked if I could come to dinner with him that night, when the show was over, and I said yes, I could. He told me to wear a little black dress and no panties, and he promised to meet me at the stage door at 10:45.

After the show that night, while everyone else gave each other warm Christmas wishes, shared plans and made arrangements to meet places, I showered and dressed to meet the tyrannical lover who ruled my world. I dried my wavy hair and drew it up into a loose chignon because I knew he loved to look at the back of my neck. I put on my smooth, pale porcelain-doll makeup, and applied the nutmeg lipstick carefully to my full lips. I put on black thigh high stockings with wide lace tops, and as he required, I wore no panties. I slipped into some patent leather pumps with high block heels, and I hoped desperately that I wouldn't humiliate myself.

Dinner with Matthew. We had never actually gone out to dinner together, not once in two and a half months. We ate at his house when we played, formal meals in his dining room and breakfasts in the kitchen. I'm sure he thought, like me, that dinner out would be too risky, would feel too much to the wistful romantic in me like a date. And he was right, I was really afraid that it would feel like a date to me, that I would fantasize, and he'd know it, and that he'd punish me for it. Maybe that was the whole point of this Christmas Eve exercise, to make me act stupid so he could torture and humiliate me. *'Tis the season*, I thought wryly. But it was my eternal goal to do what he wanted, so if that's what he wanted, that's exactly what I would do.

I walked out the stage door and there he stood in the cold air, in a heavy wool coat that made him look ridiculously handsome. He smiled, hugged and kissed me, and I'm sure to any person passing by we seemed like any other couple, a boyfriend and girlfriend, even a husband and wife, from the tender and familiar way we embraced. He led me to his car and held open the door, and I climbed in the front seat instead of the back seat I used with the driver. He kissed me again with his hand up my dress, and thrust his fingers inside me, which I accepted with a moan.

He smiled and licked off his fingers, then slammed the door and got in on the other side. He hummed some familiar Christmas carol to himself under his breath. What was wrong with the both of us, I wondered, that on Christmas Eve we were not with family or friends? No, we were both of us with our perverse, sadomasochistic lover, and neither of us thought that it was strange or sad. I had no family left aside from Grégoire, and he had Georges to sit with in front of a holiday fire. And Matthew, I assume he had no family either, because he never mentioned them, and I never asked.

He drove me to a dark and expensive restaurant, the type of restaurant with no prices on the menu. He ordered wine and food for both of us in French and I resigned quietly that I would eat whatever arrived. Of course, it was delicious, whatever it was. Of course Matthew would know the most wonderful things to eat. We both ate slowly, and for a long time we didn't talk, which was fine with me.

I didn't talk because I was afraid of saying something stupid, afraid of sounding too familiar and loving during this meal that felt like a date. He didn't talk because he was too busy staring at me, staring with eyes that made me burn. I was half afraid he'd turn me over the table right there and fuck me, lift my skirt and thrust inside while the other patrons looked on. His eyes were so alive with smoldering lust, I had no idea why he hadn't just taken me straight to his home. It had been nearly a week then since we'd been together, and we both felt that strain.

"I've missed you," he said when the waiter brought dessert. I stirred my coffee, too nervous to reply. I remembered that night long ago at the coffee house, when I'd first drunk coffee with him and he'd told me what he wanted from me.

"I've missed you too, Matthew." It was a safe, inane thing to say. Then he reached over and picked up the rectangular box he'd carried in, and handed it over to me.

It was wrapped in heavy, elegant paper, a stylized holiday print of berries and holly leaves. There was a bow on top, perfect and crimson.

"I didn't get you anything, Matthew," I said, running my fingers over the gorgeous wrappings.

"Good. I didn't want you to."

"Whatever you want, I'll do it for you later. Anything at all."

He rolled his eyes. "Don't be a dweeb. We both know you'll do what I want anyway. Just open it up. I wanted to get you a present, and now I fucking want you to see what's inside."

I smiled. He was so ridiculously charming, even when he called me a dweeb and ordered me around. I carefully undid the paper, not wanting to wrinkle it, and honestly, not really wanting the moment to end.

"Rip the fucking paper off it, Lucy. Open it up or I'll break it over your ass."

I smiled wider and looked up at him from under my lashes. I ripped off the rest of the paper and lifted the lid. I had expected something typically appropriate between us. Some new lingerie, or a paddle or a plug, but there was nothing sexual or kinky inside that box. There was a beautifully framed piece of parchment covered in spidery calligraphy and decorated at the top with a painting of a Grecian urn.

He'd gifted me with a framed copy of the Keats poem I'd quoted to him, the one about truth and beauty, and it made my breath catch in my throat. *Ode on a Grecian Urn*, it was called, five stanzas long. I stared down at the poem while he sat and watched without a word. The first two lines drew me in with their strange, appropriate sentiment:

*Thou still unravish'd bride of quietness,*
*thou foster-child of silence and slow time...*

Silence. Slow time. I thought of our hours in the basement when he only sat and stared. He'd found this for me, or perhaps, knowing him, had it crafted by some artist to his exact specifications.

*Heard melodies are sweet, but those unheard are sweeter...*
*Thou canst not leave thy song, nor ever can those trees be bare;*
*Bold lover, never, never canst thou kiss.*

As I read, it seemed every single line spoke of our strange relationship. Matthew and I were frozen in time just like the pastoral scenes on the urn that Keats described. We were frozen in a scene where we reached for one another, but would never actually touch.

*More happy love! more happy, happy love!*
*For ever warm and still to be enjoy'd,*
*For ever panting, and for ever young;*
*All breathing human passion far above...*

For us, it would always just be passion. He would love me while I was young and perfect, his unchanging ideal. And then what? Someday, the urn would be broken, would crumble to pieces, capitulate to the ravages of time. The poem was so appropriate to us that I shivered, and for a long time, I couldn't look up into his eyes.

At the end, the famous and well known words we'd discussed so long ago...

*Beauty is truth, truth beauty—that is all ye know on earth, and all ye need to know.*

The simple words that exemplified Matthew's view of the world, all Matthew desired. *You're beautiful to me. There will be only truth between us.*

I looked over at Matthew and wondered what it meant. If it was a declaration of some kind, I didn't understand it. Perhaps it had no significance at all. Maybe it was a mindfuck, a way to hurt or mock me. Maybe simply a gift to a lover with whom he'd spent so much time.

"Thank you, Matthew," was all I dared say in the end.

"Do you like it?"

"Yes. I love it. It's beautiful."

He stared at me, long and hard, but I gave him nothing, no emotional reaction. I felt we were both teetering on the edge of the cliff again.

"I love everything you give me," I said as an afterthought, and thankfully, he left it at that.

He took me back to his house afterward, and when I turned toward the basement, he pulled me instead up the stairs. "Not on Christmas Eve. I won't beat on you tonight."

"You can if you want."

"No."

Up in his room, he took off my dress as I kicked off my shoes. "Go stand against the wall," he said, stripping out of his clothes. He pushed me over to the broad white wall, the one without the paintings, and I stood there in my black stockings with my hands at my sides. He sat on the bed, looking at me, stroking his cock which was already huge and hard.

"Play with yourself. Stroke your clitty, pinch your tits."

I did what he asked, trying to look sexy. He didn't like that at all.

"Fucking submissive. Harder. *Touch* yourself." He stood up and strode over to me.

127

I moaned as he pinched my nipples, then twisted them mercilessly hard. He reached between my legs and found my swollen clit and pinched that too until I danced under his touch.

"You little cum whore," he breathed. "Come on. Come for me, let me watch you."

I reached out to him and squeezed his shoulder hard, and he let me, so I kept squeezing, just as he squeezed and worked my sodden clit. "Come on, you little slut," he prompted me again, then he pressed himself against me, pressed me to the wall and kissed me hard and violently, with more feeling than he ever had before. He hauled me over to the bed and pushed me onto my hands and knees and drove into me standing up from behind. He came just moments later, driving hard, then collapsed on top of me, his lips against my neck.

Before he even caught his breath, he gasped, "Lie down. Lie down and spread your legs." I did, the obedient slave, and he fell on me at once. He stroked my thighs, bit the top of my stockings, licked and teased me while I flew on a high of sexual pleasure and pure infatuation for the man who mastered me.

He devoured me, kissed and sucked my sore clit, licked my pussy and asshole with a fervor that made me wild. He had gone down on me on many occasions, but this time, somehow, it was even more abandoned and wild. The arousal built, throbbed, turned inside out and then exploded. I came apart, thrashing under his mouth. He held my thighs hard between his hands and began again. I begged for respite, but he allowed none. He made me come again, this time finishing by thrusting his thick fingers in and out of my cunt. As I came, he gazed down at me chanting, "Yes. Yes, beautiful girl."

He lay beside me then on the bed while I gasped for breath, completely spent, sprawled at his side. He watched me, his head propped on his hand.

"I have an unhealthy addiction to watching you come."

I looked over at him. "I've noticed. I don't mind."

He stroked my face a moment, and then leaned over and kissed me like a true lover, and I let myself kiss him back just the same. We kissed like that while time spun away, and then he broke away from me. He suddenly seemed agitated and cross.

"Lucy, can you go home now? I'll call a cab for you. You can't stay here tonight. I've got things to do in the morning. You understand."

I nodded. Yes, I did. Of course I did. I took a cab home that he insisted on paying for, and I was really okay with that. I climbed the stairs to my little apartment with my framed Keats poem clutched in my hands.

*Who are these coming to the sacrifice?*
*To what green altar, O mysterious priest...*

Matthew, my handsome and mysterious priest. And I, the urn, frozen in beauty, not permitted to change.

He was the artist, the priest, the shaman, and I was the urn, existing only to receive.

\* \* \* \* \*

That lovely Christmas Eve night that Matthew took me to dinner was an anomaly, certainly, perhaps an attempt at holiday cheer. It was nice, but I think it made both of us uneasy. We returned after the bustle of the holidays to our regular schedule and my stringent sessions in his basement continued just as before.

One morning after such a session, I came awake with the most delicious feeling. I was warm and relaxed. The bed was the perfect cozy temperature. Matthew lay beside me, an arm's length away. He rarely held me in bed even though he insisted almost always that I sleep over. I knew he didn't want me there for snuggles and cuddles. He wanted me to sleep over in case he felt like fucking me in the middle of the night, and he did wake me up to do that fairly often. Those were always nice fucks, half-conscious and quick.

But that morning, I just felt so happy and cozy. I did a hard stretch beside him. His hands came out for me at once and his sleepy arms wrapped around me. "Do it again," he whispered.

"Stretch for me." I stretched again and his hands groped over me. He nuzzled his face into the curve of my neck.

"Lucy...Happy birthday."

And I swear to God, I had completely forgotten that on this cold, luxuriously comfortable morning I had been born twenty-nine years ago.

He fucked me then, twice in a row, once from behind and once clutched close in his arms. Warm delicious snugglefucking. I came both times, to his soft encouragement, to his constant demand. *Come, Lucy, come.*

Down in the kitchen, Mrs. Kemp produced a cake for me, a small cinnamon apple cake with roses in cream cheese frosting. It had a candle on it which Matthew lit with a flourish. I laughed while they sang Happy Birthday in surprisingly lovely harmony.

All of this strange softening of Matthew around me, the affectionate kisses, the cuddles, things like the birthday cake, I was so happy he felt all right with doing these things, because it meant I had finally convinced him that my emotions were not a threat. That I no longer harbored unrealistic fantasies, that I wouldn't flip out and ask him for love. That I wouldn't expect any commitment. Things got so much easier, so much simpler after that.

After one particularly debauched session, as he kissed me before bed, he asked if I'd like to go out with him again.

"On Saturday, I'll pick you up at the theater. I'd like to take you to dinner with some friends."

*Some friends.* Friends like Davis? "Okay, Matthew."

"Why 'okay'?" he asked, mimicking my ambivalent tone. "What? Why not?"

"Nothing. I said okay. I would like to." I didn't know why he was so annoyed. Did he want me to fall over myself with excitement? "Will they know what I am to you?"

"Maybe. Do you care?"

"I guess not."

"I'll clear it up right off and introduce you as my sex slave."

I looked at him, because it was completely possible he wasn't joking. I guess my uneasiness amused him, because he laughed and pulled me next to him in the bed.

"Listen, don't think so much. I want you to come out with me. I want to see you smile and laugh and do something besides take me in every hole. You're my submissive, correct?"

"Yes, sir."

"Then you do as I say. I don't really understand the attitude."

I murmured apologies, but I felt his mood shift.

"Do you want me to put a fucking collar on you, Lucy? Would that make you feel better? Take you to dinner on a leash? Make you eat it out of a dog bowl at my feet?"

"No, sir."

"How about a toy in your ass while we dine? You'd probably like that."

"Matthew, it's fine, I'll go. I just didn't know if these were friends who..."

"Who what? Who will come back with us to the basement?" He fought with himself for a moment, over whether or not to admit it, and then I knew for certain that they were. Of course, he'd wanted to spring the whole thing on me. Now he would be angry that I'd pried it from him in advance.

"So what if they do, Lucy? What are you going to do about it? I know you're a hot little cum-crazy whore. You come like a fucking horny slut every time I fill all your holes. I thought you might enjoy a few extra of my friends."

"Yes. Yeah. I would love that, Matthew." I expected to be slapped now, for the way that I said that.

"You know what I'd love?" he said low and dangerously. "A little fucking appreciation sometimes."

I turned to him and pressed my head into his chest, and then sank down until I faced his cock. I wanted to suck him more than anything at that moment, just so I wouldn't have to participate in this conversation any more. He sighed as I put my mouth on him, and he let me suck and caress him at my own pace. For a long time he just let me have him, and while I had him, I thought about what he'd said.

I thought about going out to dinner and coming back to the basement with his friends. God, who cared? As long as it felt good. Just one more way to be sure we didn't fall in love. I was actually really looking forward to it. By the time he came in my throat the idea really turned me on. I hoped they were as beautiful and handsome as Matthew. I hoped they thought I was beautiful and desirable too.

# Chapter Ten:
# Falling

On Saturday night, Matthew didn't meet me at the stage door. He met me backstage, outside my dressing room door. Of course he had all-access granted whenever he wanted it. The amount of money he donated to the company assured that. He had a garment bag in one hand and a small boutique bag in the other, and a broad smile pasted across his face.

"My little dancer. How was your show tonight?"

"Fine," I murmured. My ankle hurt.

As soon as Ellie left he came into the dressing room with me. He helped me pull the black dress down over my naked body and it fit like a glove. He nodded in approval while I marveled at how it made me look. It fit so perfectly and so flatteringly. I had no idea how he managed it. I pictured him standing over me with a measuring tape while I slept, then calling a seamstress with all his notes.

"Yes, I had it made for you," he said.

"How—"

"I got your measurements from Jo." The costume mistress.

"I've never worn anything so beautiful. I really haven't."

"Well, it's yours now. It looks wonderful on you."

133

It wasn't a slut dress of course, not from Matthew. It fell to just below my knees. It had some beading, very subtle, on the front. It had an almost iridescent sheen to it, and the bodice laced up. It didn't lace up in some pseudo-corset way, it laced up with silk laces to a tie at the top. It was sexy, elegant, and girlish. I absolutely loved it and it moved like a dream.

But he wasn't done with me yet. "Hold up the skirt," he said, kneeling down. He reached for the shop bag he'd set down on the vanity and drew out a garter belt that made my breath catch.

It matched the dress in design and laced up in the front, and was embroidered with delicate beads. He put it on me, and of course, again, it fit perfectly. Then he gathered up the stockings and put them on next. He smoothed them up my leg so that I shivered, and then he attached the garter clasps for me. He licked me softly at the place where my ass met my thighs and I put my hand back on his head, twined my fingers in his hair. It was partly because I didn't want him to stop it, and partly because my legs were about to fail. It may sound funny to say this, but it was the first time in the nearly four months I'd known him that I'd touched his hair that way.

He stood up all too soon and said, "We'll be late."

As we sat in his car driving to the restaurant, he ordered me to pull my skirt up over my thighs. He made me masturbate myself until I came, and I was thankful that his windows were tinted black. For once, primed as I was by the erotic way he dressed me, it wasn't that hard to jack off for him. I wasn't as self-conscious and hesitant as I usually was. I thought too of the way his hair felt under my fingers for that wonderful moment, that very short moment when they twisted in his soft, blond locks.

When we arrived at the restaurant, it was busy and crowded. Lots of rich people standing around looking rich. It was loud, smoky, frenetic, and expensive of course. My eyes darted all around, wondering who his "friends" could be. He had told me nothing further of the people we'd meet, letting me work myself into a frenzy of curiosity and nerves. And I was nervous, very nervous to see the people that Matthew had decided to let play with me. Unlike Davis, I assumed these players knew what they were doing.

The maître'd led us to a secluded table, and I was surprised to be greeted by two men and a beautiful woman my age. Well, perhaps she was a bit older, thirty-five or so. The men were older than Matthew too, with gray in their hair. They weren't old men though, not at all. If they were fifty, I would have been surprised. And they turned me on. God, I hate to say it. They were sexy and virile, and potent to the core. They looked at me in the same way Matthew looked at me, as something to appraise. A thing to conquer and own. These men were dominants, and the woman was a submissive, that was patently clear to me even before we spoke.

I started to panic a little. What were the rules here? How should I act? I hung back and shrunk closer to Matthew, but he put his hand on my back and pushed me forward. They all stood up and greeted each other warmly, including me, so I was not to be ignored, the peon slave. Matthew pulled out my chair and seated me next to the woman. She was a woman who made me feel like a girl. She was voluptuous and sexy, and quietly self assured. Her body was amazing, large breasts and hips, and wide brown eyes framed by jet black, flowing hair. I wanted to cry, imagining my skinny dancer body beside hers, my babyish red curls next to her black, flowing mane.

She smiled at me though, kindly and sweetly. I took my cues from her even though we didn't talk. We were submissive sisters, that was the feeling I got from her, and I had a strong sense that later we'd be beaten side by side.

Matthew and the other men ordered dinner, and as I expected, Matthew ordered on my behalf. Over the course of time I gathered the men's names were Byron and Frank. I was shocked, however, to hear them refer to the woman as Slave. That was all they called her the entire time we dined, and I was terrified that Matthew would begin to do the same to me. I realized that I couldn't bear the loss of my name. But no, he referred to me many times as Lucy over the course of their conversations about me.

And yes, for the most part, that's what the men did, they discussed the sexual lives of their slaves. As in, the sexual life of me and "Slave" who was next to me, while we sat with our heads down and picked at the food on our plates. I didn't eat much although the food was delicious, but I listened, and wow, the things I learned. I remembered when Matthew had scoffed, "I'm ridiculously soft on you!" and by the end of dinner, I realized he had been, as Byron and Frank discussed their relationship with Slave.

Slave was apparently "full time," she didn't work or have her own domicile. She lived with Byron and Frank, who shared her every night. If one was tired or busy, the other one used her alone. They did a lot of the same things Matthew and I did, and then quite a bit more.

Slave wore a thick black padlocked collar, which she was ordered to display to Matthew from beneath the high neckline of her dress. Apparently she was also pierced and branded. I tried to keep the emotion out of my face, the way I felt about their arrangement, about the things she let them do to her. And of course, I wondered what exactly had been Matthew's point in this little meeting. Maybe these were things he wanted to do to me.

Did he want to take things further between us? Was he unhappy, or bored? Did he want me to be more like Slave? Did he just want one night of watching me worked over by Byron and Frank? Because I knew that was what was in store for me. I could tell by the lingering looks they gave me. I saw in their eyes the promise of pain to come. I was so scared. I wanted to take Matthew's hand and beg him, *please don't make me. I'm not that good.*

But I didn't do that. I stayed silent, because a part of me was curious too. A part of me was horny and reckless, and wanted to see if I could endure just one night of Slave's hell. I was pretty sure that Matthew would protect me from anything that broke his promises to me. He wouldn't let me get scars, or bleed, or get injured. He wouldn't let any of these men inside me without a sheath. So aside from that, what could I not bear?

I met Matthew's eyes from time to time, even though Slave kept hers down the entire time. *Yes, I'm allowed to look at my dominant. Aren't I a mess?* I met his eyes mostly to assuage my panic, to reassure myself that I was his and not Frank and Byron's, who seemed to regard their submissive as nothing much more than a dog.

Soon after we met, he had told me emphatically, *I'll never put you in a collar. I'll never treat you like a dog. I don't like to have sex with animals.* But Slave, apparently, ate off the floor. Slave was collared around the clock. She was walked sometimes on a leash in the garden in the walled backyard. She pissed and shat out in the yard too, and sometimes, her masters pissed and shat on her. Slave was punished in a dungeon. Slave competed in pony races and exhibitions. Slave didn't even have a bedroom. Slave slept on the floor next to one of her masters' beds.

I can't say myself what drove Slave to do this, even being submissive as I was. I wondered how long she had lived a life like this, how much longer she would keep at it, and what the adjustment would be like when she re-entered the world. The idea of what she had done completely terrified me...to give up everything, every inkling of dignity and will. My eyes strayed to her again and again. When she met my eyes, hauntingly, there was intelligence and irony there.

I suppose it's possible that it was all an act, that Byron and Frank bragged about things that weren't true. Matthew didn't brag a great amount about me, just spoke of my lithe dancer's body, of how my muscles strained under his hands. He spoke of the way I lost myself, the way I came continuously and uncontrollably for him like a mindless slut. He spoke of the way I loved to be doubly penetrated, and the way I had never yet used our safe word, even when an outsider had beaten me and drawn blood.

He said that word, *outsider*, with an air of repugnance. I think he reminded his friends too, in a subtle way, that they were not to draw my blood. He was unapologetic for his "softness" toward me.

"I like to see her dance," he explained. "I won't take her away from that."

Byron and Frank nodded, although I knew they scorned his kindness. "Of course," said Byron, "that's a choice you're free to make."

After dinner, we went to the car. We were going to Frank and Byron's house, to use the dungeon there. I sat beside Matthew half in shock, and he knew I had to ask the questions in my mind.

"Okay, you have until we get there. Ask your questions, whatever you want."

They poured out in a rush.

"How long have you known them? Have you done this before?"

"I've known them for years, Lucy, and I've played with them many times. It's perfectly safe."

"You've slept with her? Slave?" I felt unreasonably jealous.

"I've fucked her, yes," he said. "And I will tonight."

"They'll have sex with me?"

"Yes. They'll wear condoms every time." He looked over at me with a faint frown. "Of course, you trust me to keep you safe."

"Yes, I do..." I said, and I truly did.

"But you're scared."

"Yes." I looked back at him, troubled. "Do you want me to be like her?"

"No, not really. But I do think you could learn some things from her. She's been doing this for years."

"She's prettier than me," I said mournfully.

"No, just different. If I thought she was more beautiful than you, she would be mine now, instead of you."

"What do you want me to learn from this exactly?"

He didn't answer right away. "I would like you to see how somebody else asserts dominance, and how it compares to the way that I dominate you."

"Why? So you'll look better? You want me to realize that you're soft on me? I know that already. We don't have to go through all this just to show me that."

"No, it's not that at all. What I want you to learn is if what I'm doing for you is enough. If it's all you want." *Oh God, he thinks*

138

*I'm not happy. He thinks he's not enough for me.* It boggled my brain. "I guess all I want from tonight, Lucy, is to show you that what we have is only part of what's available to you. I don't want you to be mad at me later that I never showed you."

I looked out the window crossly. Did he think I was that naive? "I read *The Story of O*, and *Carrie's Story* too."

"Even so, Lucy Merritt, you're my submissive. If I want to educate you further, you're obliged to obey."

"I know I am, Matthew Norris," I answered, and that earned me an excruciating pinch on the inside of my leg.

\* \* \* \* \*

When we arrived in Byron and Frank's "dungeon," I really had to try hard not to laugh. It was such the epitome of an actual sex dungeon, it was almost too over the top. It made Matthew's stark, neutral basement room and armoire of toys look like a honeymoon suite. Slave was already naked and on her knees, with huge weights hanging down from her pierced nipples and her hands bound to a chain over her head.

I'll try to tell you everything that happened in that dungeon, but things moved so fast, it was almost a blur. They moved fast, and yet we were there for nearly three hours. I did lose myself a little bit. More than I'd expected to.

To begin with, Matthew ordered me to strip, and Byron and Frank immediately mocked my worthless body, my skinny legs and non-existent boobs. They tied my arms over my head and took turns beating and marking my ass while I watched Matthew fuck Slave in the mouth. After that, they asked Matthew if they could both fuck me at once. He agreed that they could, that I would love that, and the truth was that I actually did. They put clips on my nipples first that hurt like hellfire, then Frank lay down on a bench and pulled me onto his cock. Byron straddled the bench behind me and thrust into my ass and they both fucked me slowly in a very smooth and practiced way. And yes, it felt great, I got turned on from it, turned on enough to really come hard. Matthew sat in a chair across the room and watched with an unfathomable look on his face. Byron and Frank said nothing about the fact that I'd come, and then Slave and I were made to kneel and were both beaten at the same time.

As I cowered beside Slave with my arms cuffed behind my back, I thought that the way she took beatings was amazing. She writhed and moaned like she loved every blow. It was like the pain didn't touch her, or if it did, it was something she craved. While she moaned in my ear, I screamed and begged pitifully. When they were done striping both our bottoms, they made Slave lie down and told me to eat her out. I did, even though I'd never gone down on a woman. I tried some of the things Matthew often did on me. She moaned and twisted under me and seemed to find pleasure, but since she seemed to find pleasure in everything, I couldn't really tell if it was true. Then she was ordered to go down on me, which she did while Matthew fucked her in the ass, watching my face the whole time. I let myself drift, as Slave's cunnelingus talents put my own to sorry shame. She had me climaxing haplessly in minutes, and I stared into Matthew's eyes as I came. Up to this point, I actually found great pleasure in that dungeon, but then, after that, things took a nasty turn.

Byron commented to Matthew that I was undisciplined, childish, and self-absorbed, that I came too frequently and with too much pleasure of my own. Matthew laughed and said that was true, and Byron asked if he could gag me and punish me as he saw fit. What he actually said was, *Can I take her into my hands?* I hated that idea, because his hands would not be Matthew's, but Matthew said that he could if he wanted to, and things got totally crazy after that.

Byron began by gagging me with great pleasure. I had never worn a gag, and I'm sure that turned him on, to be the first one to gag my mouth. The one he produced was invasive. He thrust the wide phallic shape into my mouth and buckled it against my face with the straps, so I was unable to breathe deeply or swallow with any success. Matthew asked to check it, and I thought there was no way he would make me endure it, but he nodded, to my dismay, and said I was okay. Then I was blindfolded and bound to a leather-covered, X-shaped cross, bound at every point, wrists, ankles, neck, and waist. Byron, Frank, and Matthew all fucked me in the ass at that point, and I could tell from the feel of it that Matthew went last. I also didn't enjoy it at all. I was far too traumatized by the helplessness I felt.

Next, Byron lectured me a long time about how worthless I was, about how much Matthew loved Slave. He said that their slave was lower than shit but that I was even more worthless than she, because at least she was beautiful and womanly while I was unattractive and poorly trained. I could hear Slave's moans in the background, that someone was fucking her. The idea that it was Matthew brought tears to my eyes. Was this truly what Matthew wanted? The fertile beauty and utter submission of Slave? Instead he had me, coltish and pale, and more likely to cry and scream than moan with pleasure under his blows.

Byron started to beat me painfully then with a cane, and that in itself hurt like hell, but aside from that, he hit my thighs and my back. I screamed behind the gag and writhed in a panic, because those marks would show. Matthew asked sharply for him to restrict his blows to my ass, and Byron began to argue with him about the place of a slave. Matthew insisted I could not be marked as Byron wanted, and then Byron asked to beat the bottom of my soles instead. I shook my head violently, made a desperate sound of alarm, as much as I could behind the gag in my mouth, but Matthew was already voicing his denial. *Lucy is a dancer*, he said.

And those four words, I can't say what they meant to me, while I was gagged and trussed and fucked and beaten there on that cross. Yes, my name was still Lucy to him, not slave or whore, and I was a dancer, not just a piece of flesh. But the worst part of it was, what made me start weeping, was the edge of frustration in Matthew's voice that said he was being embarrassed, that he was being shown up. That Byron and Frank were rubbing it in his face. *Your girl is a piece of shit*, was basically what they were saying. I hated that I'd brought that embarrassment to him. For Matthew to be belittled on my behalf was so horribly unfair, and then for him to still stand up for me so staunchly made me want to sob.

Things turned ugly then. Byron cycled through toy after toy. Beatings and dildos and nipple clamps and beatings and hair pulling and more beating to a constant symphony of verbal abuse. Matthew and his friends had become locked in some testosterone-driven game of slave chicken, and I desperately, desperately wanted to scream *mercy*. But I wasn't able to scream anything at all. In fact, I was barely able to keep from choking on my spit behind that godforsaken gag. I thought pretty soon I'd be foaming at the mouth. If this was S & M, real S & M, I didn't want it. I only wanted what Matthew gave me, that edge of pain that was a pleasure to endure. Byron and Frank wanted to break me, smash me to pieces and then brutally smash me some more. I think Byron was trying to see how far Matthew would let him go, to see if he could actually force Matthew to stop him. And he did, when Byron said he wanted to piss in my mouth. I shook my head, frantic and disgusted, as Byron mocked me. "Do you think you have a choice?"

But Matthew muttered, "I don't think so. Bodily fluids. You know. It's getting late, we should probably go."

He came over to the cross and stood behind me, stood between me and Byron who had to pee. It felt so protective, his body behind me. I cried desperate tears that I couldn't reach back for him. Even when I had failed so miserably to live up to this S & M dream, even when he was angry and embarrassed, he still came behind me and put his hand on my neck. He touched me as if to say, *okay, now it's over*, and I wept in sorrow and shame. He unmasked me, undid my restraints, and then carefully removed the awful gag stuffed down my throat. My lips and chin were covered in drool and I swiped it away as best as I could, feeling ugly and humiliated. I couldn't have met his eyes then for anything, and fortunately he would not meet my eyes either. He brought me my dress and threw it at me. "Get ready. We're leaving."

I quickly obeyed. I knew he was disappointed in everything, me, his friends, the whole sordid scene. He didn't even ask me to thank Byron and Frank, just said goodbye to them and dragged me out the door. As he pulled me to the car, I was awash in self-loathing, and Matthew was more furious than I'd ever seen him before.

"I'm sorry, Matthew," I whispered.

"Shut up," he barked so sharply that I flinched. He opened the door and shoved me in the back seat, then slammed the door and went to the driver's side. He stood outside a minute, like he was trying to compose himself, then climbed in and peeled away from the house.

"I'm sorry—" I said again.

"Just shut the fuck up, Lucy. I mean it."

"I tried, I just couldn't—"

"Just shut up!" he yelled. "I asked you to fucking shut up!"

So I did. I sat and cried in the backseat as quietly as I could, and when we finally got to his house, let him haul me inside and rip off my dress.

He yelled for Mrs. Kemp as he pushed me to my knees.

"Suck me," he growled, tearing open his pants, pulling out his cock and stuffing it into my mouth. While I started sucking him off, Mrs. Kemp scurried in from the kitchen in alarm.

"Take this fucking dress and fucking burn it," he said, tossing it at her feet.

"Yes, Mr. Norris," she replied, not missing a beat. I did not miss a beat either. While she collected the dress from the floor, I sucked away at his cock, while he pulled my hair so hard that it hurt.

"Just suck it, you bitch. Don't be lazy."

I sucked it like I could just suck everything away, and when I finished he looked down at me furiously while I swallowed his cum. He hauled me up and pulled me towards the basement, and I fought him then. I fought him hard, but he carried me kicking and flailing down the stairs and flung me into the room, right onto the floor. For a long time he stood and looked down at me as I sobbed brokenly. His anger, his furious disapproval was something I just couldn't bear.

143

"Please, what can I do?"

"I asked you to shut up. That's what I want you to do."

"I'm sorry. I'm sorry!"

"I don't want another fucking word from you." He crossed to the armoire and got the cane, and stood over me for a minute, and then he said, "Don't bother to count."

As he started to beat me, I heard him talking low, almost to himself.

"You know why they call it *falling*, Lucy? Why they call it falling in love? Because it's completely out of your control. And I hate being out of control."

I was unable to untangle his words right then, exhausted and overwhelmed as I was. He just kept on hitting me with that cane while I writhed and drew my legs up on the floor. I felt it, but I didn't feel it. It hurt so badly, but at the same time I felt so empty by that point that my entire body was a void. It was almost four in the morning, and I was completely sure that Matthew's mind had snapped. He beat me until my own mind faltered and grew foggy, and then a word in my mind suddenly became clear.

"Mercy," I moaned into the carpet.

He hit me again. Fire and pain. *Stop him.* "What?"

"Mercy!" I screamed at him. "Mercy! Mercy! Stop!"

I heard the cane hit the wall across the room, and I heard the door slam when he stalked out of the room and left me there, and I lay there still and alone until long after dawn.

So in the end it wasn't Frank or Byron who broke me, it was Matthew himself. He broke me and crushed me and smashed me and left me lying there in jagged pieces on the cold basement floor.

# Chapter Eleven:
# Plans

I'm not sure what time it was when he came back to get me, but I was still lying in exactly the same place. I never wanted to move again, and when he tried to pick me up, I struggled and hit out at him.

"Lucy." His voice sounded tired. "Don't fight me."

He carried me upstairs and put me in the tub. I soaked in there for half an hour while he hovered around, and then he ordered me to wash my hair. When I ignored him, he washed it himself, and when he was done he had to help me out of the tub because my legs and my back were so tired and sore.

He dried me and made me lie down on the bed and again he massaged my bruised and welted ass with salve. After that he combed out my hair as I lay on my stomach. I never even lifted my head from the pillow. At some point while he did that I fell asleep, because when I woke up again, it was dinnertime on Sunday night. Matthew was there when I opened my eyes.

"Hello," he said.

I said nothing back to him.

"Lucy," he said, and then he stopped, and he didn't say anything for a long time.

Finally, he said very matter-of-factly, "Lucy, I've decided to make another promise to you. I'm never going to share you again. I decided I just don't like it."

"Oh, you decided that?" In ordinary circumstances, my tone would have gotten me slapped.

But he only frowned and said, "Yes," and waited to see what my reply was to that.

My reply was, "I want to go home."

"You're not going home."

"What do you want, Matthew? To beat me some more? To put some huge fucking gag in my mouth and make me drool and choke and then piss on me?"

"I had no idea, Lucy—"

"You're a liar. You promised me truth."

"Lucy—"

"Why did they call that woman Slave? What's wrong with them? Why are they so sick?"

"They call her that because she likes it. Because she wants them to."

"I've gone down on a woman exactly once in my life, and I'll never even know her real name."

"Her name is Gloria. And believe me, there's nothing they do to her that she doesn't completely revel in."

"Do you like her?"

"I don't care for her at all, to be perfectly honest with you."

"But you want me to be like her."

He snorted as if the idea was ridiculous. "No, I don't! God forbid you would be like her. I can't stand her. She's a total fake."

"What do you mean, fake?"

"You know what I mean." I thought for a minute and actually, I realized I did know what he meant. "She was better than me at everything, though. At the way she took pain."

"I love the way you take pain, Lucy. I live for it."

"Do you think I'm too skinny?"

"I think you're perfect as you are. I've told you that before, many times, so don't annoy me by fishing for compliments. Jesus,

Lucy, they were just trying to fuck with your mind. And were successful at it, I might add."

I kept asking questions, and he kept letting me, and the longer he let me, the braver I got.

"Why did you let them hurt me so badly? Why did you let them gag me like that? Let them mark my back?"

"I stopped them!"

"A little too late."

"Do you want to know something, Lucy? You stupid little fuck. Do you even realize why they were so rough with you? Why they turned so completely against me? You're a hundred times more real and sincere than Gloria. Gloria's a pain whore. They're never enough for her. They can't keep her happy, they can't satisfy her. She tops them from below, and honestly, soon, she's going to leave them. She's got both their nuts clutched right in her hand. I don't believe you couldn't see that."

I thought back over the evening, and his words made sense to me. It all became crystal clear. "They were jealous of you."

"Yes, jealous. Jealous of your honest, open reactions. Jealous of the fear you have, and the trust you place in me. Jealous of the noises you make that are real, not out of some porn movie."

I digested that for a moment, and suddenly Byron and Frank seemed so sad. No matter the cruelty, the fancy dungeon, the imaginative punishments, they would never be enough for her. It boggled my mind. It all seemed so sad and ugly, and not sexy at all.

"So why? Why did you take me there?"

"They wanted Slave to see you, to see if they could get through to her. They're trying to save a relationship. But I'm sorry in hindsight that I got you involved. If Byron or Frank try to contact you, you're not to talk to them. You'll tell me immediately if they do."

I snorted. "Are you afraid they'll try to steal your slave?"

"Don't laugh. They will try. You're not to go."

I rolled my eyes. "Oh, God, Matthew."

"I'm not kidding. Promise me. Swear to me now."

147

"I promise."

"Swear to me!"

"Okay, okay, I swear it."

He looked at me, frowning, and he seemed really tired. I was afraid that soon he would cut off my questions.

"Last night, when we got home, why did you do that?"

His face was suddenly hard, his expression hooded. "You are my submissive, you remember. You agree to give yourself to me. You always have the safe word, which you did use."

"You wanted to force me to use it. Why?"

"I don't have to explain myself to you."

"I know," I snapped. "But it would be nice if you did every once in a while."

"Does it matter?" His whole face changed into a frightening, furious mask. "Does it really matter why I did it? Your body is mine to use as I like. I can give you the most severe punishment I can dream up only because I felt like doing it to you. That's what you signed up for. And you can stop coming anytime, as you know."

He said that so coolly, my lips started to tremble.

"Do you want me to stop coming?"

He tsked in annoyance. "No, Lucy, I don't. What other stupid questions would you like to ask?"

"It doesn't matter. You won't answer anyway."

He scowled at me with his arms crossed over his chest. "Do you want to know why? You want to know why, Lucy? Look at me."

I did, very warily. He looked at me and his eyes narrowed, and his jaw twitched, and I thought for a moment he might hit me. He didn't hit me, although honestly, I would have preferred that to what he said.

"I need to remind myself that no matter how beautiful and perfect you are, you're nothing more to me than three holes to fuck and an ass to beat on when I'm feeling punchy. Truth, Lucy. You can thank me for it if you want, since I didn't have to tell you."

"Thank you, Matthew," I said through clenched teeth.

"You're welcome." He cocked his head, and looked down at me. "Do you know how many times I hit you last night, after we got home, how many times I hit you with the cane?"

I shook my head.

"Thirty, Lucy. You said mercy on the thirtieth stroke."

"Do you love me?"

His face got hard, and he blew out his breath.

"Are you falling in love with me, Matthew?" I repeated. I believe the term he used for it earlier, when we talked about Slave, was *topping from below.*

He squirmed, which I hated, and then he seemed to collect himself, and he actually answered me, which I hadn't expected. The problem was, he lied through his teeth.

"No, Lucy, I'm not falling in love with you. Last night I got a little jealous, a little possessive, maybe. It was hard watching them with you, knowing that they want what I have. But they wouldn't appreciate you the way I do. I guess for a moment I thought that was love, but it wasn't. Please don't deceive yourself by thinking it was..." His voice trailed off. He sighed and looked at his hands. *Don't deceive yourself,* he told me. Okay.

"I can't give you love. I won't, Lucy. I told you that from the start. I've been honest with you."

"Why not? Why can't you love me?"

"I just can't, but you have to believe that I care very deeply for you."

"I do believe that, Matthew. But you know what else I believe? I don't think you tell me the truth. I think it's you that's deceived, it's you that lies. I want to go home."

So that night, dinnertime on Sunday, Matthew had his driver take me home. I'm not sure if he waited for me to show up on Tuesday, but I didn't, or any day after that. He didn't call, which was a relief to me, and after a while the driver stopped coming so I could stop sneaking out the front. I didn't see Matthew backstage or in classes. He very gracefully let me go.

And this time that Matthew and I spent apart, I always assumed it would be a temporary thing, because I was terribly lonely without him and I couldn't imagine he didn't miss me. In fact, the more time we spent without each other, the more I came to realize all he did for me. The structure he gave my life, the affection, the hot pleasure, all of it was missed. Even the way he slept beside me, the way he would reach for me, half asleep, drowsy and hard. All those things I took for granted when we were together, it occurred to me now how needed they'd been. It seemed more and more that we were two wrongs that somehow made a right. But we needed a serious reset, and he needed to be punished for lying to me, even if, in doing so, I punished myself.

I looked often at the poem he'd given me, puzzled over it to figure out the clues I would need to understand him. He had said to me, *I can't give you love. I won't*, and it haunted me. *Why, why, why?* Why couldn't Matthew give love to me? Why couldn't Matthew give up control? Were the two things tied together? Somehow I knew they were.

Just as Matthew had warned me, Byron and Frank came to offer for me. They were waiting outside the stage door after the show one rainy Saturday, handsome and scary-looking in their rich suits and ties.

Byron approached me first, and I turned a little from him.

"Lucy, how have you been?"

"Fine." I suddenly wished Matthew's driver was here, that I could slide into that backseat and escape.

"Frank and I heard that you were no longer with Matthew. Is that true?" he asked in a strange, controlled voice.

"I don't know. We're sort of taking a break, I guess. We had a falling out."

"Was it over the night we spent together?" asked Frank. "Slave is no longer with us, you know."

So Matthew had been right about that as well, and so here they were, looking for new blood, which was me.

Byron came a little closer, and I stepped back. "If that night was difficult for you, if we hurt you, we're sorry. If you wanted to consider playing with us again, we could negotiate what we do. To a degree. How far we go."

I was already shaking my head.

"I really can't." I thought of Matthew's words to me about this. *They will try. You're not to go. Swear to me!* I wasn't to go, he'd told me that emphatically. So while I might have been tempted to consider it if I wasn't still in love with Matthew, I didn't, not even for a second.

"It can be a temporary arrangement," suggested Frank. "If you're taking a break with Matthew. Something to pass the time, just for now."

I didn't want to think about how desperate that sounded, and the look of cloaked intensity in their eyes. It wasn't as if I wasn't safe at that moment. There were dancers coming and going, and Grégoire was walking me home. He'd be out at any time. But the low voices they used to be sure no one would overhear our conversation gave an edge of menace to their words. They had backed me into a corner, for privacy, of course, but it felt more than a little like a power play. These two men standing here, looking civilized and kindly, making soft requests to me under the harsh light of the street were the same two men who had beaten and gagged me and asked to piss in my mouth.

"I have to go," I said, scooting over to the stage door. It was locked from the outside, so I had to wait for someone to come out to get back in. I stood with my hand on it, praying for anyone, anyone to come.

"Lucy, we'll go if we're upsetting you so much."

I bowed my head. They had power over me like Matthew, the same power of dominance that controlled and cowed me. The difference was, I didn't want them to have it, so I just shook my head, not trusting myself to speak. I knew if I did I'd sound guilty that I didn't want to do as they asked.

Byron tried once more, sensing my weakness. "It could be whatever you want, Lucy. Temporary or permanent. We could work out the guidelines. The idea of two men controlling you, working you, that doesn't interest you? That doesn't turn you on?"

I looked around, suddenly glad we were alone out there. Was I such a slut? Yes, the idea did turn me on. It turned me on a lot.

151

These two powerful men, handsome and virile, and horny enough to have me that they would let me set the rules. For a moment I almost let it creep into my mind. *We could work out the guidelines. It could be what you want.*

But it would never be what I wanted, because what I really wanted was Matthew. Matthew, who had forbidden me to go with them. And if I went with them, even temporarily, what if it got horribly blurred? What if I began to feel for them what I felt for Matthew? To feel that times two, that confusion and longing, I thought it would finish me off.

"To be honest with you, the idea of it does turn me on. But Matthew told me I wasn't to go with you, and even on a break, I'm his submissive after all."

Then fortunately, the stage door opened and Grégoire came out. I stammered a short goodbye to Frank and Byron. They nodded and walked away. I could see then, now that the conversation was over, the possibility of success dashed, the controlled ire they had hidden from me. They were furious that they left without what they sought. For myself, I felt an almost crippling relief. They were angry, just savagely angry in general, and they would have taken it out on me. Angry at Slave, beautiful Gloria, who had left them feeling less of the men they were, angry at anyone who might have the power to do that again. I saw now why Matthew had forbidden me to go with them. In my heart, I thanked Matthew for that.

But for many weeks more after that tense standoff, I subsisted without Matthew and sleepwalked through my life missing him every minute of the day. I spent a little more time with Grégoire, and a lot of time on my own. The days of dancing began to stretch out before me like trials. My joints became worse, my ankles ached. Then one day, one Saturday night performance, one of my ankles gave out completely and failed. It happened right in the middle of a show while I was on stage, and Grégoire felt it and compensated for it, such was his mastery of partnering. Somehow he carried me through the finishing notes of the dance until I could hobble off the stage and collapse. Some in the audience might have been fooled, but anyone who knew anything about dance would have known at once that something was wrong.

It hurt so badly I feared it was broken. Finally, now, my body was done with me. It was the beginning of the end and I burst into bitter tears. I sat there on the cold dirty floor in the wings, crying my eyes out, surrounded by mournful dancers who all empathized with me. I felt a hand on my back then, warm and firm, and I knew that warmth and pressure as well as I knew my own self.

I turned with tearful eyes to find Matthew right there, kneeling beside me with an anxious look. I wondered how he'd gotten there so quickly, and then realized he must have been watching the show. He would have known the moment it happened, the very second, because, like Grégoire, he was attuned to my body as much as his own.

By this time it had been nearly two months since I'd been with Matthew, and even injured, even devastated, I longed for him to take me in his arms. His face was so close to mine, his lips, his icy blue eyes right there. I wanted to press my body to his, cling to him and not let go.

"Matthew," I said. "Matthew." It was a plea, a prayer, a sob. It was all I could say.

He rubbed my back, supporting me there on the floor. "Lucy, poor Lucy," he said, and it was the next best thing to an embrace, the caring and concern in those words.

We had no physical therapist on staff to examine and treat my injury, so I would have to be taken to a hospital. He offered to take me for treatment, and as usual, everyone deferred to him. Then he did take me in his arms, just picked me up and carried me while I cried onto his shirt. He placed me in the front seat of his car, taking care not to jostle my leg.

"Okay?" he said, carefully positioning my swollen ankle. "Does it hurt?"

"Yes." *Yes, it hurts. This all hurts so much.* I wanted to scream out to him, *please don't leave me. Please take me home with you now and don't leave me alone again.* But I didn't, I just sat there sobbing, whimpering and sniffling like a child.

And being a rich and resourceful man, he didn't actually take me to a hospital. He called a friend who practiced orthopedics, and the friend came in to his office at that late hour especially to see me. Matthew introduced him as Rob, and Rob called him Matt, not Matthew or Mr. Norris like everyone else. The three of us were alone in the silence of his deserted office while he took x-rays and manipulated my injured joint. I still had on my dance costume, tights and shoes, and my garish stage makeup, sullied with tears. Everything the doctor did he did over the sheen of my tights, but still, his fingers were firm and sure, just like Matthew's. I wondered if this was another of *those* kind of friends. I pictured the exam wrapping up, and the doctor, who was quite handsome, producing a gag and ordering me over the table to be whipped. I imagined Matthew holding me down, and afterward suggesting they fuck me together. *She loves it in both holes. I'm happy to share.*

But no, that wasn't what happened. Dr. Rob looked over the x-rays and assured me it was only an acute sprain. He was so kind and businesslike, and seemed so trustworthy, I almost asked him for help with my other burgeoning aches and pains. But in the end I stayed silent and nodded and accepted his instructions for resting and healing my leg. He taped up my ankle and gave me some medicine, which Matthew handed back to him.

"This is too powerful," he said. "She's too little for this." The doctor nodded and handed Matthew a weaker prescription, and told him if I had too much pain, to call him back.

"She handles pain pretty well," he said with a perfectly straight face. I looked at my feet, flushing hot, and wished he would hold me close again.

After that, he took me back to my apartment. He let me limp for a while, then picked me up. He carried me up all the stairs, and I thought to myself that there was no elevator. He thought it too, and said I would come and stay at his house. He said it just like that, that I *would*, not *Would you like to?* or *If you want...*

"Just for a while, until your ankle is better. Rob said if you rested well, you'll be mobile again in a week."

He'd also told me no dancing for at least two weeks, and then only a limited amount. I felt my entire career slipping away, and my entire life.

I sat and let Matthew pack my things, and we left shortly afterward for his place. On the way, he held my hand and reassured me.

"I just want you to have a safe place to heal. I have no expectations from you." He was quiet a moment. "Not that I haven't missed you, Lucy. I've missed you a lot."

"I've missed you, too." I thought he might ask me then why I'd gone away from him. Or maybe he knew. Knew that it was, between us, an issue of truth. Now he was taking me to stay at his house, but not to play. Did I want to play? Oh, God, yes I did. I wanted him to want me, to take me, even broken as I was. But I just said, "Thanks for that doctor, he was really nice."

"An old college friend. Someone I trust. I think dancers need good doctors for all that wear and tear."

*Oh, you don't even know*, I thought.

Then he asked me point blank, "Are you dancing with pain, Lucy? Every night?"

Of course he knew. He knew my body inside and out. I played dumb. "What are you talking about?"

"I've noticed at the shows that your dancing is changing."

"How often are you coming to the shows?"

"Enough to notice a difference. And I'm more than a little worried about you."

"My dancing looks that bad?"

"To the average person, I'm sure you look fine. I probably study your body more carefully than the average person might."

It kind of felt good to know that, that he'd missed me so much he'd sat out in the audience to watch me. "I'm fine, Matthew," I said with fake conviction.

"Tell me the truth please, so I can help you." *Help me how?* I wanted to ask. Maybe money truly could buy everything. Maybe he could buy my youth and my body back. If anyone could do it, it was him. "What are your plans for when you're finished dancing?"

He discussed it so easily, the end of my career. I chose sarcasm, because otherwise I'd have burst into tears. "Plans? What are these 'plans' you speak of?"

"I'm serious, Lucy. What will you do when you're finished?"

"I don't know. I don't want to talk about this."

"Why not?"

"Because it makes me depressed."

"It's something you're going to have to face eventually."

"You don't understand. You don't know what this feels like. When I have to stop dancing, it's all over for me!"

"All over? Lucy, how long have you been dancing? Twenty-five years? There's more to life. You're what? Not even thirty years old. And you're smart and you're strong and you're beautiful. I think you should start to make some plans."

"I don't want to make plans. Anyway, why do you care?"

"I care, Lucy. You know that I do."

This is how I spoke to him, the man I loved, the man I was certain loved me, who had roused an old college friend out of bed at ten o'clock at night just to take care of my ankle.

"I'm so sorry, Matthew. I'm so sorry." I started to weep. I was still weeping when we pulled up to his house, and still weeping as he helped me in the shower, and still weeping when he put one of his soft, luxurious shirts on me to sleep in.

He set me up in a first floor guest room with the help of Mrs. Kemp. She clucked around me with exhalations of *Poor dear!* and *Poor thing!* I remembered with a pang of embarrassment how I was the last time she'd seen me, on my knees in the hallway, sucking off Matthew while he told her to burn my dress. Poor thing indeed. Of course that's how she saw me. And here I was in his house again, as broken as I ever was. When Mrs. Kemp felt I was comfortable enough, she finally left us alone, and I thought, *please, please, please.* But he seemed reluctant to come anywhere near me. He gave me a chaste kiss on the forehead and a squeeze on my arm. I cried alone long into the night. He was so near and yet so far from me. Why had I left him? It was clear now he wouldn't be taking me back.

In the morning Mrs. Kemp brought me breakfast, and I didn't see Matthew at all that day, or for three days after. He'd had a business trip to take. He came to see me when he arrived home on the third day, looking like a million bucks in his power suit and tie. If I could have, I would have crawled to him on my hands and knees and begged for sex. He took off his jacket and tie and loosened his collar, then sat down on the edge of the bed and stroked my calf.

"Have you been resting, Lucy?"

*Please fuck me, Matthew.* "Yes. I stayed in bed all day."

"Mrs. Kemp has been helping you out?" His voice was ridiculously tender.

"Yes, she's been wonderful." *Please, please, please, please.*

"Is there anything I can get for you?

*Yes, Matthew, you can get me some of those nipple clamps. Get that lube that makes me burn and use it to ease your cock into my ass. You can even get the cane for me if you want.*

"I'm fine. Really, I am. My ankle's almost better."

"Did you have dinner yet? Will you come and have dinner with me?" He said it slowly, as if he wished he wasn't saying it.

"Of course. Yes, Matthew," I said before he could take it back.

We ate that night at his formal table, dined on lamb and asparagus and really good wine. We ate by candlelight, which felt romantic, but he steered our conversation to practical things. I told him that Grégoire had been by to visit me, that other dancers were filling in for me for at least two weeks. He told me his orthopedist friend Dr. Rob would want to see me next Monday, and that he would come to the house. He asked me how the painkillers were working, and I told him they worked great and I barely needed them any more. I actually didn't really need them at all for my ankle, but I kept taking them because they helped so much with all my other pains. I didn't tell him that though. I didn't want to discuss again my soon-to-be-over career and lack of plans, especially with someone as successful and confident as Matthew. I know he would have given me anything, any money or help I needed. He would have bought me a house, a car, whatever I desired. But I didn't want him to think that was why I loved him, the way his wife and last girlfriend had loved him, only for the things his money bought.

I looked up at him constantly from under my lashes, and again and again our needful eyes met. I wondered what would have to happen for him to take me back, to have things be as they were. I still had to be with him, even if he was determined not to love me. I knew that now, that I had to be with him either way. But I didn't know how to broach that conversation especially when it seemed it was a subject he wanted to avoid.

So instead I said, "You were right. Byron and Frank came to see me. To ask me to be with them."

"I know," he said, his face hard.

"How did you know?"

"Kevin told me."

"Oh." Of course, Kevin had been there. Where? Somewhere. Close enough to help, close enough to stop me if I had made the wrong choice. "Was he there every night?"

"Yes. Some nights I was there."

"I never saw him, or you."

"You weren't supposed to."

He only had to look at me to see how much I wanted him, to see the desire in my eyes. If he had looked at me then, I couldn't have stopped myself. I would have pushed back my chair and knelt before him and laid my head in his lap like the most abject supplicant.

"I would never have gone with them, Matthew."

"No, you wouldn't. It wouldn't have been a good situation for you."

"What would be a good situation for me?"

His lips turned down a little at the edges and he chose not to reply. We finished our meal in tense and miserable silence.

If he still loved me, he was really hiding it well.

# Chapter Twelve:
# Pain

That night in bed, I let the tears come. If he wanted space between us, there would be space. It was he that controlled our relationship, and I didn't dare ask to return to him for fear he would deny me outright. Lying there in his house, his spare room, his bed, the feel and scent of him was everywhere tormenting me. I sobbed myself to sleep remembering the many intimate and pleasurable hours we'd shared, and dreamed of having them again.

I dreamed that the door opened and then closed, that I heard his measured footsteps crossing the floor. I dreamed that he pulled back the covers and climbed into the bed beside me, and then I woke with a start to find it was true. He was there beside me, real, not a dream, warm and stark naked, his cock hard like granite against my thigh. "Tell me to leave, Lucy," he said.

His hands fell on me, roving over my skin, warm and searching. His arms wrapped around me as if he just needed to feel me, convince himself that I was really there to be touched. I still had his shirt on that I slept in every night, just to have something of his close against my skin.

Again he entreated me, "Tell me to leave. Please."

"No." I trembled at the very thought of it. "No, please don't leave. Please!" I clung to him, pressing my forehead to his chest.

He pulled my face up to his and kissed me deeply while unbuttoning my shirt. He pushed it off my shoulders and down, then lowered his mouth to my taut nipples and teased them with his tongue.

"Oh, God, Matthew...please..."

I cried emotional tears as much as I moaned. My whole body felt electrified to be under his hands again. He made no sound, only kissed and loved me, running his mouth, his lips and tongue all over my skin. It was as if he wanted to memorize me with his taste buds, and his hands never once left the landscape of me. I thrust my hips against him as he caressed me. "Matthew, Matthew..."

"Shh, hush. I'm here."

"Please. Please..." I didn't know what else to say. He pulled away from me and I clutched at him, distraught, but he was back a scant moment later. He could put on a condom in record time. He put his arms around me, used his big hands to align my hips to his.

"Am I hurting your ankle?"

I think at that point I could have felt nothing, no pain or discomfort, with the measure of lust running through my veins. He thrust inside me, so slowly, rocking against me, stretching me so gradually it seemed to take a minute or more before he was fully seated inside. When he was, he buried his face in my neck and drew his hips back and thrust deep inside me again. He felt so perfect. He fit inside me so exactly, moved so expertly, the way he always had. My whole body thrummed with pleasure as he plowed in and out of me. Within moments, the arousal of every sense, every nerve converged into a shattering orgasm. I clung to him, shuddered and shook with the power of what I felt for him.

He laughed against my ear, feeling my walls contract around him. "Little Lucy, you come as well as you ever did. Come again for me. Over and over."

I did too, before he was done with me. My world was reduced to a wonderland of presses and sighs, grasps and thrusts and Matthew's lips on mine, and all over my body. How had I lived without him those many weeks? How could I ever live without him again?

When I came for the last time, he came with me and fell over me, exhausted. He held me close and sighed. I clung to him, unwilling to let him go.

"Lucy." That was all he said for a long time.

Then, "Lucy, I tried not to fall in love with you. I didn't want to. It's not what I planned." He said it so sadly, so wretchedly, my heart ached for him.

"Why is that so bad? To fall in love with me?"

"Because if you leave me...if you leave me, I won't survive it. Not you. Not this time."

"I won't leave you. I won't. Do you really love me? Please tell me, do you love me now?"

"You know I've loved you for an eternity. And it's hurt like hell, hurt much more than anything I've ever put you through."

I buried my face in his neck. "I love you too, Matthew. I want to be whatever you want. I want to make you happy."

He made a soft sound. "That's what I've always wanted for you. When I saw you at the Gala—" His voice cut off and he buried his face against my ear. "When I saw you dance at the Gala, I had to leave. I told you I had a phone call, that I missed that party because of a call. But the truth is, I was outside in my car."

"Why?" I asked. "Why did you leave?"

"Because it was too much, how I felt. The desire I felt to possess you, the drive to make you mine. I would have given my entire fortune that night, all of it, just to hold you in my arms."

"But you're holding me in your arms right now. For free."

"But then, I had no way to do that. You'd already blown off my tentative attempts to get closer to you. So I just sat in my car, insane with jealousy."

"Jealousy of who?"

"Whoever was going to get you that wasn't me. Whatever normal, vanilla man would get you and not know what treasure he had in his hands."

161

"Matthew," I said after a long silence. "Did you really know right away, that I would want what you give me?"

"Yes. I told you, I knew the moment I saw you. I knew before, when I saw those paintings." He laughed. "Those paintings are obscene."

"They're only obscene to you."

"High pornography. I don't know how everyone else can't see it, the submission in your pose."

"Maybe only you were meant to see it."

"Me and my wallet," he snorted, and I laughed.

I thought of the paintings, thought of myself posing for them, alive in the knowledge that I was being used. Used to make a painting, used for my body, used for the curves of my neck, hips, and ass. I had been Matthew's submissive in my heart, in my mind, from the second I laid eyes on him, and now, at long last, I was in the hands of my match, the man who had known even from an image on canvas how badly I needed to be controlled.

"Matthew, please don't ever leave me. We belong together."

"I know."

"Promise you'll never leave me. Please."

"I'm more worried about you leaving me. You're young, you're so beautiful. I'm an old man next to you. And you've already left me once."

"You're what? Forty years old? With the libido of a teenage boy. I think you could outfuck an eighteen-year-old."

"Not forever. I won't be able to do that forever."

"Oh, I think you will. Anyway, what about me? I'm decrepit. My joints are giving out and my career's almost through."

"Retire then and be my concubine," he teased. "Live to serve me, like Slave."

I made a retching sound. "No, I don't think so."

We lay in silence for a long while after our laughter died down, breathing in perfect cadence, our bodies entwined.

"I won't be any softer on you because I love you," he said when he spoke again. "I'll actually be harder over time."

162

I shivered with lust and excitement to hear that. Speechless with gratitude, I bit down on his neck. He drew his breath in and slapped my ass. "No biting, Lucy. I've told you that how many times now?"

I hummed and ground against him, and he chuckled at my inability to find control.

"I see some re-training will be in order, little girl. Making up for lost time."

"Yes, sir." *Yes, yes, yes.*

The next night he asked me if I was well enough to go with him to the basement.

I told him yes, I absolutely was.

* * * * *

So that's how I became Matthew's girlfriend, in addition to being his submissive and slave. He still used the favored endearments, *tramp* and *slut* and *whore*, but he added some new ones too. *Darling. Precious. My love.*

Soon after that night, he acquired Pietro's third painting of me. He wouldn't tell me what he'd had to pay to make it his. He only told me he'd wanted to own them all, and I hoped, I truly hoped Pietro hadn't been too cruel in his price.

We played down in the basement and our sessions were more fun than they'd ever been. The first night back at our games, I was beside myself with restlessness. He knew it and made me go downstairs early, to strip and kneel in the middle of the room and wait. I knelt there, horny and wet, so wet I'm amazed the moisture didn't run down my legs. I waited and imagined the things he would do to me, and by the time he came to me, I was reckless with need.

He came to me naked and already rock hard. He stood in front of me and I stared at his cock. I opened my mouth to take him inside, but he lifted my chin instead and turned my face up to his.

"I know you want me, you horny little slut. Did you touch yourself, or did you wait patiently for me?"

"I waited, sir."

"What about while we were apart? Did you ever touch yourself? Play with yourself while you were thinking of me?"

"Yes, a lot of times," I admitted guiltily. "I couldn't help it."

"Why?" he asked, with an edge of arousal. "Why couldn't you control yourself? Did you sleep with any other men?"

"No," I said, horrified at the idea. "But I dreamed of you often."

"You dreamed of me? What kind of things? What did you dream about?"

"About you hurting me." My voice trembled from the intent way he stared.

"What did I do to you in your dreams? Tell me everything."

I wanted to groan with frustration. I didn't want to talk, not right now. But I obediently told him, "You fucked my ass, and then you beat me—"

"Specifics," he snapped. "Kneel up straight and tell me a story. And remember, I'm still deciding how to punish you, so it would be in your best interest to make it good."

"You made me bend over the ottoman and you restrained me—"

"How?"

"With the cuffs. You made me part my legs, and you...thrust really hard into my ass. You really fucked me hard..."

"Did it feel good?"

"Yes, sir." His cock was bobbing in front of me. "Can I suck you now?"

"You'll suck me when I tell you to, you little cock whore, and not a moment before. What happened in your dream after I assfucked you?"

"I came without permission, and you...used your cane on me."

He smiled broadly. "The cane? Really?"

"Yes, sir."

"How many strokes?"

"Twenty," I admitted with mounting dread.

"You like being caned."

"No, sir."

"It wasn't a question. Twenty with a cane, huh? And you jerked off over that?"

"Yes, sir."

"When you woke up from your dream?"

"Yes. I was desperate to come."

"You're a naughty little whore, aren't you?"

"Yes, sometimes."

He pinched my nipples until I yelped.

"You are all the time. Open your mouth, Lucy."

Before I could part my lips fully, he thrust between them, but I was ready for him, my mouth hot and wet. I sucked him as he pulled painfully on my nipples. Then he let go and held onto my head, curling his fingers into my hair.

"I'm glad what we do turns you on, Lucy, but we have rules. You get twenty for touching yourself without permission. And you did it how many times?"

I moaned around his cock. It would have meant hundreds of strokes. Thousands.

He laughed. "Lick my balls, Lucy. Do it really nice, the way you were taught." He groaned as I ran my tongue over his sack, lapping at him eagerly. "If you do it real nice, if you suck me off good and swallow all my cum, I might have mercy on you. I might give you twenty and call it a deal."

I moaned and took his cock in my mouth again, deep throating his length. I was out of practice, but I managed not to gag.

"That's a good girl." Before he came, he pulled out and came on my mouth and my breasts. I licked his jizz from my lips the way he'd taught me, and he rubbed in the cum on my breasts while he tugged at my nipples a few more times. Then he put his fingers to my mouth.

"Lick it off. Savor it, you little slut."

And I savored every drop. I loved his fingers and the taste of his cum. I licked his fingers until they shone and again licked my lips, delicate as a cat.

"Crawl to the ottoman and bend yourself over it. How many do you get for touching yourself?"

"Twenty, sir."

"Would you like me to use the cane?"

"No, sir."

He laughed. "Noted. But I choose." I looked up at him from the ottoman, watched his mind work. "Let's try a new toy."

He returned with a thick leather strap I'd never seen before. He dropped it in front of my face, along with a condom and the itchy lube. I shivered a little.

"I'm going to fuck your ass first, Lucy, and then I'm going to beat you with this."

He slathered the itchy lube all over his cock after he put the condom on, then reached around to smooth a little between my legs. I moaned, grinding against his fingers. He chuckled. "I never make it easy, do I? Give me your hands." He bound my hands at the small of my back, then parted my cheeks and placed some more of the lube in my ass. I wiggled and groaned from the hot, invasive sting.

"You may come when I come, Lucy, not before. This assfucking is to reward your slutty little dream. When I'm done, then you'll get your punishment with the strap."

"Yes, sir," I said, but what I wanted to do was beg *please, please, please, please*! He did everything slowly and deliberately, for no other reason than to drive me mad. It had been weeks since I'd had his cock in my ass and I was desperate to feel that pleasure and pain. He had other plans though. He took his time fingering my cheeks and asshole, and then he whistled under his breath.

"So pale, so white. It's been months since I've seen you this way. Have you missed having my marks on your ass?"

The lube stung and teased inside me. I practically cried, "Yes, sir."

He played lazily with my ass cheeks, squeezing and pinching them. "Do you like it when I do this, when I play with you and touch you?"

I groaned into the ottoman. "Matthew, please!"

166

"Okay, let's try this. No toy first. Can you be open for me? It's been a while since you took me, little girl."

He guided his cock to my entrance. "Open. Relax and open." He pressed against me and I tensed a little. I'd forgotten how large he really was. He nuzzled my neck. "If you were better trained, I'd be able to slide right in. You'll learn one of these days to be ready before I even touch my cock to you. We'll just have to practice a bit more, won't we, you little anal-loving slut?"

I made a soft sound, somewhere between a thrill and a laugh.

He pushed deeper into me, so only the thick head of his cock was inside. "Relax, don't tense." He rubbed my back soothingly. "Offer your ass to me, let me come inside." And then he was sliding inside me, and I was stretching open for him. I felt the familiar burn, the full, hot sensation. "Jesus, Lucy, I love your ass. See, you're doing it, not even a toy first. You can accommodate my fat cock. You've come so far."

I moaned because his words were so nasty, so erotic. He sawed in and out of me steadily, and with each thrust, my clit throbbed.

"I'm going to fuck you a long time, Lucy. I'm going to make you so used to this, so used to the feel of getting your asshole fucked. You're going to get it fucked all the time now that we're together again, aren't you?"

"God, yes," I cried.

He held my hips in his hands and drove into me over and over, while I writhed and wiggled against him. Then he reached up underneath me and pinched both my taut nipples.

"Oh God, Matthew."

"Yes, I know you like that. But don't you come yet."

I shook my head, whimpering softly.

"Don't," he warned.

"Matthew, I can't—"

"You can, you just concentrate, you horny little cumslut. You concentrate on waiting for me. I told you to wait for me, and that's what you'll do."

I buried my face in the ottoman and I tensed, my hands behind my back clenching into fists. He fucked me roughly and again and again, jerked on my nipples. I cried out in torment, trying to hold off my orgasm at the same time it threatened to overtake me. Each moment, the strain and pleasure intensified. Finally, I heard his breath change.

"Okay, you little tramp. You may come now, because I'm about to really plow your ass."

And he did, so that I came in an explosion of sensation, my entire pelvis contracting and bucking in exquisite relief. I could feel him quaking behind me while I cried out, thrusting in me deep. He collapsed over top of me, his hard stomach muscles crushing my hands. He breathed and sighed into my hair.

"Did you like that?"

"Yes."

"Thank me then. From now on, since you like it so much, I want you to thank me when I fuck your ass."

"Thank you, sir," I breathed.

"Pathetic," he snapped, smacking my ass hard. "With some enthusiasm."

"Thank you, sir!"

"Better."

"Thanks for fucking my ass so...enthusiastically," I added, looking back at him, and he smothered a smile and grabbed my hair hard.

"Naughty. Jesus, you're naughty. Now you'll get five more, you naughty little slut."

"Yes, sir."

"Apologize."

"I'm so sorry."

He got up to throw away his condom and wash up, then he undid my cuffs and refastened them to the ottoman legs. He picked up the thick leather strap with a devilish grin and tapped it against his hand.

"This is new. I've never used it. I bet it hurts."

I buried my head in the upholstery.

"You'll count, Lucy. Twenty-five."

He warmed me up with a few cracks, and I counted each one. By the time he got to five, I was already tensing and dodging the blows, because the thick leather stung like bejeezus.

"Stop it," he snapped. "We talked about this. You just buck up and take it."

"Six." I flinched again.

"Does it hurt?"

"Yes, sir. Seven!" God, it hurt like hell.

"Does it hurt more or less than the cane?"

"Eight! Less, Matthew."

"More or less than my belt?"

"Nine! More, Matthew. Ten!" I yelped again. He was hitting me harder now. Around stroke number eighteen, I finally burst into bitter tears of remorse.

"You would have been almost done now."

"Nineteen!" I sobbed.

"You would have had just one more."

"Twenty!" Jesus, that was a hard one. He was really getting severe. I wanted it though, had asked for it, in fact.

"Little Smarty Pants."

I nearly forgot to count. He took me to twenty-five, and the last ones were brutal. My butt was on fire.

He crouched beside me, lifted my chin and looked in my eyes.

"Did it turn you on as much as your dream?"

"No," I pouted. "Not quite."

He reached back and thrust his fingers up inside me. I was ridiculously wet. "I think you're a liar." He shoved them in deeper, wiggling them, making me moan and arch my back. "Next time, I'll use the cane."

He undid my hands, yanked me to my feet, and fondled my breasts while he kissed me hard. "I'm glad that you dreamed about me while we were apart. I dreamed about you."

I looked up at him, completely enamored and sick with love. He stroked my cheek thoughtfully.

169

"Do you really like being a submissive, Lucy? I know you weren't sure. Why did you run away from me?"

"I didn't run away. I needed some time to think about things."

"Have you had enough time now? Are you sure now? Are you sure you want to be with me? I couldn't take it if you left me again."

"I won't," I promised. "I want to be here."

He kissed me, nuzzling me affectionately. "Well, run upstairs, wash up, and I'll fuck you again in bed. Go."

He came up a short time afterward, showering after me. When he came out, I was sitting on his bed brushing my hair.

"Give me," he said, sitting behind me. I handed him the hairbrush. He loved to play with my hair. The way he brushed it though...tragic.

"You have to..." I gestured hopelessly. "Brush it curl by curl."

He chuckled, dragging the brush through it.

"Or you'll make it frizz!"

He ran the brush through it the other way then, teasing it up on end.

"Stop! Stop it," I pleaded, giggling as he fought with me over the brush. We wrestled, and of course I ended up over his lap. He cracked my ass with the hairbrush, and I yelped and screeched as he tickled me in between smacks.

"Stop! Give it back to me. Ouch!"

I looked back at him, trapped under his hands.

"Give it to me. Please."

With a smirk, he tossed it into the corner.

"I like the tousled look better." He pulled me up in his lap and started to slide me down on his cock. He sighed as the head entered and went into me a little.

I pushed at him. "No."

He groaned. "Why not?"

"I don't want to get pregnant."

"Why not?"

I laughed, and looked at him reproachfully. "Matthew."

He pouted, but pushed me off him to reach for a condom. "Why don't you go on the pill already?"

"I told you why."

"Can't you get a diaphragm, or a...what the hell are those called? An IUD?"

"How about I just get a hysterectomy? Will that please my master?"

He rolled on the condom with an arch look. "Sometimes you have a smart little mouth. Makes me want to put something in it."

He pulled me into his lap again and lowered me onto his cock, caressing my back, pulling down my hips. I felt so full of him, not just full of his cock, but full of his love, his affection and care.

"Oh Jesus, Lucy. Jesus Christ." He cupped my ass in his hands, bruised and hot as it was. He pulled me closer and I ground against him, riding him, grinding my clit against him so swirls of arousal washed over me again and again. When I started getting close to coming, he picked me up and dropped me down on my back. He came over me, thrusting deep and hard inside me. I reveled in the feeling of his power, his mastery. His taut abs rubbed against my stomach and his chest hair tickled my breasts. I clung to him, drifted on the manly scent of him.

"Jesus, Lucy, I just want to fuck you sometimes. I want to fuck you forever. I want my cock in you every hour of the day."

"I'm confused," I teased. "Do you like to fuck me or not?"

He licked my neck and pulled me closer. "I love to fuck you. Frizzy hair and all. Does it feel good when I fuck you?"

"Matthew, if you knew what you felt like, how you feel when you're inside me. God, if you could feel it..."

He laughed. "I can feel it." I moaned as he drove into me. "I can feel how much you love it," he said. "I love the noises you make, like you love to be fucked." He pulled my hands up hard over my head and held them there. "Are you going to come for me, Lucy? Come hard and loud for me?" He bit my nipples while he held my hands tight. I struggled against him, just to feel that he had me held safely, that I couldn't get away.

171

"I've got you, baby. I'm going to fuck you so hard now." He pushed my thighs wider apart, practically bruising them with his hands. He pounded into me roughly and my sore ass cheeks slid up and down on the bed. I was trapped, captured, consumed by his passion. "My God, Lucy, I love you so much."

I shuddered with pleasure. How long had I dreamed of him saying those words to me?

"I love you too, Matthew," I sighed, completely transported by his hard, punishing thrusts. When I came, he came at the same time. It was like we were one, one creature, one being. I came with my legs kicking, my pussy clenching around him, his teeth buried in my neck.

\* \* \* \* \*

The next morning he woke me by parting my thighs and starting to eat me out. He licked and stroked my pussy with his tongue, sucked at my clit, parting me wider and wider to taste me.

"Turn over," he rasped. I flipped over, still not fully awake. He came over my back, the tip of his cock pressed against me, and drove all the way in, warm, pulsing flesh.

"Matthew! No!"

"I'll pull out."

"No."

"I'll pull out. Trust me."

"Please!" I knew he was clean, we'd been tested long ago, but a baby would end my career. "Please, Matthew. Please don't. If you don't want to use a condom, fuck my ass."

He stopped and pulled out of me with a groan, lying beside me on his back.

"I'm sorry," I said. "I can't let you. If I get pregnant—"

"No, it's okay. You're right to make me. I'm just being a dick." He leaned over to get a condom from the bedside table, along with some lube, which he used to ease his finger into my bottom. "I think I will fuck your ass though, now that you mention it."

He pulled me up on my knees and spread my legs wide. I trembled as he parted me and pressed the tip of his cock to my asshole. I buried my head in my hands and willed myself to relax for him. I knew he wouldn't hurt me, that he would make me come. I willed myself to accept him, and slowly, he made his way in. "Good girl," he breathed. "Jesus, what a good girl you are."

When he was fully seated inside me, he fucked me while I clawed at the bed, overwhelmed as always by the sensation of being plumbed by his massive tool.

"You like the feel of my big fat cock shoved in your ass?"

"Yes! Please, fuck me. I love it." My hands scrabbled at the sheets.

"You're a little whore."

I whimpered in agreement.

"Are you mine, Lucy?"

"Yes. Yes, I'm yours."

His hands clenched in my hair and he breathed on my neck. "Mine. You're mine." His hands roved over me and I felt his ownership deep inside, deeper even than he fucked me. Deeper than the blue of his eyes. He touched me in all the places that thrilled me, tapping my clit, pinching my nipples, until I was shuddering to come. "Oh, please, Matthew!" I howled as his cock jerked in and out of my ass, fast, slow, shallow and deep.

"You want to come?"

"Please, I want to come with your cock in my ass."

He made a growl of assent and we came together, and I basked in all my favorite pleasures. The clutch of his hands, the strength of his thrusts, his breath rasping against my ear. Afterward he held me a long time, and he asked me again, "Are you mine?"

The answer, of course, was "Yes, I am."

"Am I your dominant boyfriend?"

"I don't know. Are you?"

He frowned. "I know that you belong to me. That you're mine. You are mine, aren't you?"

"Yes, sir."

"Why? Why are you mine? How did I get so lucky?"

"I don't know that luck had anything to do with it," I said, gazing up at the three paintings that now graced his bedroom wall.

"Mmm. How's your ankle?"

"Almost completely better."

"Lucy," he said. "Do you think it's time for you to stop dancing?"

Oh, Jesus. "No, I'm fine. It barely hurts anymore."

"I think you should stop before you hurt yourself. I can tell it's not as easy as it was, even in the months I've known you."

I buried my head in his neck. "Matthew, please. I don't want to talk about it."

"I worry about you."

"Don't worry about me. Just fuck me again."

"Again? You're a greedy little slut."

He pinched my nipple hard, and caught my yelp in his mouth with a kiss. He kissed me a long time, then whispered, "Get a condom and roll it onto my cock. And yes, Lucy, I'm your fucking boyfriend. Your fucking dominant slave of love. If you ever try to top me, I'll hurt you."

I smiled as he pulled me under him. I had no desire to top him, although I had a certain power over him of my own.

"Lucy, will you always be truthful to me?"

"God, yes. Yes, Matthew, I will."

\* \* \* \* \*

But I was a big liar. I wasn't truthful to him, or truthful to myself. I slowly turned into a big, fat liar in the weeks that followed that sweet little talk, because I was in pain of the most excruciating kind.

Two decades of wear and tear on my joints had brought me to a point where the pain made it impossible to dance. So I did what any self-respecting dancer would do, which is drug myself in order to get by. I didn't go to Grégoire. He wouldn't have gone along with it. We all knew what dancers were hooked up to the pills, so I talked only to the people I had to. I took only what I needed, but that amount slowly increased, and then my flexibility started to go and the pain was that much worse.

In desperation, I considered seeing Matthew's friend Dr. Rob, who'd been so very kind to me. But I had no doubt he would have told Matthew everything. Not only that, but he would have told me to stop dancing. So I soldiered through on what pain pills I could get my hands on, and I tried, I really tried to not let things get away. But sometimes, you know, they just do.

# Chapter Thirteen:
# Lies

Hello, my name is Matthew and I'm an addict. I'm addicted to a drug named Lucy Merritt. This girl, this little dancer named Lucy fills my every waking hour with either longing, craving, pleasure, or peace.

I met Lucy back in October. It was almost May now and spring was in the air. I was sitting and waiting now for her to come to me. It was one of "our" nights, the nights when she was mine. I suppose now that she'd moved in, every night was really "our" night, but there were only certain nights I required her to play. The other nights were by choice, *her* choice, because my own choice, of course, was a perpetual "*yes.*" Most of the time, yes was her choice as well, but she wouldn't move in without a "no" choice clause, so we agreed that some days she belonged to me, and other days she would be able to choose if she was mine.

But tonight, no. No choice. I'd already planned what I was going to do to her. Some days I planned things, plotted pervertedly, other days I just went with the flow. It all depended on how much control I felt. When I really wanted her, it was better to make plans so things didn't really get out of hand. Sure, it happened sometimes, but I never hurt her, not really, and I never ever would. By some freakish good fortune, she gets off on pain, the same way I get off on watching her endure it at my hands.

I was running through my plans of depravity when I heard Kevin bang in the door.

"Mr. Norris!"

I jumped up. "Where's Lucy?"

"She's out in the car." The way that he said that, it wasn't to reassure me, it was to tell me something was wrong. "She's in the car. I can't wake her up!"

I was across the room in an instant, pushing past him.

"She was fine when I got her, and then I thought she fell asleep. But she won't wake up."

"Is she breathing?"

"Yes, she was when I left."

I ripped open the car door, and she was breathing but she was so, so still, and so very pale. I lifted her and her warmth was reassuring, but she was limp and lifeless as a rag doll.

"Get her bag. Find her phone. Call that guy she dances with. His name's Grégoire."

I took her inside and laid her on the couch. Her breathing was shallow and she was just utterly gone. I shook her and slapped her face a little, shook her harder again. Nothing. I gestured to Kevin to hand me the phone.

"Grégoire," I yelled. "What's wrong with Lucy? What did she take?"

"What? Who is this?"

"This is Lucy's boyfriend, Matthew. What the hell did she take before she left the theater?"

"Nothing. I don't know. I don't know what she took. God damn it, she doesn't tell me."

"Who would know? This is not a fucking joke. She's passed out on my sofa and she doesn't look good."

"Hold on, I'll make some calls. I'm coming over."

"Yeah, get over here, and call whoever would know."

Kevin let Grégoire in hardly five minutes later.

"Where is she? Is she okay?"

"She's dead to the world. I don't know if she's okay or not. What is she on?"

"Mariel said she thinks she took some pain pills she got from another dancer, that he bought off the street."

"What the hell are you talking about? What kind of pain pills?"

"I don't know. Some kind of painkillers. Vicodin. Something like that. Ellie said she thinks she took four."

Four. Jesus Christ.

"She should go to the hospital, Mr. Norris."

"No, I'll call someone to come here. You stay with her."

I crossed the room and called a doctor friend of mine, and he arrived and examined Lucy while we watched. During that time, she woke up a little, and he told us her heart rate and pupils looked good. He advised me to have her sleep it off, and that any pills off the street were most likely not full strength.

After he left us with instructions to monitor her, I glared at Grégoire. "She danced tonight?"

"Yeah. She was fine."

"Is she really fine, though? You're her partner. Is she really fine?"

He looked at me, and I saw the answer in his gaze.

"Who is doping her?"

"Lucy is doping herself."

"Why?"

"Because she's in pain. Because her joints hurt."

"Well, why don't you fucking make her stop?"

"Me? I'm supposed to make her stop? She doesn't listen to me anymore. Her world revolves around you now, sick as that is."

I ignored that barb. "She didn't tell me. I didn't know." I scowled at him. "They don't drug test dancers?"

"No," he said like I was an idiot. "They don't."

"You knew she was taking drugs to keep dancing."

"I suspected, yes, but I never saw her take anything."

"You never asked her?"

"I didn't want to know."

"I thought you were her friend."

178

"You don't understand. You don't know how it is! All dancers have pain, all dancers understand that, and dancers don't tell each other how to cope."

"Oh, nice. Same exact thing she said. 'All dancers have pain.' They teach that at the Dance Brainwash Academy."

"Yeah, brainwashing." He made an angry sound. "You wouldn't know anything about that."

"You have a problem with me and Lucy? We're consenting adults. You have no idea, anyway. You shouldn't talk about shit you don't know."

"Exactly. And you're not a dancer. So follow your own advice."

"Tell me what I can do then. What do I do? Can't you do anything? You're her friend, can't you convince her to stop?"

"To stop dancing?" He snorted. "It doesn't work that way. There's only one way she's going to stop dancing and that's to injure herself past the point of return. Which is not far off by the way." He stopped a moment. "Or else..."

"Or else what?"

"There is one other way. To force her to stop."

"What?" I would do anything, anything on earth to stop her from destroying herself.

"If she gets pregnant, she'll have to stop dancing. At least, she'd have to stop long enough to not be able to come back."

*Pregnant.* I shook away the thoughts that suddenly crowded my head. "She won't let me anywhere near her without a condom."

"I think if you came at her now, she'd never know."

We both looked over at her, passed out senseless on my sofa, and I actually considered it for a moment before reason prevailed.

"I couldn't do that to her. That would be heinous."

"And yet you beat her senseless and call it love."

"Beat her senseless?" I stared at him. "Is that what she tells you?"

"Believe me, she doesn't have to tell me. I see the welts, the bruises. Everyone does, they're hard to miss. Whatever. If she likes you to beat her up, that's her business. But I wouldn't get all holier-than-thou about knocking her up."

"She'd just get an abortion."

He laughed. "Lucy? I don't think so. She wouldn't even accept a morning-after pill after the rape. If he'd made her pregnant, she would have carried it."

I heard the words, but they made no sense to me. "Wait, what? What did you say? What the fuck are you talking about?"

"She never told you about that?"

"No." My mind was reeling from all the lying she'd done to me. "Why don't you tell me about it?"

"It's not my place to tell you. Why don't you ask her?"

"Because she's fucking passed out on my couch. How the fuck am I supposed to ask? I want you to fucking tell me about this time that Lucy was fucking raped, right now." I yelled so loud I think it surprised us both that she didn't wake up.

He sighed heavily. "It was, God, probably three years ago now or more. He beat her up pretty bad. An obsessive fan. He came to her place. He landed her in the hospital. He tied her up and he..." His voice trailed off. "You should ask her. Anyway, that's why I wonder why she lets you do what you do."

"I don't beat her up. Not even close. Nor do I rape her. It's nothing like that."

"Sure," he muttered. "Whatever."

"Not that I have to explain it to you."

"Actually, I wish that you wouldn't. I'd rather not know." We both turned then and looked at her, and Grégoire said shortly, "Her period was a couple weeks ago, so..."

"How the hell would you know that?"

"I know," he said. "After ten years, partners know."

I looked at him, needing help, needing something. The things I learned tonight...The things that she'd kept from me, things that had hurt her. Why? I had asked her point blank to her face, *Lucy, will you always be truthful to me?* and she'd said, *God, yes. Yes, Matthew, I will.* What a liar she was.

"I couldn't do it," I said, trying to convince myself. "It would be wrong. So totally wrong."

"She's going to injure herself soon. Badly."

"So I'll make her pregnant? That's better?"

He got up to leave. "You can do what you want. I'm just telling you. You asked me how to make her stop dancing, and that's the way. Anyway, I'll leave you alone."

I didn't want him to leave. If he left, there was a chance I'd break down and do as he suggested.

"I want to know who gave those pills to her, Grégoire."

"No. I don't know anyway."

I trailed him to the door. "I'll find out. And believe me, she's not taking one more fucking pill."

"I don't doubt that."

We stared each other down, scowl for scowl.

"What is she to you, anyway, Grégoire?"

"She's my friend."

"Good friend she seems to be with you!" I was bitter, so bitter that he knew more about her than me.

"I'm gay!" he snapped. "If you're insinuating what I think."

"Gay, that's convenient," I said, but I knew I was being ridiculous.

He rolled his eyes. "Okay, listen, I'm out of here. Call me if she gets any worse. If you're too embarrassed to take her to the hospital with all those marks on her ass, I'll do it."

I wanted to punch his fucking lights out. I really did. But he had been a friend to her for many, many years, and at one time, long ago, we had spoken as friends too.

"Good night, Grégoire," I ground out. "Thanks for coming over tonight."

"Good night," he replied, equally grudgingly, and then left me alone with his evil, evil idea.

What if I did manage to make her pregnant? The idea both attracted and terrified me in its simple grace. My mind was reeling in a million different directions. It occurred to me that I ought to have talked to Grégoire long ago. Grégoire, the keeper of all her secrets. Pain and drugs and violent rape. I thought of words she'd told me one time. *It's hard to explain, but it makes me feel safe.*

I crossed the room and knelt beside her. Her face was so innocent and guileless in sleep. Someone, some man had raped her, raped her so badly she'd landed in a hospital bed. What had he done to her? Held her down? Hurt her? Fucked her hard? All the things she liked from me. She wanted me to do them, because I wasn't him. Because when I did what I did to her, I cared about her, I wasn't her rapist. It suddenly occurred to me that that's all I was to her. Her anti-rape hero, her mental defense against what happened to her. I was the way to make it okay. So what was so bad about that? What was so bad was that she'd never told me.

I remembered how skittish she was when I first followed her. *An obsessive fan. He came to her place.* How defensive she'd been, how upset that I followed her around. Now, it all became perfectly clear.

I remembered with crystal clarity when I'd said to her, *how long have you wanted it? To get tied up, and beaten, and fucked?* She'd shaken her head. She wouldn't answer me. Then a few moments later, she'd said, *"How did you know?"* And she hadn't meant, *how did you know, how did you know that's what I want?* No, I think now she meant, *how did you know? How did you know that's what I need to feel safe again?*

I shook her gently with a lump in my throat. "Lucy. Lucy, wake up." I shook her harder. "Please wake up. God damn it, please!"

She barely responded, turning her head with a sigh, not even coming to consciousness.

Then I stood up, still looking down at her, and slowly unbuckled my belt. I undid my pants, and took out my cock and stroked it, getting it hard. Then I took off her pants and I slipped inside her. I fucked her and came inside her twice, down on the couch, still fully dressed. Then I carried her up to bed and undressed us both, and took her in my arms and came in her once more, and then, half asleep in the middle of the night, I came inside her once more again.

182

\* \* \* \* \*

It was almost noon the next day before she awakened with a groan. She lurched out of bed and managed to get to the bathroom. She vomited, over and over, then collapsed beside the toilet on the cold tile floor. I lifted her up, brushing her hair from her eyes.

"Okay, Lucy, okay. Better?"

She shook her head. "Nooo..."

She heaved again, but nothing came out, just dry, broken heaves as she held onto her head. I put a wet cloth against her hot forehead.

"Go away." She pushed weakly at me.

I got up to get her some water, and returned to hold the glass to her lips. She shook her head.

"Drink it!"

"No."

"Yes." I got a little bit past her lips, half of which she spit out when she retched again.

"Please, just leave me alone."

"No."

She tried to lie down there on the floor, between the toilet and the wall.

"No, Lucy," I sighed, pulling her up. "Drink some water. A little more."

"I want to sleep." Her words were slurred, her color was still off.

"You've been sleeping for twelve hours, you little fuck." She looked up at me then, at the tone in my voice. "Yes, you're in trouble." I picked her up and carried her back to bed. "As soon as you're healthy enough, I'm going to beat you to within an inch of your life. Now drink some water."

This time, when I held it to her lips, she drank. I looked down at her with cold recrimination.

"Where did you get those pills?"

"I don't know."

183

"I'll beat you right now if you don't tell me. If you don't tell me the fucking truth."

"A dancer. I don't know her that well. A friend of Remy's. He's not even in our company. He gets them from someone his friend knows. I don't know..." Her voice trailed off.

"Remy? Who the fuck is Remy?"

"A dancer."

"A fucking dancer. Thanks for the scoop."

"What time is it?"

"You're not dancing today."

"I have to."

"You listen to me. You're going to spend today resting, and tomorrow bent over a fucking ottoman. So lay the fuck down and answer my questions like a fucking good girl, before I tear up your ass."

"I'm tired," she said, soft and plaintive. She wasn't getting any sympathy from me.

"Does your head hurt?"

"No, I'm sleepy."

"Yes, because you overdosed on pain pills. What the fuck were you thinking? Who the fuck knows what was even in those pills? Why did you do it?"

She just moaned.

"Answer me."

"I don't know! Because it hurts."

"What does? What hurts?"

"Everything. Everything hurts, Matthew!"

"Oh, for Christ's sake." I took her in my arms. She cried weakly, her whole body pressed against mine, as if I could take the pain away.

"Lucy." I held her, rocking her as she grieved. "You have to stop dancing. You have to stop. I know it's hard. I know. But I'll take care of you, I promise."

"I don't want to stop," she whispered with a desperation that broke my heart.

"I know. But if you're hurting...if you're hurting enough to take drugs..."

"It's just for my ankle. It never completely got better. It's not totally healed, that's all."

"Then why did you go back to work?"

"Because it's my job."

"Because you're a fucking idiot. And now you've probably made it worse."

"Matthew..."

"No, you fucking listen to me. If you ever, ever fucking take another Vicodin, I will personally beat you to unconsciousness."

"I didn't know what it would do."

"Well, it's fucking addictive and you are never to take it again, do you understand?"

"Yes, okay," she said, holding her head.

"Or are you already hooked on it?"

"No."

"Tell the truth."

"No. I'm not..." I looked down at her hard but her eyes were starting to close. "I'm so tired. I want to sleep."

"Sleep then and get better, because when you're better, we're going to talk."

I watched her fall asleep, holding her close. When her breathing slowed again, I pulled her closer into my arms and I whispered against her cheek, so quietly she never could have heard. "Lucy, you stupid little fuck. Why didn't you tell me the truth?" Then I watched her sleep, still and yearning, remembering how it felt to come inside her, finally, unsheathed.

\* \* \* \* \*

She woke up again just after dark, looking much better than she had at noon. I'd given Mrs. Kemp the evening off, so I ordered sushi for her, which in hindsight was not the best idea. She sat in her chair and looked a little better when I took the raw fish away and gave her a dish of crackers and some milk.

"Eat it, Lucy," I said, and she did, slowly, looking ashamed.

"Are you going to punish me?" she asked through a mouthful of crumbs.

"Yes."

"Tonight?"

"Tomorrow."

"What are you going to do?"

"I'm going to do my damndest not to kill you."

She paled a little and looked apologetic. "I'm sorry. I know I must have worried you."

"Worried me?" It was such an understatement, I was hard pressed not to laugh. "Reckless, Lucy. You're so fucking reckless with your body. You forget that it's mine. So yes, you'll be punished. For lying and hiding things and endangering yourself. What do you think I should do to you?"

She looked down, unwilling to answer.

"You've broken every one of my most basic rules. Every one. Over a very long period of time."

"Maybe you can just forgive me."

"If I could just forgive you, this wouldn't be so hard."

She closed her eyes, pressed her fingers against them. "I hate when you're angry with me."

"Lucy, I'm so fucking furious with you. Do you have any idea how it felt, having Kevin rush in here and tell me he couldn't wake you? Do you know what it felt like to watch you all night to be sure you took your next breath?"

"I'm sorry, Matthew." She pushed her plate away, tears shining in her eyes.

"Eat."

"I can't."

"At least drink the milk. All of it."

I watched her drink it and I hated myself for wondering if she might already be growing our child. When she put the glass down, I leaned back and sighed.

"Now go upstairs, kneel on the bed, and fucking prepare yourself to be fucked."

"Yes, sir." I knew she'd be crying, full on sobbing, before she got to the stairs.

I cleaned up the kitchen, trying to hold on to my control. We had more to talk about, things I needed to hear her say. When I got upstairs she was as I'd ordered her, on all fours on the bed. I put on a condom and slathered it with lube. I put my hand on her back and pushed down her head so she arched open to me.

"Give me your hands."

She reached them back and I held them hard in one hand, and with the other, I guided my cock to her ass. Roughly I thrust the head in. I felt her adjust with a jerk. I stayed still in her, just the head of my cock for a moment, letting her stretch for me, then I started to fuck her mechanically. She sobbed, not from pain, but because I was angry. She hated when I was angry. But I hated that she kept secrets from me.

I leaned down over her, reaming her ass, and I hissed in her ear, "Lucy. Answer something for me. Do you have any idea what it feels like to be raped?"

She turned her head away, burying it in the pillow, but I turned her back to me pulling by the roots of her hair.

"Answer me, Lucy. Have you ever been raped?"

She didn't answer for a moment, then sobbed "Yes." Her eyes were screwed shut, closed up tight.

"And what did it feel like? Did it feel like this? Was that feeling of rape all you ever really wanted from me?"

"No!" she cried. And then "Stop," and that one word, *stop*, was weighted with fear.

"Why didn't you tell me? Why didn't you? You want me to stop?" I fucked her harder still. "Do you really want me to stop, Lucy? Or do you want me to rape you? Just like him? That's what you want, isn't it? What you've always wanted? You're a liar, you know. All I ever asked for was truth—"

"Stop!" she shouted, her voice hoarse with emotion. "Stop!" She struggled under me and pulled at my hands to get away. I pushed her down to the bed and I fucked her so I probably hurt her, and honestly, if she had said *mercy* then, I wouldn't have let her

187

go. I loved her hopelessly, but she was more beautiful and perfect than I could bear. I hurt her because she wanted me to hurt her, but it wasn't for the reason I thought. It wasn't because she genuinely loved me for me, that wonder of wonders that I had so foolishly believed.

"If you want fucking rape, you've got it." She sobbed and fought me until I finished and let her up. The moment I let her go, she pulled away from me, ran away from me just as I knew she would. While Kevin drove her to Grégoire's, I called him and told him to look after her. I told him it was possible that she might be carrying a child. He asked me *why? Why have you done this?* Not *why did you try to make her pregnant*, but *why are you sending her away?*

Why? God, how to explain it.

I tortured her because I hated her, and I hated her because I loved her. And because I loved her, I needed her to go away. I needed to send her running from me, for her own good and probably mine too. If she hadn't left that night, I would have punished her the next morning until she did. I would have hurt her until she left, for lying, for not being who I thought she was, for keeping so many secrets from me. Which was ironic, because the biggest lie, the biggest secret, the biggest betrayal, of course, was my own.

# Chapter Fourteen:
# Mercy

I fled from Matthew's to Georges and Grégoire's place, and they took me in without demanding any explanations. I stayed in bed for two days straight. I wanted to die, but instead all I did was sleep. Grégoire came and went, looking guilty and remorseful. I knew that he was the one who had told him about the rape, because, besides me, he was the only one who knew.

"I'm so sorry, Lucy. I'm so sorry that I told him. It came up in conversation. It slipped."

"It slipped? What the hell were you talking about to say something like that?"

"We were talking about you and why you're so screwed up."

I scowled at him. "Now he thinks the only reason I like him is because I got raped. Like I got imprinted on violence or something."

Grégoire looked at me. "Well, didn't you?"

I didn't have anything to say to that. I turned my back on him and ignored him until he left. Later that day, Kevin brought all of my things. Two small suitcases and a box of items, including the framed poem Matthew had given me. My entire life. I wanted to beg him to take me back to Matthew's, but I didn't because I was too afraid.

189

I understood why Matthew had been so angry with me. He had told me enough times about his obsession with truth. He had wanted truth and beauty, but gotten deep and encompassing lies. But to me it seemed the broad lies we told to one another were the only thing that kept our relationship alive. For him, it was the lie that he didn't love me that protected him. For me, it was the lie that I'd always wanted what he gave. Taken together, those lies made up the foundation of our relationship, and now, without them, it had totally collapsed. Those lies we lived by kept our relationship on kilter, kept us frozen in a tableau like that of the Grecian Urn, beautiful and timeless and unable to be ruined. But everything was ruined now. The beautiful, unchanging urn had been broken by the ugliness of truth.

I had felt lost the last time we'd been apart, but this time, when it seemed a permanent break, I was so much more lost than before. I missed him horribly, thought of him obsessively. I wondered hourly if he could possibly forgive my lies, if I stopped taking pain pills, which I did; if I explained to him why I hadn't told him about the rape. Surely if I just explained it all and said I was sorry, he would forgive me and we could go on again as before. But I was terrified of approaching him because if he sent me away, if he wouldn't listen, then we would really be through. So instead, I waited in hope that he would come to me. But no, he didn't, and days stretched into weeks.

My darling Grégoire was as true a friend to me as ever. I forgave him for ratting me out to Matthew because I know he hadn't meant any harm. He weaned me off the pain pills and went with me to the gym and to a physical therapist to try to salvage my joints. And slowly, day by day, the pain did get better. My flexibility returned in part, and without the pills masking the pain, I knew when I pushed too far and could stop before it escalated.

He urged me to eat well too, and take vitamins and supplements, folic acid, and calcium, and protein. He kept me out of clubs where I'd breathe in smoke and be tempted to drink, and strong armed me to bed each night at a reasonable hour. I did as he prompted because I thought it might help me heal faster and stay strong, but all that good nutrition and healthy living after many years of half-assed habits actually made me feel more nauseous and tired, ironically enough.

But I danced through all of it as we entered the summer season because I thought, as always, that this season could be my last. And as it turned out, it was my last season, because the first week in June, my Achilles tendon snapped.

I had thought I'd known pain as a dancer. In fact, I had known pain of all kinds. But the pain of that tendon giving way was more excruciating, more debilitating and terrifying than any pain I'd ever known. The only mercy was that it gave out during practice. The indignity of collapsing onstage would have made it that much worse. I was carted off to the hospital, sobbing and pleading for someone to help me, but there was no one, nothing at all, that could fix this pain.

Grégoire stayed beside me through the trip there and my admittance, and wouldn't leave my side even as they took me back to be examined. I was so far gone, so hopeless and mindless, that I was glad to have him there to answer all the questions they asked. They weren't hard questions, but there were so many of them, stupid questions that annoyed me in my pain. I was confused though, when they asked before the x-rays if there was a chance I could be pregnant, and Grégoire answered quietly, "yes."

"No," I corrected him. "There's no chance."

"There is a chance, Lucy," and his face seemed suddenly pale. The way he looked at me made my skin go cold, then prickle into goosebumps from the back of my neck all the way down my arms.

"How is there a chance, G?" I asked in a voice that was shaking on the edge of hysteria.

He swallowed hard. "Did you ever get your period last month?"

My breath caught in my throat as I thought back. No, I hadn't. But...but...that could be due to stress. It could be due to all the new vitamins and nutritious food...the vitamins and food that Grégoire had practically forced on me. Bitter tears, the tears of a friend betrayed, pooled in my eyes.

"Lucy..." he said, watching my face darken. "I can explain. I can explain what happened. It's not all his fault. It's my fault too."

I shook my head, trying to put it together. I didn't understand. I couldn't get it clear. His fault. *Matthew's.*

*It's not all his fault.*

"Am I pregnant?" I asked him. I thought of the nausea, the exhaustion that dragged me towards the earth. All this time the x-ray tech just stood there. Just a gay dancer and his partner sorting some things out about a pregnancy, a pregnancy that had happened though some unholy alliance from hell.

"Talk to me, Grégoire," I shouted.

"I'll go order a test," muttered the tech, excusing himself.

"Lucy, listen, please calm down. I'll tell you what happened but you can't freak out."

I burst into hysterical tears. "It's too late for that, it's too late to freak out now, isn't it? When? What? The night I was sick?"

"The night you took the pills, and you...wouldn't wake up."

"He fucked me? Matthew? Without a condom?" I don't know why I phrased it as a question, otherwise I'd immaculately conceived.

"He asked how to make you stop dancing, so you wouldn't hurt yourself, and I told him..."

"You told him what?"

"I told him there were only two ways. For you to injure yourself, or get pregnant."

My mouth fell open.

"I didn't think he would, Lucy! He said he couldn't do that to you. I don't know what changed his mind after I left."

My brain was reeling, the pain in my leg forgotten. I couldn't say whose betrayal was worse, Grégoire's or his. I think Matthew's was worse, because he'd broken up with me over a lie. My lie, when he had perpetuated the most horrifying lie of all. He'd been upset that I'd kept my rape from him, and yet he raped my very life, raped my very being by impregnating me with a child without my knowledge, without my permission, against my will.

I was angry enough with Grégoire, but Matthew...if he had been in the room then and someone had handed me a gun, I would have turned it on him, and I really do believe I would have pulled the trigger. I was so stunned by the audacity, the depravity of what he'd done, that I could barely draw breath.

The tech returned, and I could tell by the look on his face that they'd run a test with the blood they'd drawn, and what the result of it had been. He silently laid the lead apron over my middle and arranged my injured calf under the machine.

* * * * *

By the time I got to surgery I knew Grégoire had called Matthew, because it was Dr. Rob who smiled down at me from above.

"We're going to take good care of you, Lucy. By the time you wake up, you'll already be starting to heal."

But to tell the truth, I wasn't sure I wanted to wake up. When they put me under, there was the one liquid second of floating away. How wonderful it would be to bottle that fleeting second, to live forever in that second of drowsiness when the whole world faded away. All the confusion, the fear and betrayal. All the anger and sadness and pain. To live forever in that moment of losing it, that moment that only Matthew had ever helped me find.

But I did wake up, and yes, the pain was better, at least the physical pain. My leg was elevated and immobilized by a splint. Before my eyes even opened, I felt a hand stroking my hair and I knew, just from the pressure, that the hand was his.

"Don't touch me." I intended to yell it, but it came out a weak, raspy moan.

"Don't try to talk, just rest." His hand stopped moving but he left it there, heavy against my head. "The surgery went fine. You're going to heal completely. But you won't be able to dance. At least not the way you did. But it's going to be okay. Everything will be okay."

*Everything will be okay.* I hated him. I hated his soothing voice and his hand in my hair. I hated his arrogant assumption that everything was going to be fine just because he said so.

"What are you doing here?" I still wouldn't look at him. I couldn't. "How can you show your face to me after what you did?"

"I did it to stop you from hurting yourself. You wouldn't have stopped dancing any other way."

"Why didn't you just ask me to stop?" I asked, jerking my head away from his hand.

"I did ask you to stop. You didn't listen to me. You snuck off and got yourself hooked on pain pills to keep dancing, and started buying drugs off the street."

"You don't understand. You have no idea what it's like to be me, to walk in my shoes."

"No, I don't," he shot back, "because you wouldn't confide in me. I would have done anything in my power to help you. Anything, if I could have, if I had only known. You lied! By keeping quiet about all these things that were hurting you, you lied to me, you didn't give me truth."

"*I* didn't give you truth?" I turned on him and started to hit him as hard as I could. Of course, I was pathetically weak, and he quickly had my hands pinned.

"Enough. You need to relax. You need to be regaining your strength. You have a baby to care for now, our baby. You need to rest."

"What I need is for you to go far away from me, because you're an awful, horrible, dishonest person, and the biggest liar and hypocrite I've ever met, and the last thing I want is your fucking baby, because I never want to fucking look at you again."

My voice broke off after that long diatribe. I was exhausted but he still stood there beside me, his face tired and drawn.

"You don't mean that. You're angry now, I understand. You need some time to calm down. I'm sorry, Lucy, that things had to happen this way—"

"I hate you," I cut him off.

"You don't," he said after a moment, "and this is the most dishonest conversation we've ever had. I'm not sorry, actually. I'm excited that we're having a baby. And I don't think you hate me. I know you don't."

"I meant every word I just said. You make me sick. You really do. The way you went on and on about how important truth was to you. Do you remember how you felt when you discovered your last girlfriend lied to you for so long? That's exactly how I feel now. I really, truly do hate you and I'm not going to be in a relationship with you again, and that's the bitter truth, not that you would recognize truth if it bit you on the ass—"

"Lucy, enough. You're tired, you're angry."

"No, I'm not angry, I'm not tired. You know what I am, Matthew? I'm defeated. I'm done. My career is over. The love I had for you is gone, completely gone. I'm carrying a baby I don't want, that I'm probably just going to get rid of, and then I'll have to live with that guilt my whole fucking life even though it was your fault. But I prefer that to living with you, to having a baby with you after what you did to me, this awful disregard for me, this rape of my life—"

"Lucy," he cautioned, "do not. Do not call it that."

"That's what it is, so just...go. I'm done. There were a lot of things you did to me that hurt, but I liked them, I wanted them. But this, I don't want it. I keep waiting to wake up and find it was all just a dream."

"I know. I'm sorry. I'm really, really sorry. What I did was wrong, but what's done is done. You know I didn't do it to hurt you. And I didn't...I really...I only half thought it would work."

"But it didn't half work, because you didn't half do it, did you? You did it all the way. You came inside me while I wasn't even conscious, Matthew. What's wrong with you?"

"Four times," he murmured.

"What?"

"I came inside you four times, actually."

"Oh, four times. That's just great. Congratulations," I said sarcastically. "Your guys can swim, you must be so proud. But I'm not having your fucking baby. Not a fucking chance. No."

"Grégoire told me you didn't believe in abortion."

"I didn't, until now. Now I think maybe in cases of rape it's justified."

"I didn't rape you."

"Yes, you did! It sure as hell wasn't consensual."

"Rape is something else, Lucy. It isn't done with love. It isn't done to help someone—"

"I fucking know what rape is. Believe me, I know. No one knows better than me, because I've been there, and now I feel like I'm right back there again."

"Oh Jesus, Lucy, please."

I turned away from him.

"What can I do?" He tried to take my hand, but I pulled it away, pulled myself as far away from him as I could.

"Leave or I'll call the nurse."

"Let's talk about things again in a few days. Things might look different in a few days."

"No, things are very clear right now." I stared at the light blue wallpaper on the wall, the wallpaper that was the same pale blue color as his eyes. "I'm done. I know that. I'm sure of it. This has gone too far for me. Mercy, Matthew. Mercy, okay? Mercy makes it end, that's what you told me once. I want it to end."

Again he reached for me, and I pushed the nurse call button.

"Okay," he said. "I'll leave you alone. But don't do anything, Lucy. Don't do anything, okay? Until we talk again."

I bit my lip. I was making him no promises after all his lies.

And no, of course I wasn't going to have an abortion. I just wanted to hurt him as much as he'd hurt me. Let him believe I was going to get it taken care of, let him feel that pain of cold-hearted betrayal, the same pain I was feeling now. Just one little lie, but everything else I'd said was true. I was done with him, done with his peculiar one-sided brand of honesty. In my mind, it was completely over. Convincing him would be more difficult, but eventually he'd understand.

* * * * *

A couple hours later, Grégoire mustered up the courage to visit me. He lingered at the door like a repentant puppy, gauging my mood before he dared come near. I wished I had a rolled up newspaper to smack him with.

"I'll only come in if you promise to listen to me, to listen to my side of the story."

"What other side is there?" I snapped. "I was completely passed out."

"His side. What did he tell you?"

"Nothing. I sent him away. I have less than no interest in what he has to say."

"He didn't explain why he did it?" He was still talking to me from the door.

"I know why he did it, but it was still wrong. And you...he never would have thought of it on his own. So this is as much your fault as his."

"God, Lucy. I'm so sorry. Please don't be mad at me. I can't stand it, I couldn't stand it...if you won't be my friend..."

Grégoire's tears finally undid me. I started to cry too. It was all so sad and ugly. My lips trembled and my words came out in a rush.

"I need you now, G. I need you to be my friend, now more than ever."

I reached out and he came to me, enveloping me in his arms. I cried into his shoulder, the shoulder I'd leaned on so many times both in dancing and in life.

"I can't believe we're not going to dance together again. I can't believe it's over," I sobbed.

"Aw, Lucy, it's not over. Don't say that, not yet."

"But it is, isn't it? I'll never dance again. I can't. I'll miss dancing with you most of all, G. How can it be over? Forever? I wasn't ready for it to be over!"

"I know, sweet, I know." He crooned to me quietly, trying to soothe me. I don't know what he said. I was crying way too hard to listen. The thought of never again moving across a stage with Grégoire, soaring through space propelled by his agile hands, it killed me. I looked down at his hand patting my leg gently, felt his soft, fine black hair brushing against my cheek. The smell of him, the solid feel of him against me. I knew why I was so sad. I'd lost not one lover, but two.

Besides that, besides being alone and losing my lovers, I would get fat and awkward when I'd been sleek and graceful all my life. I'd get fat with a baby I didn't want, that I'd resent, and then I'd have to live with the guilt of giving away my flesh and blood to some strangers because I was too selfish to love it. I felt like my life was over, and nothing in my future seemed worth living for.

"It will be okay," he said when I'd calmed down enough to listen. "Everything will be okay. Maybe you can become a teacher."

"I don't want to be a teacher."

"You say that now, but you'll miss dancing. You'll miss it enough to do anything, I think. And you'll have this little one to teach dancing to." He laid his hand on my belly. "It would be a shame to waste your genes."

"No," I said. "No, never. No child of mine will ever be a dancer."

"Lucy. If you hate dance so much, why are you going on and on about how much you'll miss it?"

"You know why. You know exactly why." He fell quiet. He did understand the love/hate relationship we all had with dance. His joints were nowhere near as bad as mine, but the end would come for him too. "I can't stand to think of this baby going through this pain and loss someday..."

At that moment, as I said those words, I realized with horror that I was already protecting the thing inside me, and there would be no way to let it go. I was already attached to it, as much as I hated it. Grégoire still had his hand on my stomach, caressing it. He'd known all along.

"You'll find something to do with your life besides dance. I'm sure you will. It will just take some time, some courage." He tilted my head up and brushed away the lingering tears. "You're a brave girl. You know that you are. You always have been. And you'll be a mother now. You'll be great at it. And you'll be happy with Matthew, won't you?"

"Matthew? No." I buried my head in my hands. "I can't...I won't...G, why did you let me stay with him so long? I can't go back to him. I shouldn't. Should I?"

He was quiet for a long time.

"I don't know, Lucy. I don't know that whole story, but I can tell he loves you very much."

"I sent him away, G," I whispered in dread. "I told him he was awful and a liar and a hypocrite and that I hated him and never wanted to see him again." I burst into a fresh torrent of tears. I realized only now how painful it had been to speak to him that way, the man to whom I'd been trained to show respect. How could we ever get past the things we'd done to each other, the words we'd said?

"I can't go back to him, G. Don't let me. Please. Let me come back and stay with you and Georges, please, until I'm back on my feet." I didn't stop to wonder why I was begging so hard.

"Of course you can. You can stay as long as you need to. Maybe you both just need some time."

I laughed humorlessly. That was exactly what Matthew had said. It seemed even now the two of them were working in tandem. "You're so much like him," I said. "I don't understand how you two can be so much alike."

"I don't think I'm much like him, Lu. I think we both just care about you."

"If he cared about me, he would never have done what you suggested."

"But I suggested it, so I'm to blame also. Not that I'm arguing his side. I'm just saying..."

"Do you think I should go back to him?"

He looked away, considering. "Give it time, Lucy. You'll figure out what to do. Sometimes I think maybe, with this, you really do belong together," he said, pointing to my middle again. "But did he...what you did together...did he abuse you?"

If I was to detail half of what Matthew did to me, Grégoire would have the police down on his head, but I had reveled in all of it, all of it but what had happened at the end. Even the misstep with Frank and Byron, while I hadn't enjoyed it, had brought us closer, helped us find love.

"He never abused me, no, not in any way I didn't want. We had a...safe word," I said, my voice trembling at the end.

"A safe word?" Grégoire echoed softly.

For a minute we just sat in silence, the only sound the beep of the monitor and the steady click, click, sigh of the IV.

"Yes, a safe word," I finally whispered. "For when he hurt me too bad."

# Chapter Fifteen:
# Truth

I left that afternoon in a wheelchair to return to Grégoire and Georges's house. Georges assured me I was welcome to stay as long as I liked, and while I had every intention of landing on my feet and finding something to do to make money and get my own place as soon as possible, it soon became apparent that it was going to take a while. Rehabilitation went slowly, and I hobbled about on crutches, and had terrible nausea and morning sickness and spent many miserable days in bed.

Sometimes, vowing to pull myself together, I showered and dressed and went with Grégoire to the theater to watch the show from the wings, but it was so painful to be there and not dance, and to endure the sympathetic stares and empty encouragements of the dancers, that I soon swore it off.

I still saw Dr. Rob every other week for appointments. He came by the apartment personally so I wouldn't have to limp all the way to his office downtown. The rehabilitation was painful as he manipulated and coaxed my ankle, but even more painful was knowing that Dr. Rob was a direct link to Matthew.

I knew Matthew paid him for my care, because money never changed hands between us, and I knew also that he reported to Matthew on my progress, however slow. He must have certainly learned through Rob that I was still pregnant, that I hadn't had an abortion after all. Rob asked me question after question every week, questions that grew more involved and personal, questions I knew came straight from Matthew's mouth. I answered them, how could I not, grateful as I was for the fading pain and his patient, capable therapy.

Then one week he said flat out to me, "Matthew misses you."

The words landed on me like a punch in the gut. I'm sure I flinched, but he pretended not to notice. His fingers kept working, manipulating, stretching my healing tendon just past the point of pain. I stayed silent, partly to pretend he hadn't just said what he said, and partly because I knew if I spoke I would burst into tears.

He started to talk, uninvited, about his past with Matthew, all the mysterious and vague details I'd never known. He spoke of the impoverished, damaged family Matthew had come from, and detailed all the chances he'd taken, all the hard work he'd done to rise out of the squalor he'd been born to. He'd truly made something from nothing, built an empire of real estate from an Indiana shack. Dr. Rob had met him in college when Matthew was a struggling freshman, and Rob, a young man of privilege, was wasting his opportunities on women and partying.

"I almost died one night. Alcohol poisoning," he said. "He took me to the hospital, got medical care for me. He's a good man. He takes care of people he cares about. He cares about you."

I was really, really trying not to cry, but I was fighting a losing battle.

He pressed his point. "It's hard for him when he cares so much about you, to not be here for you. He misses you, he wants to help you. I know he'd like another chance."

I wiped my tears. Through all this, his hands never stopped. The pain, the twinge and pang of him moving my ankle was the only thing that kept me from going totally numb.

"I know you miss him too, Lucy. You're not happy. You belong with him, especially now."

"Did he tell you to say that?" I scoffed through tears. "They're the exact words he would use."

"He asked me to tell you this, yes. But I'm not saying anything I can't see for myself. You're unhappy without him, and you miss him terribly. Don't you?"

I would have answered him if I wasn't suddenly bawling too hard to catch my breath. I did miss Matthew, I missed him like madness. I missed him so I lay in bed every night and cried for an hour. I missed him so that food had no taste and art had no beauty and life had no meaning. I missed him so that I wrapped my hands around my waist a hundred times a day to cradle the only thing of him I had left.

"What do I do?" I sobbed. "What do I do?"

"Forgive him. Let him come talk to you at the very least. He wants to see you, but only if you feel in your heart you can give him another chance. He doesn't want to see you if it's only to tell him goodbye."

"But I don't know. I don't know if I can trust him again."

"He made a mistake, Lucy, and he knows it. A big mistake, with a lot of repercussions. Lifelong, life changing repercussions, and he's sorry for it. He's used to fixing things with money. He's always been able to do that. This is one situation that can't be fixed. It's been difficult for him. He's as miserable as you are. I'm an outsider, I know. It's really none of my business, but it seems to me..."

His magical hands kept massaging and moving my ankle and knee, working the stiffness away.

"It seems to me that you two being together and having to work through some issues is better than being alone and miserable for the rest of your lives. I mean, you're both unhappy. You're both lonely. You both miss each other. It seems awfully pointless to me, at least from the outside looking in."

"Ouch," I said softly as he turned my ankle to the right.

"Nearly forty percent more range on that side. You're getting better, Lucy. You won't grace the stage again, I'm afraid, but I promise you, you'll be able to dance."

"I will?"

"I'm sure of it. Not perfectly, not with the intensity and stamina you used to, but you'll dance again."

He patted my ankle and fixed me with his gaze.

"Even if it's not perfect," he said, "if you enjoy it, if it makes you happy, then it's a good thing."

\* \* \* \* \*

I thought a long time about the things Dr. Rob had told me, and by morning I'd decided to call Matthew, but I didn't do it that day or even the next. I was afraid of taking that step off the precipice, afraid of trusting him again. But I was just as afraid of living my whole life without him when I needed him so much. I was afraid to call after the things I'd said to him. I was afraid to call because of the chance, however small, that he would not take me back. And I was afraid to call because, suddenly, I was starting to show.

I know, silly vanity, but what on earth would he think when he saw me? I wasn't even five months along, but small and slim as I was, I already had a noticeable bump. My slender, muscular body was one of the main things he liked about me, and I was no longer anywhere close to sleek, with my belly sticking out strangely and my muscles weak after months of forced inactivity. Dr. Rob said Matthew still wanted me, that he missed me, but would he really want me like this? I couldn't even have a few drinks to muster up my courage, so for two nights I just stared at the phone.

"Call already, Lu," Grégoire chided me on the third night. "Enough. Pick up the phone and call."

"What if he decides he doesn't want me anymore?"

He laughed. "Believe me, that's not going to happen. He wants you back like mad."

I narrowed my eyes. "How do you know, G? Have you been informing on me too?"

"He might have called me a few times. Checking up on you. We've talked."

"You two! You both ought to be ashamed."

"Just pick up the damn phone. Do you want me to dial for you?"

I sighed. "Yes, actually. I'm shaking too hard to do it myself."

Grégoire picked up the phone and punched in the numbers. It didn't escape me that he knew them by heart.

"He loves you," he mouthed, handing it over. I waited with the phone to my ear as it rang. I hoped to get his voicemail so I could just leave a message. But no, on the fourth ring he answered, his deep silky voice in my ear.

"Hello," he rumbled anxiously. "Is Lucy all right?"

I was thrown for a moment, but then I realized I was calling from Grégoire's number, that he would assume I was him.

"This is Lucy," I managed to say, and I hated how scared I sounded. I said it again louder. "It's Lucy."

"Lucy. Lucy, what's wrong?"

"Nothing. I'm fine."

There was a short silence, a slow, soft sigh.

"I'm glad you called me. I'm so glad. I've missed your voice." He paused. "I've missed everything about you."

I was crying by then, hard enough that I almost hung up because I couldn't get any words past my lips, but Grégoire nudged me insistently.

"Talk!" he ordered, gesturing to the phone.

"Matthew..." I whispered through tears.

"Yes, honey. I'm here."

"I miss you, Matthew. I need you, I think. I'm sorry I said those things to you."

"I'll be there in ten minutes, okay? I'm leaving right now."

I handed the phone back to Grégoire, wide eyed, terrified. Frantic with relief.

"He's coming now."

He smiled. "Figures. Should Georges and I go out? Give you two some privacy?"

"No, don't leave me! Just...don't leave yet."

"I won't. I'll be here if you need me, but you and he need to talk. So dry those tears and buck up. Be brave."

205

I went to the kitchen and guzzled some water trying to calm myself. It occurred to me just as Matthew knocked that the pajamas I had on showed every bit of my strange new shape.

"Jesus," I said, hiding behind the counter. Grégoire was already opening the door. Matthew shook his hand, but he was searching the room for me. He looked as amazing as ever, his piercing eyes, his virile body, the same intent swagger as he crossed to where I was ducking behind the counter.

He took me in with one sweeping gaze. "Come here."

I straightened slowly, tried to stand and present myself to him the way he'd taught me eons ago. He pulled me into his arms carefully like I was a delicate thing, and I suppose I was. My leg still wasn't completely healed. Although his hands weren't rough or grasping, they were possessive, undeniably possessive, and I felt as soon as he touched me that I was his again.

"Lucy," he sighed so softly that goosebumps rose on my skin. His hands cupped my face, then ran down over my shoulders, my pregnancy-inflated breasts, and over the curve of my hips. They stopped on my little baby bump and his fingers spread out there, broad and warm.

"Lucy, my God. Look at you." He fell to his knees and put his head right against me like he wanted to hear the baby inside, or perhaps feel it there. My hands curled in his hair. It disturbed me to see him kneeling at my feet, the supplicant for once, the one without the power. I wanted to give it back to him immediately. *Take me, Matthew*, I wanted to say. *I'm yours.* The moment I'd seen him in the doorway I'd known I was his and that I always would be as long as I lived. Dr. Rob was right, we belonged together. *If you enjoy it, if it makes you happy, then it's a good thing...*

He stood up and looked deep in my eyes, and I looked back at him just desperate with love. He kissed me, hard, gentle, soft, deep, just kissed me and kissed me and kissed me again. He drew me close until I was wrapped tightly in his arms, body to body, and the little round body between us both.

"I'm sorry," he whispered, breaking away from my lips. "I'm really so sorry for what I did. You're right. It was terrible, and hypocritical of me. It was the worst kind of dishonesty, when I demanded the truth."

He sighed and took my face in his hands, his thick, gentle fingers threading through my curls. "I owe you truth," he continued, "so here's the truth. I'm happy you're growing our child. I'm sorry that I didn't give you a say in it. I hope you'll forgive me for that. But I won't ever leave you again, Lucy. I love you, and I can't really live without you. I'm going to marry you and we're going to have a baby. And that's, finally, the whole truth of it." By this point, tears were running down my face and he put his cheek against mine so it grew wet too, then he rubbed it against my hair. His fingers tightened in my curls so I felt it, felt that insistent pang of pain. "I'm sorry if I hurt you, Lucy. I don't know how else to love. But I promise I'll take care of you forever, if you'll just give me the chance."

"I thought you didn't love me because I'd been raped. What about that?"

He shook his head against my hair. "I didn't understand. I just didn't understand why you didn't tell me."

"I didn't because I thought you wouldn't hurt me the way I wanted to be hurt."

"Is that why, though? Is that the reason you want to be hurt?"

"I don't know," I said, crying against his shoulder. "Does it really matter, Matthew? Does it really matter in the end?"

He thought about that for a long moment, then sighed so I felt his breath against my ear.

"I think the only thing that matters is that, from now on, we tell each other only truth."

I clung to him and he held me and soothed me while I soaked his shirt with tears.

"I'm...I'm afraid," I stammered, my voice trembling.

"I know it," he said, smoothing my curls. "I know."

* * * * *

So back I went, from Grégoire's to Matthew's, that very night. Matthew insisted he wouldn't sleep another night away from me and our child, and I was overjoyed to have my master back giving orders again. He came to my little room and helped me pack up everything, my very few things in my two suitcases. His eyes lingered on the Grecian Urn poem.

"Do you know why I gave you this?"

"No, Matthew, I don't. Maybe because it talked about truth and beauty, and it was meaningful to you."

"You were meaningful to me. Even back then when I was still in denial of how I felt about you. How much I loved you. Did you love me back then?"

I didn't even consider lying.

"Yes, I loved you long before then. Desperately."

"Me too," he said. "I loved you from the start. I loved you when we sat in that coffee shop talking, and you blushed and stammered and tried so hard to tell the truth. I loved you when you danced that night at the Gala. I loved you that day we spoke in the hall, when you tied your little shoes up without looking down once."

"You loved me then? You didn't even know me."

"But I did, Lucy. Just like you knew me."

I sat beside him and we looked at the poem together.

"If you had told me the truth then," I said, "I would have run away. If you had told me all that was going to happen between us."

He laughed. "I still would have caught you. I wouldn't have let you get away."

We said our goodbyes at the door. I thanked Georges and Grégoire with tears in my eyes for the love and support they'd given me when my life had been off the rails. But now I finally felt I was back on track again. I hobbled to Matthew's house and he carried me up to his bedroom and there were Pietro's paintings of me just as before, all three in a row.

I stared at the paintings while Matthew slowly undressed me, ran anxious fingers over me like I might still try to get away.

"I'm yours, Matthew," I whispered. "Please take me. Like you used to."

"I don't want to hurt you."

"You won't."

And he didn't, even though he loved me for hours. He made love to me until I was falling asleep in his arms and still he made me come, made me thrill with his mouth, his fingers, his cock inside me. We fell asleep still connected, and I woke up the next morning in his insatiable grasp.

So life went on between us, thrilling and wonderful as ever. I rested during the day while he worked. Mrs. Kemp spoiled me rotten, coming and going and clucking over me constantly. Kevin drove me wherever I needed to go, and Dr. Rob came to see me as always. I thanked him gratefully the next time I saw him for giving me the courage to call.

Matthew and I stuck to our pact to tell only truth to each other. We had long revealing talks in his bedroom—well, *our* bedroom now—while I lay cradled in his arms. My old life, dancing and the secrecy of pain, was replaced by a new world of honesty and warmth. And love. We'd talk for hours with his hand resting on my swelling belly, and the baby grew and began to move inside me while my leg knit together like new.

And of course we found ways to make love, to have sex, to fuck, to do the things we had to do. It wasn't always easy, and it was downright awkward as I grew bigger, but he still fucked me and beat me and bedeviled me until I came. Matthew hired a private obstetrician who came to the house, and who was let in on our games so there would be no need to explain away the marks. On the plus side of this open communication, the physician was able to offer frank advice of how far we could go and still be safe. "The baby is exceedingly well-cushioned," Dr. Stein would say to Matthew with a wink, "so if she misbehaves, you give her hell."

It was one of those nights when my ankle was almost completely better that Matthew stroked my face and said, "So, now, Lucy, can I be your dominant husband?"

"You call that a proposal?"

209

He pulled out a ring that made my jaw drop. "Lucy Merritt, marry me." An order, not a question, of course.

"And be your submissive wife? Let me think it over." I pretended to for all of three seconds. "Yes, Matthew, I will."

He kissed me a long time, then he whispered to me.

"Lucy, will you always be truthful to me? Forever?"

"Yes, Matthew," I said. "I promise I will."

And I really meant it this time.

* * * * *

We had a wonderfully beautiful wedding that Matthew's money threw together in a week. His rich developer friends attended, and the dancers from my company. They wished me well but they looked at me with fear in their eyes. *She's through. Someday I'll be through too.* But being through wasn't as bad as I'd feared. As time went by, I missed dancing less, and settled into the wonder of being Matthew's wife.

I was quickly becoming Matthew's huge, bloated, whale-like wife, but he seemed to love me just the same. And being Matthew's wife was a full time job, much to my pleasure and occasional pain. We played almost every day, and every night, and I'd never known such happiness in my life.

We found out eventually that we were going to be having a boy, so we began to shop for blue and boyish things. It was one such time, when we were out shopping downtown, that we ran into Joe. We were getting coffee, and a huge pastry to feed my pregnant hunger, when I looked up and saw his eyes on me, on my massive waistline, and Matthew at my side.

"Hi, Joe," I said. Matthew's eyes shot to him. "Matthew, this is Joe. We almost got married once."

Joe had the grace to look sheepish. He had a ring on his finger. "Kim and I got married. And I see you did, too."

"This is my husband Matthew."

Matthew and Joe shook hands, in that way of two men who've loved the same woman.

"Nice to meet you," Matthew said. "I guess I should thank you for being foolish enough to leave her at the altar."

I nudged him, rolling my eyes.

The awkward conversation ended shortly afterward and we said our goodbyes. As soon as he was out of earshot, Matthew taunted him under his breath. "Idiot," he muttered. "Vanilla fuckboy."

"Matthew, be nice. His loss is your gain."

"And yours too," he whispered, eyeing me lasciviously.

I laughed. "How can you look at me like that, when I look like this?" I pointed down at my huge belly, round and swollen.

"I think you've never looked sexier. I bet Joe did too. I can't wait to take you home and fuck you."

"Stop!" I laughed, looking around at the people passing by us, oblivious to what he said. "You're such a perv. To even think of fucking a woman this pregnant—"

"What are you talking about? We'll be fucking up until the bitter end. Did you hear that, baby?" he said to my stomach. "If the womb's a rockin'..."

"Don't talk to our baby about sex," I giggled.

"I'll be pushing the doctor out of the way to get at you in the delivery room."

"Matthew."

"Those stirrups will come in handy. I'll be hunkered down there with my mouth between your legs."

"Oh God," I laughed. "Please shut up. You're so sick!"

"You made me that way. You're the one who did this to me and you know it. I was doomed the moment I laid eyes on you."

Yes, we spent many fun, wonderful afternoons shopping and preparing for our lives to really, really change. We fixed up a nursery for our soon-to-be-born baby on the top floor of the house, the longest possible distance from the basement where we played, for obvious reasons.

In the early hours of New Years Day a little over a year and three months since we'd met, we had a healthy, darling baby boy.

He had light blue eyes and red curly locks of hair, and we named our beautiful baby Keats.

# Epilogue

His deep voice whispered over the monitor. "Little Lucy, I'm coming for you."

I laughed. So he'd successfully gotten Keats to bed. I was in the basement room, kneeling by the sofa. A moment later he was at the door.

"Did you hear me?"

I nodded with a smile. It was a little ritual we used to test the monitors each night. A whispered message to whoever waited below, more provocative some nights than others.

He came to the sofa shedding his clothes. He looked down at me, taking control without words. As always, I gave myself over to him easily and thankfully. He sat in front of me, spreading his legs and guiding my mouth to his cock. I sucked him. He pinched my nipples each time he wanted something different, for me to lick his balls, or rim his ass. I stroked my lover and my husband all over, and he came on my lips and on my tongue.

"Beautiful little whore. Savor it. Swallow it all."

I did, with grateful exuberance. He watched me, then pulled me over his lap. He started to spank me and I moaned from the pleasure of the contact. I squeezed and kissed his leg, and then I nibbled.

"No biting, Lucy," he said with an especially sharp crack.

I jerked under the harsh sting and he gripped my arm more firmly behind my back. He spanked me soundly and I reveled in it. No matter how many times he did it, I still wanted more. When my ass was deep pink and burning, he stood me up and walked me to the center of the room.

"Stay," he said, and I complied, although I shifted a little from one leg to the other, trying to cope with the discomfort of my reddened ass and the increasing arousal in my pussy and clit.

He looked at me sternly on his way back from the armoire.

"Behave yourself. Stand still." Over his arm was a fine silk garter belt and some matching black stockings. I shuddered a little in delicious anticipation. It was going to be one of *those* nights.

He knelt at my feet and fit the garter belt to my waist, then laced it up in the back. He smoothed it down over my hips and my bottom, then picked up the first of the black stockings in his hands.

"Turn," he told me, his voice low and raspy. I did, and pointed one toe. He gathered the stocking up with deft fingers and smoothed it up my leg with a delicate touch that belied his strength. He carefully hooked it in the front and the back, working the tiny garter clasps with a skill born of practice.

"Your other foot." He did the same, gathering the stocking up, pulling it up to the top of my thigh, and hooking the clasps. He held my foot in his hands, massaged it. "Point."

I obeyed. He caressed my pointed foot while I stood perfectly still. "I thought dancers were supposed to have ugly feet," he said.

"I'm not a dancer anymore."

"Of course you are. You always will be." He picked up my other foot and I pointed it in his hands. He ran his fingers over the arch and across the top.

"How beautiful you are, Lucy."

"Thank you, Matthew."

His fingers moved up higher, splayed across my ankle and then up my shin. He shifted to crouch behind me until I could feel his hot, steady breath on the back of my thighs. With both hands he smoothed the back seams, running one finger up the center of each calf. I tried to stand still but I was so hot, so wet. I tried to stand still and be a good submissive to him.

I felt his mouth brush against my outer thigh, and then at the lacy sheer top of the stocking, he placed a kiss. He nibbled, softly biting the pale skin outlined by garters, and wherever he bit me, he licked and tasted me too.

"Down, lie down." He pulled me down to the floor right there where I stood. He parted my thighs and licked above my stocking tops, and I flexed my thighs in that way I knew drove him wild.

"Your hands," he growled, and I gave my hands to him. He grasped them tightly in his own. His questing mouth settled between my legs, and the second he put his lips on me, I arched under him, the warm erotic sensation too much to bear.

"Lucy," he chided. "Be a good girl. Don't you come yet. I'll punish you if you come."

I shook my head and gritted my teeth as he laved me. Lick, caress, nibble. Each point of contact sent lust through every teeming nerve. He went on and on, teasing me to insanity.

"Matthew, please."

"No." His deep voice vibrated against my clit. He nipped me softly, thrusting his fingers inside me.

"Please, Matthew, please, you're going to make me come."

"I said no," he growled, feigning impatience. "You obey me or you're going to pay."

I felt him smile against my clit as he closed his teeth on it and very intentionally sent me over the edge. I came with a howl, shaking and bucking. He licked me hard across my entire aching slit, then looked up at me with a devilish grin.

"You're so naughty, such a naughty girl. I don't think you'll ever learn."

He hauled me up, looking down at me masterfully, then kissed me long and hard so I tasted myself on his lips. He ran his rough hands over my bottom, squeezing and pinching it.

"You've already had one spanking tonight. You're going to be sore."

"I'm sorry, sir. I'm sorry I came without permission."

"I know you're sorry, but my rules are very clear."

I loved this man. He hauled me to the armoire and I stood beside him and watched him choose which instrument to punish me with. He chose the thick leather strap that really smarted. "Over to the wall, Lucy. You know what to do."

I went to the wall and put my hands on it, and rested my forehead against it. I thrust out my ass just the way he liked me to, and he tapped it lightly with the strap.

"Part your legs." I did, but not very wide. He popped me then. "More. Don't fuck around."

With a sharp yelp I parted them wider. "I'm sorry, Matthew."

"Hush. Just stop dawdling, it annoys me. Spread your legs and stick your lovely little ass out to me. You know by now how this works."

I did as he asked, my trembling legs spread wide, my ass ready to accept whatever punishment he wanted to mete out. That night, he was in a mood to beat me hard, and he landed some good ones that had me hopping up on my toes.

"Keep your legs spread. Stand still or I'll add more strokes."

I whined because it was a really hard strapping, but I tried to resume the position he liked, that had me spread wide and open to him. My hands clenched into fists against the wall as I counted each stroke and struggled not to reach back.

"Don't you dare take your hands off that wall," he said. "If you cover yourself, you'll be a very sorry girl."

"Yes, sir," I moaned. My ass was on fire. The leather strap was thick and it hurt like hell. I ended up getting an extra five for fidgeting. By the time he finished, I was wailing and tearful, but I was wet too, and ready for him.

Until he told me to do otherwise, I held the position. I wanted to press my legs together to ease the throbbing in my clit, but I didn't dare, and he chuckled, knowing exactly what I felt.

"You horny little cum whore. You're supposed to be feeling punished."

"I do feel punished."

He smacked my ass with the strap. "Don't contradict me, Lucy. Watch your tone."

"I'm sorry, sir," I said with all the submissive deference I could muster in my current state of quivering lust.

He stood behind me, close behind me, and I waited for his instructions. I hoped they were the basely sexual kind.

"What do you want?" he asked.

I answered him honestly. "I want to come."

"You like when I redden your naughty little bottom?"

My clit pulsed with each word he said. "Yes, sir."

"You're such a dirty little slut, aren't you? I bet you'd like me to plug your ass and then fuck you until you scream."

All I could do by that point was make a little strangling sound. He crossed to the armoire and returned with some lube and a toy. He lubed my ass while I braced myself against the wall, trying to stand still. He pressed the toy against my tight hole and I felt it invade me. It was a big one, but by then I'd been well trained. I pressed back against it, opening to its girth. I let it slide into me, long and hard and thick. I may have moaned softly when he rubbed the small of my back.

"Good girl. I bet you love how that feels."

He turned me, his big hands on my waist, and I looked up at him, my eyes glazed over with need. He smiled as he lifted me, braced me against the wall, and settled me down on his cock.

I groaned in my throat from the wicked sensation, his huge cock filling me, rubbing against the toy in my ass. He pressed against me, pressed me right to the wall, and his hard chest and abs were like steel against my skin. I wrapped my legs around his hips and arched against him. He drove in me over and over, all the way to the hilt.

For a while, he held my hands behind my back, but at the end he let them go, and I wrapped them tightly around his neck. I was filled with him, filled with love for him, filled with thankfulness for his care and his mastery.

"Come for me, Lucy," he urged me.

With a stifled cry of joy, I obeyed.

217

# About the Author

Annabel Joseph is a multi-published BDSM romance author. She writes mainly contemporary romance, although she has been known to dabble in the medieval and Regency eras. She is known for writing emotionally intense BDSM storylines, and strives to create characters that seem real—even flawed—so readers are better able to relate to them.

You can find Annabel's site and sign up for updates at www.annabeljoseph.com, or "like" her Facebook page at www.facebook.com/annabeljosephnovels.
You can also find Annabel on Twitter (@annabeljoseph).

Annabel Joseph loves to hear from her readers at annabeljosephnovels@gmail.com.

# An Excerpt from
## *Comfort Object* by Annabel Joseph
Copyright 2009 Annabel Joseph

On Monday night Jeremy picked me up at my door like a true gentleman, and I didn't invite him in although I had worked all day to ensure my apartment looked chic and organized from his vantage point at the doorway.

*This is about a job. It's about a job,* I kept reminding myself, but a part of me couldn't stop thinking about how personal a personal assistant might get with a person she helped. Especially if that person was someone nice and handsome and perfect and unattached like Jeremy Gray.

I somehow managed not to simper about how incredibly handsome he looked in his suit and tie, or how totally awesome his big movie-star SUV was. I tried to hide how sexy I thought it was when he tossed the keys to the valet, and how wet it made me when he swept into the restaurant and all the bigwigs started kowtowing to him. I was even able to subdue my impulse to jump him when he led me to the table with his hand just barely touching my back. I felt like a princess when he pulled out my chair. Finally we were seated at our private table, wineglasses in hand.

"You look lovely," he said, raising his glass to me.

I tried to look appropriately modest. Sure, I had agonized for almost two days over the simple black dress I had on, the low-heeled but stylish black pumps I wore. Businesslike yet hip and fun. Isn't that what a personal assistant of Jeremy Gray's would need to look like? I knew he was single now, but his last girlfriend had been really beautiful and fun and stylish, just like him. It was like a currency. Style and desirability. I wanted him to want me for the job.

We small talked awhile, mostly him asking questions. *Where are you from? How did you end up in L.A.? Previous jobs?* I edited of course, feeling slightly guilty about it. Would he hire me if he knew I'd worked at a private BDSM club for the last five years? And was it totally dishonest of me not to mention it? There was always a chance that something about my former job might come out and make him look bad. But I didn't think so. BDSM people were nothing if not universally, protectively discreet.

And Jeremy was so encouraging and funny. God, I desperately wanted to work for this man.

The food arrived, but I was almost too freaked out to eat it. My hand shook as I reached for my wineglass. Of course he noticed.

"Are you nervous? Don't be. I've already decided I want you for the job."

"You have?"

"If you want it, yes, it's yours. I decided it a while ago. That first night I met you actually. When I came in late and you really just wanted to go home, but you were nice to me instead."

I smiled. "I try to be nice to everyone. It's one of the worst things about me."

"No, not at all. I think it's great, Nell. I really do. And I hope you really are available to travel, and you really do think this job would be a good fit, and that you'll find my salary is fair." He told me a number then that made me choke on my salad.

"I know it sounds high." He paused as I tried to compose myself. "But I have to admit, I haven't been completely honest with you yet about the demands of the job."

"You must have a lot of stresses and inconveniences to deal with on location."

"I do. It's extremely difficult to go to one of these shoots, constantly traveling, working, doing PR, all the little things. I really need someone with me who I can depend on. I mean, it's a complicated job, but it's really very simple. I just need someone to get me what I need when I need it, to keep me happy and focused and able to work."

"Sure," I said, but the look on his face was weirding me out a little. He reached for the small portfolio he'd carried in.

"I brought this paperwork along, just for you to look over. You don't have to sign anything or agree to take the job right now. This just sort of lays things out for you, what your duties, tasks, expectations would be." He opened it up and handed me a long, single-spaced document in dense legalese.

"To start, this is your typical confidentiality agreement. These are, unfortunately, a necessary evil in my business."

Yes, I thought, my old business too. I had signed many a confidentiality agreement in my old line of work.

"I understand," I said soberly. "Of course you can count on absolute discretion on my part."

"I'm glad to hear that. So perhaps, before we go any further, you might just sign this document. Because the rest of these papers contain more personal details about the day-to-day demands of the job, and somewhat more personal details about me." He looked at me expectantly.

"Of course," I said. "If you like."

I signed the paper after scanning it to be sure it read just like all the other ones I'd signed. By this time the food was getting cold, but I was too spellbound by his attention to eat another bite. We were going over *papers*. I was about to learn his *personal details. Oh my God.*

"Now, Nell," he said with what almost sounded like a sigh. "Let's talk seriously about the job.

Jeremy slid the papers across the table. "Why don't you just read them? Let me know if you have any questions."

There were five or six full pages of job description. I smiled, resting my head on my hand. Okay, the high salary made sense now. I began to scan the first page, also written in something akin to legalese.

"I guess you keep your lawyers busy with all these papers and contracts," I said.

"Yes, I do. But I think it's important to have everything perfectly clear and written down in black and white. It's easier for everyone involved."

"Yes, of course."

The document began with more verbiage about privacy, discretion, the outward appearance of normalcy. *Outward appearance of normalcy.* Okay, that was a little weird.

Near the bottom, it got even weirder. *The applicant will tender public displays of affection as needed...*

*The applicant agrees to cooperate with photo opportunities and/or candid interviews regarding the love relationship of Jeremy Gray and the applicant with a positive, convincingly affectionate tone...*

I stopped reading, my pulse suddenly beating in my ears. "I don't... I'm not... Okay. I'm a little confused."

"About what?"

"So...this sounds like I'm supposed to pretend to be your girlfriend."

"Yes, that is part of the job. A big part of the job actually. The public part."

*The public part.* I wondered what the private part amounted to. I flipped over to page three, page four.

*The applicant agrees to provide sexual relations on demand, to include vaginal, oral, and anal sex. The applicant agrees to comply with regular blood testing and remain monogamous while in the employ of Jeremy Gray, excepting group sexual encounters at the discretion of Jeremy Gray, to include but not limited to m/m/f, f/f/m, f/f/m/m, m/m/m/f encounters.*

*The applicant understands that she will act as submissive and/or sexual slave to give comfort and relaxation in private, and function as a loving and affectionate girlfriend in public, and under no circumstances will behave in any way that exhibits or suggests her submissive status in public.*

*The applicant understands the protocols and expectations of the dominant and submissive relationship and agrees to comply with all requested protocols in private, to include obedience, sexual subservience, and constant availability.*

*Sexual subservience and use may include but is not limited to sexual intercourse, the use of erotic toys and aids, the use of multiple partners and multiple penetration, the withholding and control of orgasms, sexual objectification, and diverse sexual practices, which the applicant may or may not find repugnant.*

The papers fluttered from my fingertips. There was more, much more, but I had seen enough. The knot in my throat made it impossible to speak, and I couldn't look at him, so I simply stood and started to walk. Walk away, walk outside, walk home. I didn't care. I didn't care as long as I was walking away from him.

But of course he followed. He took my elbow, and we waited for his car. He helped me in like nothing in the world was wrong, tipped the valet, started driving. I fumed beside him on the seat. How dare he? Just because he was some big-time movie star, that gave him the right to try to hire me as his personal slave? To spring his contract on me, to humiliate me?

"Nell, listen…"

"Please, just take me home."

"Talk to me."

I turned on him. "What do you want me to say? You said you wanted an *assistant*. Someone to help you, keep you organized—"

"It does help! It does keep me organized!"

"You lied to me! Do you have any idea how humiliating this is? You wanted to hire me to be your sex slave. You might have mentioned that sometime before now—"

223

"And if I had, what would you have done? The same thing you're doing now. Pretending to be outraged and running away—"

"Pretending? No, I'm really outraged, Jeremy! This...this setup, those documents—it's all sick, reprehensible—"

"Reprehensible? A little perverse, yes. But this is what you do, isn't it?"

He looked over at me, but I refused to meet his eyes. I clamped my mouth shut and crossed my legs more tightly. So he was hot. So what? He didn't turn me on. *If that's true*, a voice inside me whispered, *why are your panties so damp?* I huffed again to myself and stared out the window.

"Look, let's cut the drama. Okay?" Jeremy said. "I know that you're for sale, and that you're available. I know you're a professional."

"You know that how?"

"Because I already have a personal assistant who does things for me. Like find other types of assistants."

"Let me guess." I seethed. "His name is Kyle."

"Yes."

"You and your assistant are the reason I'm out of work!"

"Yes, but I never intended you to be out of work very long. I wanted you to work for me."

"Why this song and dance? Why didn't you just come to me at the club?"

"Come to you at the club? I'm Jeremy Gray. I'm a little bit famous, in case you hadn't noticed. I don't think you or Mistress Amelia or any of the other clients there would have appreciated the paparazzi camped at the door."

"It was your two thousand dollars! You sent him there to— what? Try me out?"

"I sent him to find someone for me. He knows what I like, what I'm into. Yes, he tried you out."

I thought of our daring, exquisite night of pleasure, now reduced to Kyle's tawdry work assignment. "That's just...repugnant."

224

"Repugnant. Another nice word. Kyle's good at what he does. I asked him to find someone intelligent this time. I know you're not stupid, Nell. I know your mind isn't closed. I know you understand the lifestyle, and I know you've lived it. Put yourself in my shoes. How do you get what you need when you're in the spotlight twenty-four-seven? When cameras and gossip rags and web sites are recording your every move?"

I couldn't wrap my mind around it. It was just so depraved. I knew rich, superstar actors lived hedonistic lifestyles, but this was just plain sick. "Your last girlfriend—she was this too? A *personal assistant?*"

"Yes, she was. She signed those same papers you just read. We worked great together for a while." He said it like it was perfectly reasonable. He was crazy. He pulled up to my apartment. I wanted to get out, to slam the door in his face and go upstairs and shower until I could feel clean again.

But I didn't. I sat still, still as he did, and for some reason I asked him, "What happened? Why did she quit?"

He sat a moment in silence, biting his lip. "They all leave eventually. You will too."

I snorted. "No, I won't. Because I'm not going with you in the first place. I'm sorry that you're in this situation, I really am. But I'm not... I can't—"

"All right," he said. "Before you make any final decisions, I want you to think about this. You're out of work. Your real work. Waitressing can't be paying the bills. You're good at what you do. I'm good at it too. And I think you and I would get along. I know I went about this the wrong way, and I see that I've made you angry. It was never my intention to humiliate you or hurt you. Trap you, maybe. But only to make you consider things. So don't run away so quickly. Take a few days to consider—"

"The only thing I'm considering now is whether I'm going to take out a restraining order on you and your creepy bitch-boy Kyle. Good night." I got out, slammed the door, and went into my apartment without looking back. I don't know how long he stayed there, parked out in front. I was afraid to look. I was afraid to admit I cared.

I was afraid, because under the blazing anger burned a small ember of desire.

**Comfort Object is the first book in the Comfort series, available in paperback on Amazon.com and in ebook format wherever romance ebooks are sold.**

**The Comfort series is:**

**#1 *Comfort Object* (Jeremy's story)**

**#2 *Caressa's Knees* (Kyle's story)**

**#3 *Odalisque* (Kai's story)**

**#4 *Command Performance*
(Mason's story)**

Made in the USA
Monee, IL
01 June 2023

35111001R00125